FIGHTING FOR SCARLETT (SPECIAL FORCES: OPERATION ALPHA)

PREY SECURITY: ATHENA TEAM
BOOK ONE

JANE BLYTHE

Cover designed by Q Designs

Dear Readers,

Welcome to the Special Forces: Operation Alpha Fan-Fiction world!

If you are new to this amazing world, in a nutshell the author wrote a story using one or more of my characters in it. Sometimes that character has a major role in the story, and other times they are only mentioned briefly. This is perfectly legal and allowable because they are going through Aces Press to publish the story.

This book is entirely the work of the author who wrote it. While I might have assisted with brainstorming and other ideas about which of my characters to use, I didn't have any part in the process or writing or editing the story.

I'm proud and excited that so many authors loved my characters enough that they wanted to write them into their own story. Thank you for supporting them, and me!

READ ON!

Xoxo

Susan Stoker

ACKNOWLEDGMENTS

I'd like to thank everyone who played a part in bringing this story to life. Particularly my mom who is always there to share her thoughts and opinions with me. My wonderful cover designer Amy who did an amazing job with this stunning cover. My fabulous editor Lisa for all the hard work she puts into polishing my work. My awesome team, Sophie, Robyn, and Clayr, without your help I'd never be able to run my street team. And my fantastic street team members who help share my books with every share, comment, and like!

And of course a big thank you to all of you, my readers! Without you I wouldn't be living my dreams of sharing the stories in my head with the world!

CHAPTER ONE

January 7th
10:59 P.M.

Something snapped Scarlett Madden awake.

Bolting upright, she scanned her dark bedroom.

Nothing moved amongst the shadows, and as much as she strained her ears, she couldn't hear anything either.

A dream?

That didn't seem to be particularly likely. Sure, her childhood had been rough, but it wasn't abusive per se, and working for the world-renowned Prey Security she'd seen a lot, but her job was mostly lab work. Nightmares had never been a problem for her, and she doubted she'd randomly had one.

Couldn't remember one anyway.

She'd just been asleep and now she was awake, and the feeling in her gut said something was off.

While she was a romantic when it came to matters of

the heart, in all other aspects of her life, she was every bit the logical, sensible, practical scientist. If she felt like something was wrong, she was going to make sure she was prepared if she was right.

If she wasn't, then, no harm no foul.

Inching her way closer to the side of her bed where her cell phone was sitting on her nightstand, she tried not to make any noise. She'd grab the phone, then send out a text while she snuck over to her walk-in closet where her weapon was locked in its box.

Positive she was overreacting, Scarlett tamped down on the fear that was rolling around in her stomach. No one was in her house, maybe something had bumped into the window, and that had woken her up. Or it could be the neighbors, they had been known to have huge fights in the middle of the night. She'd had to call the cops a couple of times because she'd been worried one of them was going to wind up in the hospital. Or it could have been a car hitting something in the street. A couple of weeks ago, someone had knocked down all the garbage bins driving drunk.

Or the whole thing was just her imagination.

This was going to turn out to be nothing, and the other women on her team were going to tease her about it for the rest of their lives.

Still, better to be teased than dead.

Just as she reached a trembling hand out to scoop up her cell phone, she heard it.

Footsteps.

Definitely not her imagination.

Someone really was inside her house.

Trying to pretend she wasn't panicking was completely off the table now. Scrambling, she grabbed the phone and darted across the room and into her closet. Of course, it was the first place any intruder was going to look for her, but all she had to do was text one of her colleagues at Prey, grab her weapon, and then she could hunker down and defend herself till backup arrived.

Defend herself.

She'd never once in her life been in a position where she had to defend herself.

As a kid, she'd had to be mentally prepared for the psychological warfare her family loved to play, but she'd defied them and refused to join the military, instead choosing to fight evil with her brain. Sure, she knew how to shoot and had been taught almost as soon as she could walk. And she knew plenty of self-defense moves, too.

But knowing them and practicing them in a gym wasn't at all the same as actually having to use them in real life to protect herself.

Just as she reached up on tiptoes to grab the gun lock box, Scarlett heard the door to her bedroom ease open.

They were so close.

She only had seconds to do something before she wound up just another statistic.

If her parents could see her now, they'd be appalled. They had always accused her of being too weak, too soft, of not having what it took to be a warrior. While she would have sworn that their narrowmindedness could no longer affect her it seemed she was wrong. Seconds away from death—if she was lucky a quick death, if not, it would be rape and death—and she was worrying about the fact that as far as her family was concerned, she was nothing but a great big disappointment.

Unlocking her phone, she started typing out a text one-handed as she pulled the gun box down, grabbed the key, and squeezed herself into the back corner of the closet. Hiding behind her long winter coats, Scarlett barely breathed as she heard footsteps cross the room.

There were only so many places you could hide in a bedroom. Under the bed and in the closet had to be the top two, and she had no doubt that if someone had gone to all the trouble of breaking in here, they weren't going to leave just because she wasn't sleeping tucked in under the covers.

Her walk-in closet led through to the attached bathroom, which she was sure the intruder would check next. If he didn't thoroughly search the closet, she might buy herself a little time, but not enough for help to arrive.

With the gun box open, she picked up the weapon.

It felt much heavier than usual in her shaking hand.

Could she do it?

Could she shoot to kill if it was the only way to protect herself?

Scarlett honestly doubted that she could.

Wasn't even sure she could shoot to disable the intruder long enough for someone from Prey to show up.

Had it been a mistake to text her team rather than call 911?

Pure instinct had been driving her. The people at Prey were the best and she trusted them implicitly. But now that she thought about it, the cops probably could have gotten here quicker than one of her colleagues.

It was too late to second guess her decision now.

The door to her walk-in closet opened, and two huge black boots walked in. Of course, Scarlett knew that the boots were attached to a person, but right now, they were all she could see. All she could fixate on.

They were huge.

The largest pair of shoes she had ever seen.

How big was the man they belonged to?

Big enough to crush her like a bug, she knew that much.

Slowly, the boots moved through the wardrobe. The gun in her hand shook. She was holding her breath. Her pulse pounded so loudly she was quite honestly shocked that the intruder didn't hear it.

After walking to her bathroom and looking inside, the man turned and headed back toward the door. As badly as she wanted to let out a breath of relief, she knew she wasn't even close to being out of the woods yet. It was obvious she had been in her bed, which meant he knew she was somewhere in the house. He'd search it and find her.

Then ...

She didn't have to know exactly what this man had planned to know it would be bad for her.

Just as he was about to re-enter her bedroom the intruder stopped.

The shoes turned around until they were facing her again.

He knew she was in here.

The breath she had been holding shuddered out of her. She lifted the weapon and pointed it at the man.

Do it, Scarlett.

It might be her only chance.

If she hesitated, it could be too late.

Life and death.

You have to do it.

What were the chances that the intruder wasn't armed? None. Zero. Zilch. If he didn't have a gun, he'd have a knife or something equally as capable of killing her.

At the exact same second, she found her courage and fired her weapon at the man who had broken into her home in the middle of the night, he must have fired too.

Pain burned through her arm, causing her to drop both her weapon and her phone as her good hand instinctively went to press against the searing agony.

Voices shouted.

Footsteps pounded through her house.

But …

Prey couldn't be here yet.

Could they?

"She shot him!" a voice shouted.

Definitely not Prey.

Scarlett didn't recognize the voice.

"A kill shot," a second man said.

There were at least three men who had broken into her home. What did they want? Why were they doing this to her?

"Scarlett Madden, put your weapon down and come out," a third voice ordered.

They knew who she was.

How did they know who she was?

This wasn't random.

They'd come for her.

Specifically.

But why?

Tears of pain, fear, and frustration rolled down her cheeks, and she scrambled to pick up the weapon she had dropped.

No way was she coming out. If she had to, she would shoot every single one of them. Just because she hadn't followed in her family's footsteps didn't make her weak, or pathetic, or any of the other insults that had been slung at her over the years.

"Boss wants her alive," a fourth man said, and a couple of muttered curses followed.

Then the next thing she knew, five men were storming into her closet, grabbing at her, dragging her out of her hiding place, and pulling the weapon she'd only just reclaimed a grip on out of her hand. It was tossed uselessly onto the floor beside her cell phone.

Training flew out of her mind. Scarlett just fought like her life depended on it.

Because it did.

Throwing punches and kicks, she was sure she connected a couple of times at least. Not that it did any good. There were five of them to one of her.

Something sharp pricked the side of her neck.

Her vision grew fuzzy, limbs heavy, and then, poof, everything just ... disappeared.

* * *

JANUARY 8TH
8:38 A.M.

"WHAT THE HELL?" Tate Laurier exclaimed as he and his Navy SEAL team walked in for a mission briefing.

Taped up to the board was a picture of a woman he knew.

Not just knew, had slept with.

Not just had sex with, but been unable to forget about afterward.

That wasn't normal for him.

At all.

While he was hardly a playboy, he had a strict one-and-done policy when he was with a woman. Easier to avoid heartbreak that way. Watching his dad grieve long and hard after his mom had died, he had sworn off the whole idea of relationships and forever.

Not even love guaranteed forever.

No way was he going to willingly invite that kind of pain into his life. Losing his mom had been hard enough, he wasn't going to risk falling in love and possibly losing a partner as well.

The woman on the board was the only woman he'd ever slept with and thought about afterward. For months. Almost three of them. That's how long it had been since he'd had sex with Scarlett Madden, and he still wasn't over it.

Couldn't get the damn woman out of his head.

And he didn't like it one bit.

But he didn't want her out of his head bad enough that

he wanted her to be the focus of an op because that meant something had happened to her. Something that needed his kind of skill set.

Looking from him to the photo pinned to the board and back again, his CO asked, "You know her?"

"Yeah. I know her," Tate replied as he took a seat at the table. And now he might never get a chance to know more about her. Months of doing his best to forget her sweet giggle and shy smile, her warm milk chocolate brown eyes, and long silky black locks. The woman had made an impression on him because she was the opposite of who he usually slept with. She had white picket fence and happy ever afters written all over.

Everything he didn't want.

Everything he couldn't give her.

So, he'd ignored her calls and texts. Even went so far as to pretend he didn't remember her when they'd accidentally bumped into one another at the supermarket one day.

Humiliating her by pretending he hadn't even remembered her name or that they'd met hadn't felt good.

In fact, it was one of the things he felt the most guilty about.

Sleazy, slimy, dirty.

Problem was, he should never have touched her in the first place, but there were no do-overs in life. Tate had known from the moment he laid eyes on the giggling woman dressed up as Little Bo Peep at a Halloween party at a local bar he frequented that she wasn't for him. Too sweet, too good, too pure. The kind of woman he had no business taking into his bed when he was neither sweet, good, or pure.

"This going to be a problem?" his CO asked.

"No." The word came out automatically, but if Tate were to think about it, maybe it could be a problem. Unlike with any other woman, he wasn't completely clearheaded when it came to Scarlett. Despite knowing that he absolutely did not want to fall in love and get married, he couldn't seem to rid the woman from his thoughts.

If it was just getting himself off replaying that night in his mind it would be one thing. But it was more. The woman intrigued him, brought out a protective side of him, worse, a softer side.

He could do this though.

Treat her as though she were any other op he and his team were sent on.

Before his CO could press him on it, and he knew the man well enough to tell that he wasn't convinced, the door to the room opened, and a group of men followed by three women walked in.

What was going on?

Tate would have sworn that the men belonged to Prey Security. Were they involved in whatever was going on with Scarlett? It wouldn't be the first time that a SEAL team would work with Prey, but he couldn't figure out what Scarlett could have gotten messed up in that would necessitate a joint Navy Prey mission.

"I'm sure you've all heard of Owen "Fox" LeGrand," their CO said, nodding to the man who had joined him at the head of the table.

Yeah, every SEAL knew of Fox and his team. They were all retired SEALs who had gone to work for Prey. Prey Security was legendary in the special ops world. While the company also worked private security for wealthy clients, their covert ops made them well known in the special forces' community.

The expression on Fox's face was tight, as were the expressions on the five other men and three women who had come in with him. Tate recognized the other men. Ryder "Spider" Flynn, Eric "Night" McNamara, Logan "Shark" Kirk, Grayson "Chaos" Simpson, and Charlie "King" Voss. All six men were married with families, and he had no idea how they had managed to make family life work knowing what they did about the world and the evil that permeated it.

While he knew the men, the three women sitting in the room he'd never seen before. The former SEALs looked angrier, but there was fear in the women's faces, and he wondered who they were to Scarlett. Not family, because there was no way they would be allowed here without high enough security clearances. So, who were they?

"What's going on?" he asked, anxiety mounting inside him. What had happened to Scarlett? And why did he care so much?

Fox's dark eyes met his and narrowed slightly, but the older man didn't comment, just moved his gaze to take in the entire gathering. "Scarlett Madden is part of Prey Security's Athena Team," he said, pointing to the picture of Scarlett on the board and then to the other three women.

Shock would have knocked him over if he wasn't already sitting down.

Scarlett Madden worked for Prey?

The sweet, innocent woman he had known he was corrupting just by taking her into his bed worked for the best private security company in the world?

How was that possible?

And how had he not seen beneath the pretty pink veneer to the skilled warrior beneath?

Gullible just like his father.

Anger slowly bubbled to life inside him, knowing he'd been played. For months now, he'd been obsessing over Scarlett, thinking she was all soft and perfect, too good for him, and all that time she'd been lying to him.

Okay, *lying* was a stretch. He hadn't told her much about himself either. They'd laughed and talked, shared some food, then headed back to Scarlett's house to spend the night.

"She works for Prey?" he asked, needing to hear it said again.

Fox's eyes narrowed again. "Do you know Scarlett?"

"You're Tate Laurier," one of the women said. She was a little younger than the others, with long chestnut brown hair and large brown eyes. With her head tilted to the side, she examined him, and he very much felt like a bug under a microscope.

If these women knew his name, then it was obvious Scarlett must have talked to them about him. But what exactly had she said? And more importantly, what was she doing for Prey that had garnered the Navy's attention?

"What happened to her?" he asked, ignoring both the

older man's question and the young woman's observation. Angry with Scarlett for not telling him she was part of Prey—unjustified as it might be—didn't mean that his anxiety had disappeared.

"Last night a little before midnight, Scarlett sent out a text to Lucy," Fox said, nodding to a blonde with light blue eyes. "It just said help. Athena Team does not work in the field, they are primarily a team of scientists who work on processing forensics for Prey. They also do some development work for us. While they are all trained, they rarely have cause to use those skills. Lucy alerted me, and since I live about ten minutes from Scarlett's house, I went straight there. I found her back door open, a dead body in her bedroom, along with a puddle of blood in the walk-in closet. There was no sign of Scarlett."

Kidnapping.

Not random if it had been more than one man and she'd been taken.

If it was just some sicko, he would have done what he wanted with her and then killed her.

Fox stood with a piece of paper in his hand and went to the board, pinning up a picture of what was clearly a dead man. The shot between the eyes was a direct kill shot. Scarlett might not spend a lot of time in the field, but she had skills.

"I'm sure you're all familiar with this tattoo," Fox said, pointing to a mark in the hollow of the dead man's neck.

As soon as he saw it, Tate knew what it was.

A small gun surrounded by a ring of dynamite.

The symbol of one of the world's most dangerous weapons traffickers.

Why had the notorious Raul Castillo sent a team after a woman who worked in a lab at Prey? Made zero sense.

"There's more," he said, looking to Fox, who nodded tightly.

"We also discovered an email that indicates someone might be trying to sell the wonder drug Athena Team have been working on," Fox informed them.

There was no need for the man to say more.

The person who was trying to sell the drug to a notorious arms dealer was none other than Scarlett herself.

CHAPTER TWO

January 8th
2:14 P.M.

How soon was too soon to lose your mind after being kidnapped?

There was no such thing.

Right?

At least Scarlett hoped so because she was already dangerously close to losing her mind, and she'd only been here for …

Who knew how long.

But it couldn't be all that long.

Or she was praying it hadn't.

Whatever she'd been drugged with had knocked her out completely, long enough for her to be transported from her home to this dungeon.

Yep.

An actual dungeon.

It was like she had stepped onto the set of a movie. The walls were made of stone as were the floors. There were no windows, and it was simultaneously cold and stuffy. There were dark stains on the stone that she didn't have to use her imagination to figure out where they'd come from. Three of the four walls of her prison cell were stone, and the fourth—the front one—was made of metal bars that ran from the floor to the ceiling.

Trapped.

No way out.

Panic bubbled up inside her, coming out in a hysterical laugh.

See.

Losing it.

Had to be.

Because all she could think about was her childhood and her parents' "training exercises". While they were both in the military and away on deployments more than they were home, when they were home, they liked to teach their kids how to survive once they joined the military themselves. Which they had believed was a foregone conclusion.

Only she and her twin brother, Zander, hadn't wanted to join the military.

Living with their grandparents until they died when she and her brother were thirteen, they had then been put in foster care. Their parents weren't going to give up the careers they loved just because somebody had to raise their kids.

In an effort to finally gain their approval—and by extension, their love—Zander eventually caved in to the pressure and joined the Army. Smart, hardworking, dedicated, and loyal, her brother excelled and became a member of the elite Delta Force.

Eighteen months had passed since her brother had been killed in action.

Leaving her all alone in the world.

Now, she was even more alone.

Imprisoned here without her team, without her Prey family. Neither her parents nor her grandparents would be impressed that she had wound up working with a whole bunch of military types. In their minds, she was just proving how weak she was. All those men and women had served their country, fought to protect the innocent, to eliminate evil, and she sat in a nice, air-conditioned lab doing work they would believe was beneath her.

More light suddenly filled the dimly lit cell she was locked in, and the sound of footsteps told her someone was coming.

Time to face the music.

Scarlett prayed some of what her parents had taught her more than a decade ago had managed to stick.

Because she was going to need every ounce of strength and training she'd ever had if she was going to survive.

You sent the text to Lucy. She knows you're in trouble. Prey will come for you. They never leave anyone behind. They'll come. All you have to do is stay alive until they get here.

The mental pep talk did little to encourage her, and by

the time two men appeared outside her cell, she was shaking so hard that her teeth were chattering.

Way to show you're not afraid, Scar.

Funnily enough, her rebuking herself rather than encouraging herself calmed her enough to control the worst of the shaking.

She *did* know that Prey would come for her. They'd scour the world for her. Eagle Oswald himself—retired SEAL and founder and CEO of Prey Security—would call on every single contact he had to find her and bring her home.

That was what family did.

They didn't abandon you, treat you like you were a nuisance, get angry that you wouldn't live your life according to the plan they had for you, and then disown you. Her Prey family would never turn their backs on her.

Not for anything.

Knowing that meant she could face the two men who had unlocked her cell and stalked toward her. Just because she didn't work in the field didn't mean she didn't recognize the look in their eyes. They were excited to have a prisoner and looking forward to hurting her.

This was the first time she'd seen anyone since she woke up on the floor inside this bare little cell. Now that she got a good look at the men, she realized with a sinking feeling of hopelessness that she knew who they were.

The tattoos.

A gun surrounded by a ring of sticks of dynamite placed in the hollow at the bottom of their throat.

These men were Raul Castillo's men.

Raul Castillo was a notorious weapons trafficker. He had money and power, and he lived deep in the Mexican jungle surrounded by his own army. While he hadn't specifically been on Prey's radar in an active case, he was wanted, and she knew Eagle would love to add him to one of Prey's success stories.

Why had Raul had her abducted?

Did he intend to use her to force Prey's hand to get something he wanted?

That seemed unlikely.

If the man wanted to blackmail Prey, there were better people to abduct to do it than her. One of the Oswald kids would cause a much bigger wave if they were taken. Then again, if one of the Oswald little ones were taken, the fury of Prey would be ignited much greater than by taking her.

Two meaty hands grabbed her arms, one of them closing around the gunshot wound she'd gotten back at her house.

Pain screamed down from the wound, and Scarlett had to clamp her teeth together to stop the scream from escaping and giving these men exactly what they wanted.

They wanted her in pain. They would relish her suffering. The only leverage she had was to pretend she was unaffected by all of this.

Sure, easy, Scar, you can totally convince these men you're a tough girl. They'll totally believe it.

Rolling her eyes at herself only reinforced her belief that she was the opposite of tough and had already succumbed to panic and fear and lost her mind.

"Where are you taking me? Why am I here?" she asked, aiming for haughty but failing miserably.

Ignored by the two men confirmed her belief that she was nothing but the weak, pathetic mess her parents had always accused her of being. She couldn't survive whatever they had planned for her.

Turned out she wasn't taken far from her cell, just walked past a few more cells, all of which were empty as far as she could see, into a room at the end of the passageway. A chair sat in the middle of the room, blood stains beneath it. Hanging on the wall was a range of implements designed to torture someone.

Panic got the best of her, and any pretense that she could do this flew out the window as she struggled.

"No, please. Don't put me in the chair. I don't know why I'm here, I don't know anything. Just let me go and I won't tell anyone you kidnapped me," she begged.

Of course, she was ignored, and despite her desperate struggles, she was easily shoved into the chair. Metal cuffs locked around her wrists and then her ankles, securing her to the torture chair.

Tears streamed down her cheeks. She tried to fight against the cuffs, knowing it was pointless as she continued to plead for her life. "Let me go. Please. I haven't done anything, I don't know anything, I just want to go home. Please. Please. Let me go home."

"I do *so* love it when a lady cries," a voice spoke, and Scarlett looked through her tears to see Raul Castillo himself standing in the doorway.

Dressed in black suit pants with a crisp white shirt

rolled up to his elbows, he looked completely out of place in this torture chamber.

Begging was pointless.

It would only turn him on more.

Still, Scarlett couldn't seem to stop herself. "Please, I just want to go home. I don't know anything, I didn't do anything, I don't understand why I'm here."

"On the contrary, you know exactly what I'm after," Raul told her as he closed the short distance between them, stopping right in front of her.

That made zero sense.

What could she possibly know that would be useful to a man who dealt in weapons?

She was a lab geek. She ran forensics for Prey, and she and her team worked on various side projects out of pure interest.

"I ... I ... don't ... I don't understand," she said, no longer able to catch her breath as she began to hyperventilate. Panic clawed inside her, squirming and wriggling through her body as it took control of her.

This couldn't be happening to her.

It couldn't.

"You're here because of the Reactivator," Raul told her.

Scarlett froze.

Because of the Reactivator?

That made no sense.

More tears flooded her cheeks. "I don't understand, the Reactivator isn't a weapon." The opposite in fact. It was a drug she and her team had been working on for almost two years. There were several aspects of it, but basically, it was designed to help injured soldiers survive in the field. The drug worked to slow bleeding, encourage faster healing, dull pain, and add extra adrenalin to the patient's system to keep them on their feet.

While nowhere close to being finished and ready for trials, Scarlett was hopeful the drug would indeed end up doing what it was designed to.

Meaning it would be a game-changer.

But it wasn't a weapon.

So why was Raul Castillo interested in it?

"I want that drug, Ms. Madden. Not only is it worth a fortune for those who intend to use it as you had planned, but it could also be engineered in reverse to make a weapon that would inflict unimaginable suffering."

Technically, that was true, but it would take years to create a drug that would do that, it wasn't as easy as Raul was making out, you didn't just make it in reverse. Even aside from that, there was no way she was going to give this man the formula for the Reactivator. Athena Team had created it to do good, not to be sold to the highest bidder and used against the people they'd wanted to help.

Bad news for her.

She wasn't telling him how to make the drug which meant all those torture devices hanging from the walls were ones she would become intimately acquainted with.

A wicked grin filled Raul's face as he followed her line of sight. "Oh, I'll use every one of those on you if I have to. Sooner or later, you'll talk. Pain is a very powerful motivator."

With that, he reached out toward the ragged hole in her arm and pressed his thumb into it.

Agony burned through her body, and Scarlett couldn't

hold back an ear-piercing scream as her body tried instinctively to get away from the pain.

Only there was nowhere to go.

How was she going to do this?

* * *

January 10th

7:12 P.M.

His mood had been getting progressively worse since he walked into the briefing room and found out the woman he hadn't been able to get out of his head was a traitor to her country.

Like father like son.

Okay, so his father hadn't fallen for a traitor, but then again, Tate had always had a penchant for outdoing everybody around him.

At first, as a kid, it was because he always felt like he was competing for his parents' attention. As an only child, one would assume all attention would be focused on him, but his parents' love for one another was so big, so deep, so powerful that they had a tendency to get caught up in it and forget about everyone else.

Including their son.

Then, it had been about trying to pull his dad out of the depths of the grief-filled depression he had gotten stuck in after losing his wife. Only eight at the time, little Tate had been afraid of losing the only parent he had left and thought if he was stronger, smarter, more helpful, and more obedient than any other kid around, his dad would have to notice and be a dad again.

After that, it was because he needed the self-reassurance that he was worthy. That just because his parents loved each other more than they loved him, and his dad couldn't get over losing his wife, he still had value.

That determination and single-minded focus had served him well. He'd graduated high school early, then college, then worked hard to make it through training and become a SEAL. Not an easy feat, and one he was proud of.

But all the determination and single-minded focus in the world couldn't stop him from falling for a woman just like the one who had finally pulled his dad out of his hole of depression.

A liar.

A betrayer.

A backstabber.

A selfish, self-absorbed woman who didn't care who she hurt as long as she got what she wanted and was fully prepared to throw anybody under the bus.

At least his father's ex-wife was nothing but a lowlife drug dealer. After getting his father hooked on drugs, when she got caught dealing, she shoved all the blame onto him. Spending all his time high, his father had been unable to properly defend himself and was now serving a ten-year prison sentence while his scheming, lying, now ex-wife claimed she was nothing but a poor, abused spouse.

Tate wasn't pretending his father didn't have faults, but he wasn't abusive.

At least his former stepmother had only wiggled her way out of a drug trafficking charge, unlike the woman he hadn't been able to forget. She was prepared to backstab her own team and sell something that could have been used for good to a weapons dealer who was indirectly responsible for thousands of deaths.

There was not a doubt in his mind that right at this second, Scarlett Madden was currently sitting in Raul Castillo's jungle mansion relaxing and enjoying herself, believing that she had gotten away with it.

Well, she was sadly mistaken.

They would take her down.

He would take her down.

And once she was in custody, he would personally take it upon himself to make sure she was punished to the fullest extent of the law.

Although he'd rather she got the punishment all traitors deserved.

Death.

Sitting in a jail cell for the rest of her life was too good for someone who would take a drug that could mean the difference between life and death to soldiers in the field, and sell it to someone who would find a way to use it against her country.

The last two days had been spent trying to get a location on Raul Castillo's jungle mansion. They had an approximate location, but the man was rich, the kind of rich that afforded him the benefits of being able to pay off anyone he liked, including law enforcement and politicians.

When he wasn't buying people off, he was ruling

through fear, and no one was willing to give up the man's exact location.

Not that he and his team wouldn't find it.

Prey were helping, too, even if they didn't seem to want to believe what was right in front of their faces. It wouldn't be the first time they'd had a traitor in their midst. In fact, Fox himself had almost lost his now-wife Evie when a traitor at Prey gave up her location when she was hiding from a mob boss who wanted her dead.

"We might have a lead on Scarlett's location," Spider suddenly announced.

Like a switch had been flipped, the room suddenly went completely silent. Nobody even moved.

"Where is she?" he asked, breaking the spell. He wanted to get the hell out there and start looking for the woman who had fooled them all. Tate wouldn't be able to relax until she was sitting in a jail cell somewhere. Knowing she was out there, had maybe already received her payment from Raul and disappeared to some tiny corner of the world where she thought she would be safe, was eating him alive.

She'd be wrong though.

If it took him the rest of his life, Tate would hunt her down and see that she was made to face the sins she had committed.

While his team never took their eyes off Spider, all the Prey people turned to shoot him glares. He was prepared to take their frustration, he got it. They were upset, they'd been blindsided here, just like he had been when his father had called him from jail. But he wasn't the bad guy. That was Scarlett. And it was the job of all of them to find her and see that she was punished for her choices.

"We compiled all the data we have on Raul Castillo, and we've managed to narrow it down to a fifty-square-mile section of jungle in central Mexico," Spider replied tightly. It was clear he didn't like this, but like it or not, it was happening.

The cards had already been dealt by Scarlett herself and now they all needed to scramble and play their hands.

That was all he needed to hear.

Now he and his team could get out there. Shouldn't take them all that long to clear an area of jungle that size. Wasn't like he could imagine a man as wealthy as Raul Castillo living in some tiny little hut that would be hard to pick up.

Already pushing back from the table, he nodded. "We'll keep you updated."

"Wait," the brunette he knew was Cassidy said, also shoving away from the table. "You can't go out there like that, like you're about to take down a terrorist."

"Scarlett didn't do what that email implies," the green-eyed blonde, Ella, agreed, also standing up.

"You don't know her like we do. There is zero way she would do this," the blue-eyed blonde, Lucy, quickly added. "Scarlett is good, sweet, and kind. She has the biggest heart ever and truly cares about people."

Looks could be deceiving.

Tate knew that better than most.

He had actively encouraged his father to pursue a relationship with the woman who wound up destroying his life. That was guilt he would have to live with the rest of his life, and if Athena Team tried to get in the middle of this, they, too, would have to live with the guilt of knowing they contributed to what Scarlett had set in motion.

"I get it. You guys are close. But sometimes we don't see what's right in front of us," Tate said gently because he truly did understand where they were coming from. "But facts are, there is a dead man tattooed with Raul Castillo's mark in her apartment, killed with her weapon, and an email that suggests she's selling the Reactivator to the weapons dealer."

"But she texted me that she needed help," Lucy protested.

"Or she was trying to set up an alibi not knowing about the email that had been found," he suggested. "Likely, she hoped everyone would believe she had just been kidnapped, and while they would look for her they would eventually give up. Maybe she has a whole plan to eventually fake her death. I don't know. None of us do. But what we do know is Scarlett is tangled up with Raul Castillo. That fact is indisputable."

"Scarlett said you were a real jerk," Ella muttered. "She still has no reason to do any of this."

"Actually, she does," he countered. Over the last forty-eight hours, he'd gathered every bit of intel he could about his target. And what he'd learned suggested Scarlett did indeed have reason to sell the drug to the enemy. "Grew up abandoned by her parents who prioritized military careers over her and her brother. Grandparents, also military, were strict and uncompromising. Placed in foster care after their deaths when neither parent would give up their career. Then she lost her brother, who also abandoned her to join the military only a few months after you began working on this drug. I'd say if anyone has a reason to dislike the military and sell a drug that could save the lives of soldiers it would be Scarlett Madden."

CHAPTER THREE

January 11th

12:35 P.M.

HER CONFIDENCE that rescue was just on the horizon was starting to wane.

Scarlett shivered as a wave of pain rolled over her.

Lying on the cold, hard, unforgiving stone floor of her cell was not the place to be when you were littered with cuts and bruises.

At least she didn't have to worry about infection. Yay. Raul was keeping her pumped full of antibiotics. He didn't want her getting sick and dying on him before he got what he wanted out of her.

Not that she was giving it to him.

Whatever he dished out she, would *have* to take. Honestly, there was no other option because she wasn't going to betray her team and Prey and hand over a drug that had the potential to save millions of lives.

But Prey better hurry up and find her because she wasn't sure how long she could last.

So far, she'd been roughed over, nothing too serious, for now, but she got the feeling that Raul was trying to feel her out, find out the best method of getting her to talk. Scarlett had taken harder hits in the gym when she was working out, so she'd managed to keep her mouth shut and taken the punches, walking away with a litany of bruises but nothing broken.

Next, Raul had upped his game, he'd had her stripped naked and strung up from the ceiling and whipped until she could feel her blood running down her skin. Again, she knew he hadn't pushed as hard as he could have. While her back felt like it had been ripped open, she knew it definitely wasn't as bad as it could have been, not that it was at all pleasant.

None of this was pleasant.

Not even close.

Actually, it was as close to hell as she had ever been.

And she had no idea how she was going to handle whatever came next.

Problem was, she had no experience in withstanding torture. Her parents and grandparents were mean, they didn't love her or her brother, and they'd definitely mistreated them and pushed too hard too many times to count, but they weren't psychopaths.

As children, she and Zander had lived on a strict diet. There were no fun snacks, no chips or pretzels or popcorn. No candy or chocolate or cake. Not even a birthday cake. They also worked a strict exercise routine, a workout early before school and one when they got home. Then there were drills to run, and lessons in shooting, and martial arts training. Plus, all the chores and her parents and grandparents expected her and her brother to remain honor roll students in every subject.

Life hadn't been fun, but she had never feared for her physical safety, and she had no idea how to do this.

Why hadn't Prey come for her?

They had to be looking, she trusted her team and her colleagues implicitly. Prey was more of a family to her than her own had ever been, and she knew they wouldn't leave her hung out to dry.

When she heard footsteps approaching, Scarlett instinctively curled herself into a ball, making herself as small a target as possible. It was stupid, and it wasn't going to achieve anything.

Wishing she knew what she was doing, that she could handle this, that being tortured for information with no end in sight was something she was capable of surviving wasn't going to make it true.

This *wasn't* something she could do for much longer.

What happened when she reached the end of her rope?

Giving over the information on the drug was not an option which meant her only option was … taking herself out of the equation.

Was she strong enough to end her own life if it came down to it?

From the tears trailing down her cheeks and the way her body shook like it had been encased in a block of ice, Scarlett feared that she wasn't.

All these years spent believing she was strong for not being forced into becoming who her parents wanted her to be, for forging her own path in life had evaporated. She wasn't strong, she was every bit as weak as they had always believed her to be.

There wasn't enough strength left in her at the moment to get up onto her feet, so she simply stayed where she was. The guards didn't speak as they came to her and grabbed her roughly, of course making sure to grab her around the gunshot wound. Just because infection wasn't going to become an issue didn't mean the wound didn't throb along with the rest of her aches and pains.

A small cry escaped despite her attempts to smother it, and she hated the grins on the guards' faces, their satisfaction in causing her to show her pain.

Once again, she was taken back down to the room that, in her mind, was called the torture chamber and shoved again into the chair in the center of the room. Another small cry of pain fell from her lips as the metal cuffs were secured around her wrists and ankles. The skin there was torn and bloody from rubbing against the rusty metal as she strained and struggled against the bonds.

When she was rescued—*if* she was rescued—the wounds would leave scars. Scars that she would see every single day, a constant reminder of what she had lived through.

But as Raul strolled into the room, dressed impeccably as always, her hope died a little more. With every passing minute, her hopes for rescue seemed to disappear. Of course, she knew that Prey weren't miracle workers, and nobody had an exact location on Raul's jungle mansion, but surely they would have found something by now.

Weren't they coming?

Didn't they care about her?

Were they going to leave her behind like everybody else always did?

"How are you today, Ms. Madden?" Raul asked, his tone polite, conversational, like she was his guest here.

With a weary sigh she met the man's dark, soulless eyes. "We're not friends, Mr. Castillo, and I'm not here voluntarily, there's no need to pretend you care about anything other than the fact that I'm in pain. And yes, I can confirm that I am one whole throbbing mess of agony, and I'm sure it will be worse when you finish whatever you have planned for today. But as much as I hurt, I'm not going to give you the formula for the Reactivator."

That much Scarlett was certain of.

If it came to it, she *would* find the strength to kill herself rather than give over the information the weapons dealer wanted.

"You offend me, Ms. Madden," Raul said with a chuckle. "I am not always going to inflict pain, and any pain that has been inflicted so far was brought upon by yourself. You could have just told me what I wanted to know, and you would have been gifted a quick death once you created the drug for me."

If that was an invitation to spill her guts, she wasn't accepting it.

When she remained stubbornly silent, Raul continued, "Among other things, I am a collector. Yes, I deal in weapons, it is a lucrative living and one I enjoy. Besides the money, I find I enjoy the thrill and excitement of it all, the danger, knowing at any moment I could be caught or killed. But I have other interests and collecting unusual drugs is one of them. Your Reactivator is one I would relish having in my collection, but there are a few others that I find amusing. This one in particular."

A nod at the man beside him had that man lifting a syringe filled with something clear. Scarlett didn't have to know that whatever was in that drug was something horrific. Something terrifying.

There was nowhere for her to go, though, when the man walked toward her and pierced the skin on her upper arm, pushing the plunger and administering whatever concoction the syringe contained.

"What did you do?" she asked, panic hitting her system with a massive dose of adrenalin. "What did you give me?"

Raul chuckled. "Pain isn't the only motivator in the world, Ms. Madden. This beauty of a drug was given to me by a friend who works in a different trade. Flesh. Women. Sex. There are many men who enjoy it when a woman struggles, when she is not a willing participant. But many enjoy it when a woman begs and pleads for more, when she is insatiable, they love to feel her coming around them. Think of this drug as a large dose of arousal. I have yet to see it in action, but I have heard the reports. Women screaming and crying as they beg a man to have sex with them. I've heard they remain aroused for hours and that if their needs are not taken care of, it is extremely painful for them. How long do you think you will last, Ms. Madden, before you are pleading with my men to relieve your pain, to give you the orgasm your body craves even as your mind rejects the idea? How long until you are willing to offer anything to get some relief from the arousal coursing through your system?"

* * *

JANUARY 12TH
5:48 P.M.

WHERE ARE YOU, little traitor?

Are we getting closer?

Tate was pumped high on adrenalin and anger as he and his SEAL team slunk through the Mexican jungle.

They'd been there for going on thirty-six hours and knew they were closing in on their target when they'd finally located a road.

Well, not so much a road as a track barely recognizable unless you were looking for it. But since he and his team were there looking for signs of a hidden mansion, they'd spotted it as soon as they'd gotten close.

Now they were following along parallel to the road while still maintaining hidden within the cover of the trees. If someone was monitoring the road, they'd be spotted, but Tate was banking on the fact that Raul Castillo thought he was safe tucked away out there.

Ego had been the downfall of many a man—or woman—who had crossed his path, and he had zero doubt that it would be the downfall of Scarlett Madden as well.

Chances were, she also believed she was safely hidden away out there.

Game's up, sweetheart.

While he would love to be the one to personally destroy the woman who'd had him tied up in knots for almost three months, his orders were to retrieve her and deliver her back home. He was not to engage, he was not to confront her with what they knew because the plan was to try to get her talking once she was in custody. If he pushed too hard, she might be able to escape, but once she was cuffed and in an interrogation room, she would have no choice but to realize she was all out of options.

There was at least one good thing to come out of this mess, and that was Raul Castillo had officially become a big enough problem that it was time for him to be eliminated. Tate was hoping this was going to be a two-birds-with-the-one-stone kind of situation, and he'd walk away with both Scarlett and Raul, but the priority for this op was Scarlett.

They already had a read on Raul, but Scarlett was somewhat unknown. If she was willing to sell this drug, what else had she or would she be willing to sell? To work at Prey, you had to have a high security clearance, which meant she could have already, or been planning to, sell any number of secrets if the price was right.

Traitors had no conscience, they were out for self and self alone, and Tate was looking forward to watching the look on Scarlett's face when she realized this time she wasn't coming out on top.

Just as he noticed the thinning of the trees and the shape up ahead of them that looked like a large building, he heard the unmistakable sound of the whir of helicopter blades.

As he watched, a helo rose above them, taking off into

the sky away from what was quite obviously Raul Castillo's hideout.

Damn.

The man was escaping.

Had they somehow tripped a sensor, alerting those in the mansion that someone was approaching?

Seemed possible given the timing.

Double damn.

Was Scarlett also on that helo?

Shouting orders into his comms to his team, Tate took off at a dead run toward the mansion ahead of them.

They were approaching the building from what looked to be the back because he could see a large pool and an outdoor dining patio area behind the large wire fence. A fence that was likely electrified.

As he broke through the tree line, someone immediately began shooting at him.

It took him less than a second to identify the direction of the shooter and fire off a round of his own.

A faint thud told him he'd hit his target and dropped the body, so he spared no more time on the guard. He had to find a way over that fence because he saw her.

Scarlett.

Standing naked by the pool.

Had the woman been out there, lounging around and enjoying herself, when they'd set off the alarm?

Looked like her buddy Raul had left her to the wolves and fled.

Not that he was in any way aligning himself with the weapons dealer, but in this moment, he sent up a silent thank you that Raul had left Scarlett behind when he left.

"Not so nice when someone betrays you, is it now, sweetheart?" he whispered as he snagged a branch and tossed it at the fence. Sparks flew as it hit, and with his assumption about the fence confirmed, he ran toward a nearby tree.

There was no time to figure out how to get the electric fence turned off, he had to get in there and get Scarlett before she fled.

Why wasn't she running?

She was just standing there by the pool.

Frozen in shock?

From what he knew, Scarlett had zero field training. Maybe she was overwhelmed by the shooting going on around her and didn't know what to do.

It took him mere seconds to climb up the tree closest to the fence. He'd have to jump, hope he missed the barbed wire topping the fence, and it would be at least an eight-foot drop, but he didn't have any other chances.

He wasn't letting Scarlett get away.

Flinging himself forward, Tate jumped from the tree, somehow managing to clear the top of the fence, and landed with a bone-jarring thud on the other side.

"I'm over. Going to get target," he informed his team as he took off toward Scarlett.

It wasn't until he got closer that he realized why Scarlett wasn't moving.

It wasn't because she was in shock or panicking because of a lack of field experience.

It was because she couldn't move.

Someone had tied a large rock to her leg. It was too big

for her to pull around with her which meant she was stuck there.

For a moment Tate faltered.

Why was she outside, naked, by the pool with a rock tied to her leg?

Made no sense.

There would have been no time for Raul to organize for her to be disposed of and get himself onto a helo if they'd set off a sensor.

Which meant he had already been planning on disposing of her.

Had she been double-crossed?

Would serve her right if she'd given her intel to Raul, and he had promptly decided to be done with her.

"Scarlett," he called her name as he got closer.

Immediately, her head whipped around in his direction. Was he mistaken or was that relief on her face as she spotted him sprinting toward her?

Before he could examine her expression, she cried out, and the next thing he knew, she was falling into the pool. The weight of her body falling was enough to drag the rock, which as he was closer now, he could see had been balancing right on the edge of the pool, down with her.

Water splashed everywhere as Scarlett thrashed, but she was weighed down with her head beneath the surface.

Drowning.

She was drowning.

Unless he got her out, she'd die.

"Oh no, you don't," he muttered as he reached the pool and dived into the water after her. Scarlett didn't get to die now. She was going to stand and face justice and suffer the consequences of her actions.

As soon as he reached her, Scarlett began to grab at him. For a moment Tate thought she was trying to shove him away as though that would somehow stop him from getting to her, but he quickly realized she was panicking and thought he was her savior.

Not your savior, sweetheart, not even close.

I'm about to become your worst nightmare.

I won't stop until I make sure that justice prevails and you're punished for what you did.

Unable to do anything with Scarlett panicking like that, he moved behind her, locked her arms to her sides as he wrapped one of his own around her chest and pressed her against his body. Then, with his free hand, he pulled out his knife and sliced through the rope attaching the rock to her leg.

With Scarlett free, he swam them both back to the surface then lifted her up and onto the tiles, keeping a hand on her as he pulled himself out in case she decided to try something stupid and make a run for it now that she was free.

But that wasn't what she did.

The opposite in fact.

Water streamed down off both of them as Scarlett threw herself into his arms, wrapping herself around him as though she were a small child who'd had a nightmare and needed to be comforted.

Automatically, his arms wrapped around her, and that was when he noticed. Her back was littered with raw, open wounds. There were bruises on her pale skin as well, and her wrists and ankles were also covered in open wounds.

Looked like she had been tortured.

But that made zero sense.

What the hell was going on here?

CHAPTER FOUR

January 12th
6:06 P.M.

FINALLY.

Finally, someone had come for her.

Scarlett was so relieved that all she could do was cling to her savior and weep. Huge, wracking sobs that made her chest ache.

Someone was here.

Someone had come.

Someone cared.

Relief was so overwhelming that in this moment nothing else seemed to matter. Not that she'd been kidnapped, not that she'd been tortured, not that there was currently a firefight going on all around them.

Nothing.

Just this.

Someone had come for her because she mattered.

Maybe not to her parents, or grandparents, or possibly even her twin brother, but she mattered to her Prey family, which meant the world to her.

"What's this?" a voice snarled, and a hand brushed lightly across her back, making her flinch as pain came screaming back.

Then the voice clicked, and Scarlett froze. The voice didn't belong to anyone at Prey, but she recognized it.

Slowly, she lifted her head—which suddenly felt much too heavy—from the shoulder of the man whose arms she had been sobbing in. Her savior was dressed all in black with paint smeared over his face, but she would recognize him anywhere.

For months, those eyes had haunted her dreams. Months.

Despite her assurances to him the night they'd spent together, she wasn't a one-and-done kind of girl. She wanted the whole fairytale romance. Wanted to fall in love and live happily ever after. Wanted fun dates and roses, holding hands, long walks along the beach, and lying in the sand staring up at the stars. She wanted someone she could talk to about anything in the world, someone who would understand her.

Wanted to be loved.

Stupid maybe, but she'd felt this weird fluttery feeling in the pit of her stomach as soon as their eyes met. Even stupider she'd thought he'd felt it too. His amazing eyes—one brown, the other a beautiful blue-gray—had flared to life like he was experiencing the same weird feelings she was.

That was why it had hurt so much when he'd never

called or texted. And the time they'd bumped into one another at the grocery store, and he pretended he didn't know her, that they hadn't spent an amazing night of lovemaking and sleeping in one another's arms, hadn't just been humiliating, it had hurt her.

Gutted her.

Tate Laurier didn't work for Prey, he was a SEAL.

Why had Prey sent in a SEAL team to get her instead of coming after her themselves?

All at once, that wonderful high she was riding … vanished.

"T-Tate?" she murmured, voice hoarse from all her screaming the day before. "Wh-what are you doing here?"

Something flashed across his face that she didn't understand. It almost looked like he was … angry with her?

What would he have to be angry about?

She hadn't done anything wrong.

Maybe he thought she'd talked? Told Raul Castillo about the drug? Could he even know that was why the weapons dealer had taken her?

"What are these?" he growled again as he brushed a hand down her back, not bothering to avoid the gashes from the whip.

Wincing, she shifted slightly to get away from his touch. Well, she tried to shift away, but Tate's hands clamped around her biceps, right over the bullet wound from the night she was abducted, and she sucked in a pained breath.

"Why do you have cuts on your back? Why are your

wrists and ankles all torn up? Why did you have a rock tied around your ankle?"

The rapid-fire questions were too much for her stressed-out brain to answer. She was tired, she was in pain, she was afraid, and all she wanted was to be surrounded by people she loved, but instead, she was with a man who she'd had sex with and then been tossed aside like trash.

If anyone should be angry here it should be her.

Okay, he didn't have to offer more than their agreed upon one night, and she could have imagined that he had felt anything at all for her beyond lust and attraction, but he hadn't had to be cruel about it.

Assuming he was angry, she might have said something she shouldn't, Scarlett gave her head a small shake. "I didn't tell him anything," she whispered.

There was no exclamation of agreement or reassurances that he knew she was loyal to her team and would never betray any of them. Instead, there was an almost … suspicious pause. Like he doubted that. Doubted her.

Still, he didn't say anything, and for that Scarlett was eternally grateful.

While she would have loved to be able to brush away his hand when he gripped her elbow and pulled her to her feet, she knew she was running on empty and needed his help. Her skillset was woefully inadequate to deal with any of this, and if she wanted to get home alive, she needed his help.

Even if he seemed reluctant to be here.

Thinking that he didn't really want to be here rescuing

her made Scarlett feel horribly guilty. Whatever their history he *had* come, risking his life in the process.

Reaching out, she rested a hand on his forearm, frowning when his other hand moved slightly, shifting his weapon as though he thought she was about to tell him she'd noticed an imminent threat. "It's okay, I didn't see anything, I just wanted to say thank you for coming to get me. I thought I was going to die in that hellhole."

His unusual eyes looked at her, but there was no hint of the warmth she'd felt that night they'd spent together. If she didn't know it had happened, she would have been tempted to think she had dreamed that whole thing up.

The man she'd spent that night with was funny, smart, gentle, a tender lover, and easy to talk to. He was warm and open, and they'd had fun together. The man she'd seen afterward and the one here right now were the opposite. Cold, hard, and dangerous.

This man reminded her of the ones who worked for Raul.

A cold shiver rocketed through her, and for the first time, Scarlett realized she was still naked. Of course, she'd known she hadn't been given clothes after she'd been whipped, and the only way he could have seen some of her wounds was because her body was bare for all to see, but somehow, it hadn't sunk in until this moment.

Suddenly feeling small, vulnerable, and oh so very exhausted, she swayed and then wrapped her arms around herself, doing her best to shield what she could.

Instead of offering her something to cover herself like she thought he would have, Tate merely grabbed her hand

and dragged her toward the house. "You do exactly what I tell you when I tell you to do it, or else," he growled.

Taken aback by the viciousness in his tone, Scarlett flinched. "I'm not stupid, Tate," she murmured. "I know this is your skill set, not mine. I won't do anything to get either of us killed."

He merely huffed, then began to drag her along with him.

Moving much too fast for her shorter legs to keep up with even if she wasn't teetering on the edge of complete exhaustion, Scarlett did her best to shove everything else away and concentrate on the fact that she was going home.

So what if Tate wasn't pleased he'd had to traipse through the Mexican jungle to find a woman he had slept with and obviously regretted it. At least at the end of all of this, they'd be home.

Well not home to her house.

After what had happened, there she never wanted to step foot in the place again. She'd put it on the market as soon as she could and look for another place to buy.

Assuming they were going to the house to meet up with the rest of his team when they bypassed the building and instead headed down toward the front gates, she wondered what was going on.

"Aren't we going inside?" she asked. Not that she particularly wanted to go back inside the house, but she did want to get somewhere she didn't feel as exposed.

"No."

Ooookay.

More than a single-word answer would help.

What exactly was Tate's problem?

So, she might have wanted more than one night with him. Did that really make her such an awful person that she deserved to be treated like this?

Reaching the end of her rope, Scarlett dug her heels in. "What does that mean? I don't understand. You got Raul Castillo, didn't you? Why can't we go inside and wait for whatever ride home you and your team have organized?"

With what could only be described as an irritated grunt, Tate spun around, grabbed her off her feet, threw her over his shoulder, and took off at a dead run toward the front gates of Raul's estate.

Why did she get the feeling that something more was happening here than she was aware of? Tate's anger seemed directed specifically at her, not the situation, and not the weapons trafficker who had abducted her.

It shouldn't hurt so much.

Scarlett knew that fairytales were just that. Stories.

They weren't real.

In real life, you didn't fall madly in love, you didn't form an instantaneous connection with a man you didn't know just because you locked gazes with him.

There were no happy endings.

There was nothing but loneliness.

* * *

JANUARY 12TH

6:31 P.M.

. . .

What game are you trying to play with me, little traitor?

As he ran with Scarlett draped over his shoulder, Tate felt uneasy. A sensation he hated. He liked to be in control of himself and his environment, and when something happened to shake up that control, it always threw him.

Right now, nothing seemed to be adding up.

Scarlett certainly wasn't acting like she had been at Raul Castillo's of her own free will. The wounds on her body told a story, and it wasn't one of a woman who had decided to betray her team and her country and sell secrets to the enemy.

If she and Raul had a business arrangement, then why had she been tortured?

Those wounds on her back couldn't be self-inflicted. Not possible. And the ones on her wrists and ankles were similar to those he'd seen before when a victim had been restrained and tortured.

And she had been about to be murdered, horribly, when he and his team had shown up. There was no reason Raul would have had to do that if Scarlett had been there to do what she'd said she was in the email that had been found.

Had she gotten cold feet?

Decided that she couldn't go through with it after all?

From what they knew of Raul Castillo, the man wasn't a sadist, he didn't get off on torturing people. More businessman than anything else, Raul appeared to do what he did because he liked the money, excitement, and living his life on the edge. There were no accounts of him crossing those he did business with, it was one of the things that made him so successful. You knew what you were getting with him. While he might rip you off price-wise, he wasn't going to double-cross you. Raul wanted to have a good reputation with his potential clientele.

The idea of him going off the deep end with Scarlett made zero sense.

Then again, none of this made sense.

Having put enough distance between them and the mansion, Tate slowed to a walk, checking around them to ensure they were safe. Once he was convinced they hadn't been followed and could wait things out until the extraction time in the early hours of tomorrow morning, he stopped.

While he'd heard her small grunts and moans of pain as he ran full out through the thick jungle, Scarlett hadn't protested, hadn't asked him to stop, hadn't complained. She'd just hung off his shoulder like she didn't have the energy to do anything else.

There had been a moment when he first got her on her feet, when he thought she was going to try something stupid. Something like trying to kill him in a desperate bid to escape her fate.

But she hadn't.

She'd thanked him.

Thanked him.

Why would she do that?

Did she regret her choices and was happy to go home and face the consequences, even if they were life in prison because at least she was alive?

As much as he'd like to believe that this was all some big misunderstanding, it was there in black and white. In Scarlett's own words, she'd said she wanted to sell the

Reactivator and had negotiated a price of just under five million dollars.

No matter that there was a part of him that wanted to protect her, wrap her up in his arms, and soothe the suffering she had endured, he had to remember that she was not to be trusted. She was a traitor, she'd betrayed her team, Prey, and her country.

Whatever game she was playing he wasn't going to fall for it.

With that in mind, he set the woman on the ground in front of him and immediately felt gut-punched when he saw her beautiful face was streaked with tears.

She made no move to hide the fact that she'd been crying, but he could see the pain in her big brown eyes. There was confusion and a tiny hint of anger, maybe at being caught. But it was the relief that made him want to second-guess everything he knew to be true.

Why was she so relieved to have been found?

The only logical explanation was that she was an innocent victim, but he knew that wasn't the case.

Acting.

That had to be it.

She was trying to con him.

Nice try, sweetheart, but it's not happening.

Instead of saying that aloud, he merely pulled his pack off his back, unzipped it, and rifled through it in search of his first aid kit. Traitor or not, Scarlett was injured, and he'd need to attend to those wounds if he wanted her fit and healthy to stand trial once she was returned home.

When he had his kit open and everything he needed laid

out, he turned to find Scarlett standing right where he'd put her. There was a glassiness to her eyes that he didn't like, and she was worrying her bottom lip just like she had that first night when she'd been all adorably nervous.

At least he'd thought she was nervous, now he wasn't so sure. The woman had mad acting skills, he'd give her that.

"Need to clean your wounds. Out here they're just asking for infection to set in." It was only seven hours to exfil, but he wasn't taking any chances.

"Raul was giving me antibiotics," Scarlett whispered as he knelt before her, took one of her hands, and began to clean her wrist.

For a second he stilled. Why would the man order injuries to be inflicted on her but then give her antibiotics to keep her healthy?

He wouldn't.

Another lie.

Seemed like Scarlett just couldn't help herself.

Offering a grunt as a reply, neither spoke as he cleaned and bandaged one wrist and then the other. Scarlett didn't attempt to help him in any way, but she also didn't try to move away. Her winces were small, and although he could see her perfect white teeth biting into her pale bottom lip, she didn't make a single sound even though he knew he was hurting her.

Much as a part of him would like to say he was rough as he dealt with the traitor's injuries, he wasn't.

Couldn't make himself be.

In fact, he flinched along with her as he made sure

each open wound was clean before slathering it with antibiotic cream and wrapping them in bandages.

When her wrists and ankles were done, he skimmed his hands up over her hips, wishing her skin wasn't every bit as soft as he remembered. Every bit as soft as he'd dreamed about. It was like silk, and his fingers glided over it. Not even the dark mottling of blacks, blues, and purples could diminish its beauty.

Although seeing the marks on this woman, knowing they were caused by someone hitting her, filled him with a deep-seated rage that was as annoying as it was ridiculous.

Whatever was going on, Scarlett had gotten herself into this mess, she had no one to blame but herself if things had gotten out of hand.

Still, his touch was gentle as he turned her so he could work on cleaning the wounds on her back. They were brutal, angry, and red raw, they'd leave scars, permanent reminders of what had happened. After years as a SEAL, Tate knew the wounds were caused by a whip, and rage bubbled inside him at the thought of Scarlett being subjected to something like that.

It didn't seem to matter what his head knew about this woman, his body could only remember the amazing night they spent together and craved more. All he wanted to do was wrap Scarlett up in his arms and kiss her until the tears shimmering in her eyes disappeared.

Irritated with himself, Tate quickly cleaned each of the wounds and smeared them with the cream. Then he pulled out a vial of painkillers and a syringe. While, in theory, he liked the idea of Scarlett suffering for her crimes, he wasn't a monster. She'd been beaten and whipped, she was in pain, he was giving her the damn drugs.

"You allergic to anything?" he asked, doing nothing to hide the bite in his tone.

Looking over her shoulder at him, Scarlett's eyes grew wide when she saw the syringe in his hand and tried to scramble away from him.

Thinking she was going to try to make a run for it, he gripped her wrist in a hold he knew had to hurt her. Not his intention, but he wasn't letting her go. "Just painkillers," he told her, wondering if she'd been drugged while she was with Raul, and that was why she looked on the verge of freaking out.

Actually, she was beyond freaking out.

He wouldn't have thought it possible for her skin to go a paler shade than it had been when he found her, but it did. She was more gray than white, and she was panting and struggling to get out of his grip, which was ridiculous, she wasn't getting away unless he let her, and he had no intention of doing that.

"I … d-don't … need … th-them," Scarlett stammered, on the verge of hyperventilating.

"Need them or not, you're getting them." He had no time for a bout of hysterics. All he wanted was to wait out the next few hours, then get on that helo, get home, and hand his prisoner over to face her fate.

Yanking Scarlett up against his body so he could hold her in place much the same way he had in the pool, he swiped the bicep that hadn't been shot with an alcohol wipe, then administered the drug.

As soon as he disposed of the syringe, Scarlett seemed to calm down. At least, he thought she had, but when he sat her down on a large rock and knelt in front of her, he realized she was holding her breath.

"What are you doing?" he demanded, not in the mood for more games.

She merely shook her head and waited. After what had to be a full minute she finally relaxed, puffing out the breath she'd been holding. "It's okay, I'm okay," she murmured, although more for her own benefit than his, he suspected.

"You'll be thanking me for those painkillers in a minute because I'm going to have to stitch up your gunshot wound." Despite it likely being the cause of the blood that had been found in her closet, the wound still looked open and unhealed five days later.

Scarlett just nodded and then tucked her chin to her chest, her other arm wrapping around her middle as she waited for him to tend to the wound, and once again he was struck by how not right this whole situation felt.

Whatever was going on, whatever he was missing, whatever was running through Scarlett's head right now, one thing was for certain. He was not letting the little traitor out of his sight, not even for a second, because he didn't believe she wasn't playing him and had some sort of trick up her sleeve.

CHAPTER FIVE

January 12th
7:24 P.M.

HONESTLY, Scarlett couldn't care how badly it hurt stitching up the gunshot wound that had been poked and prodded so many times while Raul was holding her prisoner that she was surprised there wasn't a huge hole going all the way through from the entry wound to the exit one.

Pain she could handle.

Pain was nothing.

Pain was easy in comparison to …

Nope.

Not going there yet. Or ever.

Because she had zero plans to include Raul drugging her in her report when they got home. It didn't serve any purpose. While she had begged and pleaded just as Raul told her she would, she hadn't given up any intel.

Nobody needed to know about it.

Although, when Tate had pulled out that syringe for a second there, her mind had thrown her back into that dungeon torture chamber. Chained up, drugged, and afraid, the arousal that had coursed through her body was unlike anything she had ever experienced before.

Desire was normal, and being turned on was normal. She'd dated before, been engaged twice, and thought she was in love more times than that. There had been plenty of times in bed she had thought she would die if she wasn't given an orgasm immediately, but it had been nothing close to what that drug had induced.

It was like being set on fire. The throbbing between her legs had been so strong it was painful. The need to orgasm was like a physical being low in her belly trying to claw its way out.

Only there had been nothing to quench the fire raging inside her.

No matter how much she begged and pleaded for release, no one had touched her. They'd just stood around and laughed at her torment, a few of them had gotten themselves off to the sounds of her breathy moans, the thrusting of her hips seeking relief that wasn't there. A few had squirted the evidence of their own orgasms onto her naked body.

Hours.

Her torment had lasted for hours.

Scarlett had no idea how she hadn't blurted out the formula for the Reactivator for an orgasm that might bring her a little relief.

"Why are you still hyperventilating? It's done," Tate snapped.

Blinking, she looked down at her arm where a small, ragged row of black stitches closed the entry wound. Since Tate had a roll of bandages in his hand, she assumed he had likewise stitched the exit wound.

Trapped in her memories, Scarlett didn't remember a single thing about him stitching up the wound.

"You didn't flinch once. You were too lost in thought," Tate accused like he had the ability to read her mind. "What were you thinking about hard enough that you didn't even notice your wounds being stitched?"

"Nothing," she lied, praying he believed her. People knowing she had been tortured was one thing, but she didn't want them to know how she had begged Raul Castillo's dirty, despicable men for orgasms her brain hadn't even wanted, only her body had craved them.

From the look on his face, he did not believe her.

Nothing she could do about that.

There was no way he could possibly know all the things Raul had done to her. As long as he believed she had just been physically tortured then neither he nor anyone else would have cause to think there had been more to it.

His eyes narrowed, and he looked angry all over again. How could he be so angry with her and yet touch her so gently? Maybe it wasn't her he was angry with? Maybe just at the whole situation?

Too tired to attempt to figure it out, between being tortured and in pain and half-starved, she'd had little sleep since being kidnapped. A hot shower, a hot cup of tea, and a long sleep in a nice comfortable bed. That was what she craved right now.

"What time is the exfil?" she asked.

Something danced through Tate's eyes that she couldn't interpret. "Oh two hundred."

"What location?" If the worst happened and they were split up, Scarlett wanted to make sure she knew the coordinates of the exfil, or at least the general direction, since she didn't have anything on her that would help her find it. Which reminded her she was still naked. Just because Tate had seen her naked the night they spent together, it didn't mean she was comfortable with him seeing her body now. They weren't together, he'd been rude and cruel to her after their time together, and he didn't seem to want to be here now. The imbalance of power with him fully clothed and her completely bare was making her uncomfortable. "Umm, do you have something I could wear, please?"

A grunt was the only response she got, but thankfully, he packed away his med kit and pulled a long-sleeve black T-shirt and a pair of pants from his pack.

When he handed them to her, she snatched them up greedily and quickly pulled the T-shirt over her head. It was several sizes too big, but she didn't care, it covered her body and gave her back a little of her sense of control over herself and her surroundings. Likewise, the pants were way too big, so she rolled them up several times, both at the cuffs and the waistband. Not perfect, especially if they had to run, but better than nothing.

Much better than nothing.

With clothing taken care of, that brought her to her next pressing need.

Embarrassment made her cheeks turn red. "Umm, I'm just going to go over there and ..." Scarlett trailed off, not wanting to say out loud that she had to go pee.

With eyes narrowing, the look he threw her was close to a glare, and she had no idea why he was being such an angry, callous jerk.

Did he have no compassion for what she'd just been through?

Even if he hated her, she was a human being who had been abducted and tortured. Surely, he could keep his personal feelings out of it long enough to get her home. Then, if he chose, he could go right on back to hating her.

"I'll go with you," he said, already hefting his pack onto his back.

What did he need that for?

She was only going to go behind a tree to get a little privacy. After being paraded around the basement naked for days, then out through the house to the pool so Raul could threaten to have her drowned if she didn't tell him what he wanted to know, a little privacy didn't seem like a big deal.

Too exhausted to argue, she merely nodded and headed for the trees.

Maybe she was being too hard on Tate. She only knew bedroom Tate, not in the field Tate. Maybe he was always this aggressive on an op. Other than assuming they were in Mexico because that's where Raul was rumored to reside, she knew nothing about their location, the number of men here, or anything else pertaining to the op.

"Could you umm … close your eyes?" she asked when she reached for the waistband of her borrowed pants. Tate might be just trying to be vigilant since she was injured and unarmed and his responsibility right now, but she didn't want him watching her pee.

For a moment, she thought he was going to refuse, but then his eyes closed, and she quickly shoved her pants down and squatted awkwardly to do her business.

It wasn't until she was yanking the pants back up that she realized she had never asked. "Raul? Did your team get him?" If he was in the SEAL's custody, she wouldn't have to worry about him coming after her again, and maybe she could survive this whole ordeal with her sanity intact.

"Nope. He bailed in a helo," Tate answered, opening his eyes and pinning her with a harsh stare she didn't understand.

"Left?" Now that she thought about it, she remembered being out by the pool and everyone, Raul included, suddenly running off, leaving her standing there. Not long after that, Tate showed up and saved her life. Somehow, Raul had known the SEALs were coming before they had arrived and fled so he wouldn't be captured.

"Yeah, left you behind."

Thankfully. Because if he'd taken her with him, she might never have been heard from again.

Fighting a yawn, Scarlett did her best to push away her hurt that a man she'd felt such a strong connection to was treating her so poorly, especially when she needed a little coddling right now. "So, what next?"

Giving her a long, hard, assessing look, Tate finally

hooked a thumb behind him. "There's a cave just back there. We're going to wait in there for a few hours. You can get some sleep and then we'll head to the extraction point."

"Then we can go home," she said with a happy sigh. She couldn't wait. All Scarlett wanted to do was put this whole nightmare behind her.

Tate gave her a weird look. "Yeah. Home."

"I can't wait."

A grunt was the only response she got.

"Lead the way to our cave, a nap sounds perfect."

"You go first," he said quickly, and she could have sworn his hands tightened on his weapon like he was almost afraid to let her out of his sight, even for a second.

Which made zero sense.

Not that any of this made sense.

How did Raul even find out about the Reactivator? No one outside a few people at Prey knew anything about it. Why would any of them pass that intel along to a known weapons trafficker?

Right now, she didn't have the energy to figure it out. Once she got home and got some rest, she, her team, and Prey would figure it all out.

JANUARY 13TH

1:02 A.M.

THIS WOMAN WAS MAKING him question everything.

Tate knew the facts and had read the email for himself. In it, Scarlett offered the sale of the Reactivator for five million dollars.

Those facts were not in question.

Yet everything about Scarlett and her demeanor screamed that she was innocent and had no idea what was going on.

The problem was, for every benefit of the doubt he wanted to give her and prove her innocence, there was a counterargument.

She'd blanked out while he was stitching up her gunshot wound—medical treatment wouldn't be high on the priority list once she was taken into custody, and he didn't want the wound getting infected—which could have indicated she was reliving her trauma. Or she could have been figuring out a plan on how she was going to handle the fallout of her decisions.

When she had learned Raul Castillo was not in custody, she had seemed relieved. But was it because she thought she was safe now or because no one was around to contradict whatever story she was going to weave?

She was obviously confused by his anger toward her, although she was yet to confront him on it, but even that wasn't proof of her innocence. Scarlett had no idea the email had been found, she probably thought she had wiped her trail clean.

Even the fact she had immediately curled into him the second she fell asleep could show that she had nothing to hide, or she could be attempting to play him, hoping she could manipulate him into being on her side.

Not going to work, little traitor.

What was working was her making him doubt himself and his abilities. Tate had never had this problem before, doubted the intel, or doubted a target he was sent in to retrieve or neutralize.

But Scarlett made him doubt everything.

To the point where he was considering if it was time for him to get out of the game. Maybe he'd been in too long and was starting to lose what had made him a good SEAL.

Because every atom in his body screamed at him that Scarlett was innocent.

Only she wasn't.

What good was he going to be as a SEAL if he could no longer trust his instincts?

Instincts kept you alive, kept your team alive, and brought you home safe after completing a successful mission.

Without them he was useless.

One night of sex with this woman and everything he had always believed he was good at had been thrown out the window.

Frustration at himself only stoked the fires of his anger at Scarlett. And then again at himself because he had done absolutely nothing to move her when she had snuggled into his side, draping herself across his chest just as she'd done that night.

He hadn't pushed her away then and he didn't now.

Stupid.

Did he need to be beaten over the head with it?

Scarlett Madden had sold out her team, employer, and country. She'd been lying to him from the beginning, and he had no doubts that her attempts to reach out were because she thought it would be helpful to have a SEAL on her side.

I'm not on your side, little traitor. Not ever.

It was time to wake Scarlett if they wanted to get to the exfil point. Actually, he should have woken her fifteen minutes ago, but for some reason, he'd been unable to disturb her sleep when she so obviously needed the rest.

Now they were out of time, Scarlett could sleep on the plane. She would if she knew what was good for her because once she got back Stateside and was taken into custody she wouldn't be getting much rest.

"Wake up, Scarlett," he ordered as he shook her a little rougher than was necessary.

"Tate?" she mumbled as she blinked sleepily and stretched.

Damn. Why did she have to look so good in his clothes? Why did she have to look so good, period? Even exhausted with dark smudges under her eyes, dirty with tangled hair, and cuts and bruises littering her body, she looked gorgeous.

Too gorgeous.

Was she used to using her body to get what she wanted?

He had a feeling she'd grown up every bit as lonely as he had, but what was she prepared to do to gain a little companionship?

"Time to leave," he snapped, annoyed that no matter how many times he reminded himself that this woman was the enemy, that she had betrayed him and their country, his body couldn't seem to get the memo.

Too many months spent lusting after her.

That was the problem.

“Okay,” she agreed. “Can I pee first?”

Before he’d let her go to sleep, he’d made sure she was hydrated. He was surprised she’d managed to sleep for a few hours without having to get up given how much water she’d drunk.

Watching her guzzle down that water from his bottle, then lick the last drop off her plump bottom lip had thrown his system into a frenzy. His body had gone haywire, and all the blood had dropped south as he remembered those lips and what they felt like worshipping his body.

“Umm, you can stay close if you're worried about someone finding us,” Scarlett continued when he didn't answer.

It’s not Raul’s men I'm worried about, little traitor, it’s you doing a runner.

“Make it quick,” he snapped. When she didn't move, he growled, “Hurry up.”

Turned out it was only his common sense that was worried about her running because while he did stand, he didn't follow her as she scrambled to her feet and scurried off behind a tree.

Scarlett wasn’t going to run.

For all his talk of no longer trusting his instincts, he knew for certain she wasn’t going anywhere.

Maybe she honestly thought she was going to get away with this.

Less than a minute later, she popped back around the tree and stood there waiting for him. In his much too big for her small frame clothes, she should have looked ridiculous, but she didn't. She looked far too sexy for her own good.

It was a mile to the extraction point, and he'd already let her sleep later than he should. With the near-pitch darkness of the thick jungle, Scarlett was going to struggle to see where he was going without the benefit of the night vision goggles he was snapping on as he turned off the flashlight.

"I don't have spare shoes, but you need something to cover your feet," he muttered, irked that he cared about her comfort after what she'd done.

"It's okay, I'll be fine," Scarlett assured him, but he ignored her and dug through his pack to find a spare pair of socks. Again, they'd be too big and wouldn't offer much protection from the terrain, but they were better than nothing.

Once his pack was on his back and his weapon slung across his shoulder, he went to her and knelt at her feet.

She sucked in a breath as his hands swept across her ankle as he pulled a sock onto one of her feet. When he looked up at her, she was chewing on her bottom lip again, looking near angelic in the green glow of his NVGs.

Why did she have to act all sweet and innocent when he knew it was just that? An act.

Quickly, he slipped on the other sock and then stood. It would be hard walking side by side through the jungle, but he didn't want her behind him, and he was the one who knew where they were going so he had to lead.

With a sigh, he knew there was only one way they could do this even if he didn't want to.

"Hold onto my waistband," he ordered, stepping in front of her. "And don't let go." Despite what he knew about her, he didn't want to shoot her if she tried anything stupid.

Not that it seemed she wanted to.

Scarlett quickly looped her fingers through his waistband and clung to him with such trust he once again was swamped by the feeling that this woman had no clue what she was in the middle of.

Not wanting to go over the same thoughts he'd had for hours as he watched Scarlett sleep, Tate set a punishing pace as they headed for the exfil location.

To her credit, Scarlett kept up despite the exhaustion that had only been kept at bay by her nap. She didn't complain or waste energy she didn't have peppering him with questions. Just trusted that he knew where he was going and would get her safely home.

Your trust is misplaced, sweetheart.

While he would get her home, she was hardly going to be safe once she got there. Given the charges she'd face, she would be held indefinitely without access to the usual safeguards for suspects. Scarlett would be living out the rest of her life behind bars in a maximum-security prison. If she was that lucky. Otherwise, she would be squirreled away at some black site hardly anybody knew about.

Feeling sorry for her was stupid. Nobody had forced her to make these choices, she'd known the risks and gone ahead anyway. There was not a single person Scarlett could blame for her predicament other than herself.

So why, when they reached a small clearing and he

saw the helo sitting waiting for them, did he feel a rush of protectiveness?

Of pity for this woman's fate?

Once they were onboard, all eyes swung in their direction, a litany of non-verbalized questions filling his teammates' eyes.

Obviously sensing the hostility directed squarely at her from the rest of his team, Scarlett inched closer as though he were her only form of protection.

I'm not going to save you, little traitor. You're on your own in this mess you created.

CHAPTER SIX

January 13th
4:56 A.M.

WHY DID everybody seem to hate her?

By the time the helo touched down back home, Scarlett was more confused than she'd been when she first realized it was Tate and not a Prey team who had saved her.

It was weird, and she had tried her best not to take it personally, but it was like she had the plague or something. Not only did no one on Tate's team seem to want to get too close to her, but they had also remained on edge the entire flight.

Now, sure, she wasn't a field operative, the lab was where she was most at home, but she was pretty sure that once a team was on a helo flying home, they didn't sit with their weapons at the ready as though a threat was about to jump out at any second.

Although she hated to admit it and certainly didn't understand it, it was almost like they believed *she* was the threat.

Which was totally crazy.

As far as threats went, she had to be bottom of the barrel. Scarlett was pretty sure Raul Castillo would back that up.

The helo landed at Prey's West Coast office, and it felt good to be back on solid ground. Metaphorically speaking since she had no problem with flying. But she was back home now, and she needed to be surrounded by the people who loved her for a little post-kidnapping coddling.

When she stood and looked out the window, Scarlett was surprised to see that none of her team was there waiting for her.

Weird.

None of the retired SEAL guys who ran the West Coast office were there either.

Double weird.

Her team was like the sisters she had always wished she had when she was a lonely little girl, and they had grown even closer after she lost her brother eighteen months ago. The guys were absolute surrogate brothers, and she loved them dearly and their families, too. Call her a loser, but she'd rather babysit their sweet little kiddies than go out to a bar or a club.

A home and a family, people who were hers forever, who could never be taken away from her, that's what she wanted above all else.

There was a moment where she thought the man who

stood so close to her back she could practically feel the warmth emanating from him might be the answer, but obviously she'd been wrong.

Oh well, lesson learned.

But she wasn't giving up.

Happiness, family, love, it was out there somewhere, and she would find it. One day she'd belong somewhere, be loved by people who accepted her for who she was and who would never walk away from her.

The tension continued to pulse through the helo as she stepped down, aware that Tate and his team remained close and attentive as though they were still on duty.

Deciding to ignore their strange behavior, it wasn't really important right now, she started toward the door leading to a lift that would take them down off the roof. Scarlett startled when two men dressed in crisp black suits approached.

For a moment, the contrast of their black suits and white shirts made her think of Raul and panic sparked to life inside her.

Instinct had her taking a step back, but she bumped into Tate who was still standing close, and his large hand clamped around her bicep, right over her gunshot wound, making her wince.

"Ma'am, please come with us," one of the suits said, his hand hovering above his weapon, and with a shocked gasp Scarlett realized that every single man on the roof with her either had a weapon pointed at her, or their hand close enough to draw their weapon.

Panic grew.

What was going on?

Why were they treating her like the enemy?

Where were her team, and her Prey guys?

There wasn't a single friendly face, and the uneasy feeling that had been growing inside her ever since she was met with Tate's open hostility flared so strongly that she was almost positive she was about to throw up.

"Don't make this harder on yourself than it has to be," Tate murmured above her.

Harder than it had to be?

That made no sense.

"What's going on?" she asked, hating that her voice trembled. Showing weakness in front of men like this was not a good idea, but she was too scared to rid the shakes from either her voice or her body.

Nobody offered her any answers, and the two suits came up to flank her, walking her between them across the roof and into the lift. Tate and his team didn't follow them, and honestly, she didn't want them to.

Whatever lingering feelings she'd had for Tate were gone.

He wasn't on her side.

He was the enemy.

These men were too.

Were they Raul's?

Did he have the kind of reach to have her … taken into custody?

Is that what was happening here?

Okay, she hadn't been cuffed, but it was more than obvious that she was considered a threat.

Instead of being taken to the main office levels or the lab, they stopped at the floor used for interrogations. If she had any energy left for humor, she would have reminded herself she was lucky she hadn't been taken to the level that contained holding cells. While nothing like Raul's dungeon torture chamber, they weren't pleasant rooms, and she didn't want to find herself locked in one.

Marched down the hall, she was taken into an interrogation room and left alone as the two suits disappeared. The hard metal chair only aggravated her beaten and tortured body, and her dreams of a hot shower, comfort food, and a soft bed seemed to drift further away.

No one from Prey was here, although since she was in the building, they had to know she was here.

That hurt.

Abandoned.

Again.

The people she needed never seemed to be there for her when she was at her lowest.

In the last few days, she'd had the safety of her home shattered, killed a man, been drugged and abducted, held captive, tortured, beaten, whipped, and drugged again. Was it too much to ask to at least have someone who cared about her here at her back?

Although she guessed their absence only proved they never really cared about her.

When the door edged open, Scarlett forced away her fear, ready to demand answers, but it wasn't the suits, it was Dora Hibbert, the office receptionist.

Not who she had expected.

Creeping into the room, the woman quickly set a steaming cup of tea and a sandwich on the rickety metal table. "Sorry, it's not much, but I'm sure you must be starving. I made you some tea, I know how much you love it."

Touched by the only little bit of kindness she'd been shown, Scarlett promptly burst into tears. "Thank you," she managed to get out. "Do you know why I'm being treated like this? Do you know what they think I did?"

A hand touched her shoulder, squeezing gently. "I don't know, but whatever it is I know you didn't do it. You're the kindest, sweetest, most generous woman I have ever met. You're nice to *every*one. You care about everyone. I have to go, I'm not supposed to be in here, I just … couldn't let them keep you here with nothing to eat or drink."

"Thank you," she whispered again, doing her best to get her tears under control. She was obviously in hot water, but she had no idea why. If she was going to be accused of something, she couldn't show any weakness, and tears were a definite weakness.

After offering her an encouraging smile, Dora slipped away, and Scarlett quickly forced down the sandwich, knowing that as part of the interrogation she was about to be subjected to, she would be denied water, food, sleep, and painkillers.

Ten minutes later, the door to her interrogation room opened, and the suits strolled in. They both eyed the empty sandwich wrapper and the cup of tea she clutched in her hands, but neither commented.

"Ms. Madden, we need you to answer a few questions," one of them said.

Gathering strength she hadn't had to reach for in a long time, Scarlett set down her cup of tea and met their gazes squarely. She hadn't done anything wrong, she had the money to pay for a lawyer if she needed one, and she had plenty of practice facing problems alone.

She had this.

Or at least, she'd pretend she did until she convinced herself it was true.

"Why am I here?" she demanded, pleased her voice came out strong and steady.

"What is your relationship to Raul Castillo?" one suit asked.

Feeling the blood drain from her face, Scarlett curled her now trembling fingers around the edge of the table, letting the bite of the sharp metal keep her sane. "My relationship to him? You make it sound like we're lovers or something." Her stomach rolled and she pressed a hand to it in the vain hopes of keeping the sandwich down. "The man is a monster who kidnapped me, tortured me, and demanded I give him the formula for the Reactivator. Which I did not do," she said, proud that it was the truth. "I don't know what you think I did, but I do know I'm happy to do whatever it takes to convince you you're wrong because a dangerous man wants a drug I helped create, and no way is he getting his hands on it."

* * *

JANUARY 13TH

5:04 P.M.

HE SHOULD HAVE LEFT ALREADY.

Gone home and washed his hands of this entire situation.

Yet Tate was still there. Still in the Prey building, still watching the feed from the camera set up in Scarlett's interrogation room, still feeling like something wasn't right.

Leaving with the rest of his team felt like … leaving Scarlett to the wolves.

Knowing that she was getting what she deserved, and that if she had been tortured because she'd been double-crossed then it was her fault, didn't seem to make one iota of difference.

When he'd tried to go home it was like his body physically could not leave the building as long as Scarlett was being kept in an interrogation room.

The weirdest sensation.

After Scarlett had been taken into custody, he and his team had debriefed in an empty conference room. Then they'd grabbed their stuff and headed to their vehicles parked in the underground garage. Only as soon as he got in the car his hands got all sweaty, his pulse sped up, and it seemed near impossible to draw a full breath.

Almost like he was having a panic attack.

Absolutely as annoying as it was weird.

Lying to his team that he wanted to stay because something in his gut was telling him something was off felt wrong on so many levels. You didn't lie to your team, not if you wanted to make it home alive. Trust was imperative in their world, you had to know the guys watching your back had you one hundred percent. It could mean the difference between life and death in the field.

But his ability to trust and accept others' trust in return had been shattered by his father's recent ordeal, and he found that lying had been easier than it should be.

No one had questioned him when he'd said he was going to stay and see what happened and headed back inside. Just because no one had questioned him didn't mean he didn't see the questions in their eyes.

Had felt those unasked questions the entire ride back home.

They knew something was up between him and Scarlett, and they were wondering why he was interested in a traitor.

Only Scarlett had consistently denied being a traitor.

She'd shed a few tears, and her body had shaken, whether from exhaustion, fear, or pain he wasn't certain, but she had answered every question, maintained her innocence, kept her back straight and her head up, taking on each increasingly harsher interview session.

Was it possible she was really innocent?

The email said otherwise but …

Scarlett didn't act guilty.

Her profile didn't match with someone who would sell sensitive information for money either. They'd done a deep dive into her past when they were given this mission, and from the background check none of this added up.

Scarlett and her twin brother had been mostly raised by their paternal grandparents up until the age of thirteen while their parents served in the military. Their grandfather was also former military and it looked like Scarlett's life had been rough. Not abusive, but not a warm, loving environment to grow up in either.

After their grandparents' deaths and their parents' refusal to accept the offered honorable discharges, she and her brother went into the foster system. While there were no reports of abuse suffered, Scarlett and her brother were both bounced about often, sometimes winding up in a home together but oftentimes separated. Again, a lonely place to be even if not outright abusive.

As an adult, she had bucked against family pressure and gone to college instead of enlisting. That had gotten her shunned and contact with her brother had dwindled to virtually nothing after he did enlist. She'd been engaged twice before. She was lonely and from all reports a romantic at heart.

Bottom line was Scarlett Madden was desperate to be loved.

The exact reason he never should have touched her.

She wanted a family and a happy ever after, he wanted to remain single.

But it was her very profile that said she wasn't the kind of person who would do what she was being accused of. People desperate to be loved and accepted didn't usually throw away the only connections they had for money. Because love and acceptance were more important to them than money.

Was she possibly coerced into selling the formula for the Reactivator?

The idea had been bouncing around inside his head since they'd been sitting on the helo. It would explain why

Scarlett had been tortured—and the evidence on her body meant nobody could argue with that fact—and why she had been grateful to see him when he came to rescue her. Maybe she'd tried to go through with it and then found that she couldn't, and that was why Raul had turned on her.

Or maybe he was just reaching because he … wanted … her to be innocent.

Sighing, Tate raked his fingers through his hair and then rubbed at the tight muscles in the back of his neck. Tension had his entire body feeling like it had been twisted into knots.

When the door to the room he was holed up in watching the feed from Scarlett's interrogation room opened, he lifted his eyes to see who it was.

Chaos and King walked into the room. Both of them looked as exhausted and stressed out as he felt. Despite what Scarlett probably thought, everyone at Prey seemed to be on her side. Even with evidence to the contrary, nobody seemed to believe it. Every single person had wanted to be there for Scarlett, comfort her, reassure her, make sure she knew they believed in her, but the best thing they could do for her right now was let someone neutral handle the situation.

None of the Prey people could be neutral when it came to her.

Hell, he couldn't even be neutral when it came to Scarlett, leaving him feeling angry and helpless.

"Why are you still here?" Chaos growled. Despite the fact the man had a reputation of being easygoing and lighthearted, a lover of practical jokes that he sometimes took too far, right now, Chaos looked every bit the lethal warrior he was behind the jokester veneer.

Since there was no good answer he could give to that, Tate merely shrugged.

"She hasn't wavered in her story once." King said it as a challenge, but Tate had no intention of refuting it. That was true. Her story had zero inconsistencies no matter how many times she was asked to go over things. Either she had her lies memorized or she was telling the truth.

King had been a notorious playboy up until he met and fell in love with Faith Johnson, now Faith Voss. All it had taken was for him to meet the woman who would own his heart for his entire life to change. King and Faith were now happily married with a two-year-old daughter Indigo.

Was that how easy things could change?

Was it possible for falling in love to make everything different?

If he wasn't intent on lying to himself, would he admit that he already had feelings for Scarlett even if he'd done his best to shove her away?

Refusing to allow himself to continue down that path, Tate straightened and looked the two men in the eye. "Did you get the results of the polygraph?"

There had been no hesitation on Scarlett's part when she had been asked to take the lie detector, she had readily agreed. Eagerly even.

While not admissible in court because it was much too easy to fake it, passing the test would go a long way in helping convince everyone outside of Prey that something else was going on.

Instead of answering, the two men shared a look, and Tate felt his stomach drop.

If Scarlett had passed they would have been shouting it from the rooftops.

All that anger that had been dimming these last twelve hours as he listened to and watched Scarlett insist she was innocent over and over again suddenly flared back to life.

Of course she hadn't passed.

Of course she wasn't innocent.

She was a liar and a manipulator just like his former stepmother had been.

"She failed," he growled, surprised at how much that seemed to hurt. Maybe there had been a part of him that needed to know the only woman to ever have made him feel anything at all was not a traitor.

Anger sparked in King's gray-blue eyes. "Only one question. And not any to do with her guilt."

"Then what?" he demanded, completely confused. If she had passed when asked about her guilt, what had she lied about?

"A question regarding her torture," King replied.

There was genuine pain in Chaos' voice and his light green eyes when he spoke. "When asked if she gave up any information while being tortured there was a slight indication that she wasn't being completely truthful."

What did that mean?

Had Scarlett gone there intending to sell information or not?

If she hadn't, had she given intel up under torture?

Did this mean she was guilty or innocent?

And why the hell did he care so much?

CHAPTER SEVEN

January 14th
5:13 P.M.

"You're free to go."

Scarlett startled as the suit entered her interrogation room, this time leaving the door open behind him and uttering the words she'd been longing to hear.

Only they didn't mean as much as she'd thought they would.

Maybe because it was clear from his expression, he still thought she was guilty of making a deal with the notorious weapons trafficker to sell the Reactivator.

Rubbing tiredly at her temples, where a headache raged, Scarlett nodded and shoved to her feet. She was still dressed in Tate's borrowed clothes with no shoes on her feet. In the hours she'd been locked in there she'd been given nothing more than a couple of bottles of water to drink. The last time she'd eaten was the sandwich that

Dora had snuck in for her, and the painkillers from before they got on the helo had long since worn off.

Tired, in pain, hungry, and defeated.

Yep.

That pretty much summed it up.

Since she didn't know their names and had nothing to say to them even if she did, Scarlett merely shuffled on her ruined socks toward the door. Her body was stiff, muscles cramped from hours of just sitting, and right now, she didn't even care that the last time she'd been in her house she'd been shot and kidnapped, she just wanted to lock herself away from the rest of the world.

When her purse was shoved into her arms, she stared at it surprised. Must be more exhausted than she thought if she hadn't even considered that she would need her phone, keys, and wallet if she was going to get home.

Somehow, she made it to the lift and out onto the street. She used her Uber app to arrange a pickup and thankfully, the driver seemed too shocked by her disheveled appearance to attempt conversation.

Conversation was the last thing she wanted. Company too. While she might have needed her team and Prey family to rally around her earlier, now the sting of their betrayal ran too deep. Her team were the last people she wanted to see right now. If they thought she was capable of betraying not only them but their country, by giving an enemy an edge in war, then they had never been true friends to begin with.

It wasn't until she had paid the driver and hauled herself out of his vehicle that she realized the lights were on in her house.

Scarlett froze.

Just because nobody else believed her didn't mean she didn't know the truth.

She hadn't sold any information, she'd been kidnapped by Raul Castillo and tortured for that information. But even with the pain she'd gone through, she hadn't told the trafficker what he wanted to know.

Which meant he could come back for her.

Did he have more men in there waiting for her?

Before she could panic and try to call back the Uber, the front door to her place was thrown open and three women came bursting out.

Lucy Elrod, a month to the day younger than Scarlett's twenty-eight, with long blonde hair and light blue eyes, she hadn't allowed her epilepsy to rule her life. Cassidy "Cassie" Caddel, twenty-three, with brown hair and eyes, an actual genius who had graduated college before she hit her twenties with several degrees. Ella Whitlock, a twenty-seven-year-old musical prodigy with blonde hair and pretty green eyes.

Athena Team.

The people she loved the most in the world.

Her own little family where she finally felt like she belonged.

All ruined now.

When the three women ran toward her, Scarlett instinctively took a step back. She didn't want them there, didn't want to have more accusations thrown at her, especially by the people she thought would always have her back.

But they hadn't.

Their absence when she had been held for well over a day spoke volumes. Actually, it told her all she needed to know. They weren't her friends, they weren't the family she'd always wished for. They were nothing. And the last thing she wanted was for them to be there when she already felt raw and exposed.

Hurt flashed over Cassie's face, Ella looked confused, and Lucy looked angry.

"Are you okay?" Cassie asked, taking a tentative step forward even though Scarlett had wrapped her arms around her middle and stiffened, ready to run the second they hurled accusations at her.

"Of course she's not okay," the ever-practical Lucy said. The anger had faded a little, but it was still there, Scarlett could sense it.

Tears blurred her vision, and she did her best to hold them back. She was just so tired of having everyone's anger directed at her when she hadn't done anything wrong. After living through a horrific ordeal, all she wanted was someone to show her a little warmth and compassion. Heck, she'd take just a little ounce of kindness, but nope, all she kept getting was anger, and she was way too exhausted to deal with it.

"We were so worried about you," Ella said softly. The woman was all warmth, softness, and goodness, and even though Scarlett was closest to Lucy, Ella had always held a special place in her heart because of the light she shone so freely, so of all their betrayals hers seemed to hurt the most.

"Listen to me," Lucy said in that take-charge voice she used when she was close to the end of her patience.

Although she didn't want to, Scarlett found her gaze snapping to meet her friend's. The anger still glowed brightly in Lucy's blue eyes, but there was something else there, too. Something that made her long for the impossible. Something much too close to compassion for her to handle right now, so instead, she only stiffened further.

"We did not believe for one single second that you did what that email says you did," Lucy spoke clearly and firmly.

"Not for a second," Cassie echoed.

"Is that what you thought? That we believed you would do that?" Ella asked, hurt in her voice, and her green eyes filled with tears that turned out to be the straw that broke the camel's back.

Right then and there the meltdown that had been steadily building inside her since she woke up and realized someone was inside her house just detonated.

There in the street, Scarlett burst into noisy tears, her entire body shaking with the force of her sobs. Yeah, she had shed some tears when Tate had saved her from drowning in the pool on Raul's estate, but those tears had been filled with relief. Then she'd thought she was saved and her ordeal was over, little did she know it hadn't even come close to really beginning.

Now the pressure on her was too great. Too much had happened too close together, and she'd had no one by her side to help support her.

Arms wrapped around her, but her tears blinded her. Still, she didn't offer any resistance as her team somehow managed to get her inside despite the fact she was crying so hard her chest ached, and shaking so badly it felt like she was going to fall apart.

"Y-you didn't th-think I b-betrayed you?" she stammered as she was gently eased onto the couch, a warm fluffy blanket wrapped around her.

"I'm a little offended you would even think that," Lucy said in that straightforward way of hers.

"B-but you weren't th-there," Scarlett cried. If they believed she was innocent, why did they leave her to face the wolves all on her own when she was nothing but a helpless sheep in comparison to what she was up against?

"We wanted to be there, Scarlett," Cassie told her. "But we weren't allowed. Orders were everyone from Prey had to keep their distance. We all believe in you, the guys, too, they're super mad at being forced to stay away. They wanted to be here when you got home but we told them it might be too overwhelming for you after everything you've been through."

"Plus, we were a little selfish and wanted you all to ourselves," Ella added. "We got your back. Always."

"Someone not emotionally invested in you had to be the one to clear you," Lucy added. "Which is why orders were all Prey people had to stay away. It killed us. We've been terrified ever since I got your text asking for help."

"So, y-you don't think I w-was trying to sell o-our drug?" she asked, needing to hear it again if she had any hope of believing it.

"Not in this lifetime," Lucy answered.

"Not in any lifetime," Ella clarified.

"Like Ella said, we got your back," Cassie said. "All of

us. You know Prey is a family and we know you would never betray us like that."

"But there's some email I supposedly sent." Worried they didn't know all the details and that was why they believed in her, she dropped her gaze just in case they were about to back away from her now they knew.

"You didn't send that email," Lucy said fiercely.

Relieved, Scarlett felt like a weight had lifted off her shoulders. "I didn't," she agreed. "But somebody did."

"Someone who's trying to frame you," Cassie said, stating the only logical conclusion.

"But who? And why? And how am I going to prove it?" Just because her team believed in her didn't mean she was anywhere close to clearing her name.

* * *

JANUARY 14TH

5:50 P.M.

THERE WAS one thing Tate knew about Scarlett Madden with absolute certainty.

The woman had absolutely no idea how to pay attention to her surroundings.

He'd followed her out of Prey's building, watched her get into an Uber, got into his car, and tailed her on the drive home.

Of course, he was tailing her because he wanted to see where she was going to go and if she was going to meet up with anyone, nothing more personal. Likely the same reason she had been released rather than held in a cell where she belonged. So far, she hadn't cracked, hadn't changed so much as a single detail from her story, and if they wanted to get more proof of what she'd done, they needed to shake things up a little.

If Scarlett felt like she was being believed, then she would slip up.

When she did, he would be right there waiting.

No one else had tailed her, and he had to wonder if despite there being a discrepancy with her polygraph, maybe she had been cleared. After all, it wasn't beyond the realms of possibility that someone had set her up.

Despite being in prison serving a ten-year sentence for dealing drugs, his father was completely innocent. Well, his dad had turned into an addict, and he had married a dealer, but he was not guilty of the crimes he'd been charged with.

Could the same be true for Scarlett?

Knowing firsthand how badly it sucked to know the truth and have no one believe you, a surge of guilt had him tightening his grip on the steering wheel.

If Scarlett was innocent, he owed her a huge apology.

Major apology.

But that was still a big if as far as he was concerned.

Not that her team seemed to agree.

As Scarlett climbed out of the Uber, looking so utterly defeated, and so very small and vulnerable that he almost got out of his car and went to her, the door to her house was flung open.

Apparently, none of the four women had any idea they were being watched if their behavior was any indication.

There was not a single glance around, no attempts to hurry and get inside, no concerns that perhaps a sniper was waiting to pick them off, or a team of Raul's men close by.

If by chance Scarlett was telling the truth, then there was a leak at Prey who had set Scarlett up and had their own plans to sell the Reactivator to a dangerous weapons trafficker. If there was a leak at Prey, then no one on Athena Team was safe.

Raul Castillo was not a man to be messed with, and once he set his mind to something he was going to follow through. Either he would come after Scarlett again or he would target one of the other women.

Tate watched as Scarlett stiffened when her team came barreling toward her, taking a step back. Because she knew she had betrayed them and was feeling guilty? Or because she was hurt that they hadn't been there for her?

His dad had been lucky, Tate had always been there for him, always supported him, and made sure he had a good lawyer—not that it had ended up doing any good—but so far, Scarlett had been facing this alone. Her own problem if she was suffering the consequences of her own choices, but hell if she was suffering for something outside of her control.

Another wave of guilt surged through him as he watched Scarlett break down.

Noisy tears burst out of her, her sobs audible even from inside his car parked across the street and one house down from Scarlett's place.

Whatever words were exchanged amongst the women

he couldn't hear, but he did see them bustle Scarlett inside.

Before Tate even realized what he was doing, his hand was on the door handle, ready to follow them.

The problem was, he wasn't following because he wanted to keep a visual on a suspected traitor.

Never had been.

It wasn't why he'd gotten in his car to tail Scarlett home, and it wouldn't be why he spent the night right there, watching her place.

The reasons he was there were a whole lot more personal.

He was there because he felt an … all-consuming need … to watch over Scarlett.

It was ridiculous and he hated himself for it, because chances were, she was guilty of the things she had been accused of, but there was that tiny niggling piece of doubt in the back of his mind that kept whispering, *what if*?

What if Scarlett was innocent?

What if she'd been kidnapped?

What if she'd been horribly tortured?

What if, instead of attempting to support her, he'd been cold and callous after rescuing her?

What if it really had been a rescue and not a retrieval of a target?

What if she'd been left alone to answer hours of questioning when what she needed was care and comfort?

What if he was the villain in this story and not her?

It was that last what if that irked him the most. Tate had always felt like the outsider, the one in the wrong even when he knew he'd never done anything wrong. He hadn't asked to be born to parents who would have preferred to remain childless so they could focus all their time and attention on one another. He hadn't been responsible for his mother's death and yet his father checking out had made him feel as though he somehow were. And he wasn't responsible for the mess his dad had gotten into when he remarried, even though there were times his father had implied that if it weren't for Tate and his quote "pressuring" he never would have remarried and betrayed the deceased wife he still loved.

Was his own recent history with his dad being framed, the betrayal of the stepmother he thought would breathe new life back into his family, clouding his thinking? It simultaneously made him think of Scarlett as just another traitor, while making him feel like she was innocent.

When his phone buzzed with an unknown number, Tate debated whether or not to answer it. His CO hadn't approved this little stakeout, not that he'd told anyone where he was going and what he was going to be doing, but his team knew there was something with him and Scarlett, they just didn't know he'd slept with her then been unable to forget her. The last thing he wanted was to be either directly ordered to stop following Scarlett, or for his team to be sent out on another mission.

He needed answers, needed proof one way or the other.

All numbers from anyone he knew were programmed in his phone, but wondering if it was the agents who had interrogated Scarlett, he answered the call.

"Tate Laurier?" a voice asked before he could even say hello or ask who it was.

"Yeah. Who is this?"

"It's Eagle Oswald."

The legend himself. The former SEAL who had been forced into retirement after an op went badly wrong and he lost part of his leg was almost a mythical being in the special forces community. Using the billions he and his siblings had inherited when their parents were murdered to start Prey Security, Eagle had connections everywhere, was respected by everyone, and had a reputation for being used to getting his own way.

Why was the man calling him?

There was no way Eagle could know that he'd slept with Scarlett a few months back. Nobody knew. Tate didn't go blabbing about his sex life, and even if he did, there was something about Scarlett that felt different, he definitely hadn't spread the word that a woman had managed to affect him in any way.

"What do you want?" he asked, unable to think of a reason why the legend that was Eagle Oswald would be calling him.

"Are you outside her house?" Eagle asked. So far, the man was yet to make a physical appearance, but he had no doubt that the founder and CEO of Prey was keeping himself apprised of the situation. In fact, Eagle was likely the one who had given the order that Fox and the guys, as well as Athena Team, were to keep their distance from Scarlett. Tate just couldn't figure out if it was because Eagle believed Scarlett was guilty, or if he wanted a clean investigation to clear her.

If it was the former it filled him with the uncomfortable feeling of wanting to rip the man apart for doubting Scarlett.

Which absolutely made him a hypocrite because he doubted her too.

"Why does it matter where I am?" he demanded, unwilling to answer without knowing more about Eagle's motivation.

A chuckle came down the line. "I'll take that as a yes. Don't take your eyes off her."

Before he could open his mouth to ask why, the line went dead. His gaze moved to the house, where the lights were shining brightly, and he could just make out shadows moving in the front room.

A ball of anxiety rested heavily in his gut.

Was he worried *about* Scarlett because she was a danger to her team and her country? Or was he worried *for* Scarlett because she had been dragged into something dangerous?

How did he get an answer to that question?

And what did Eagle Oswald know that he hadn't shared?

CHAPTER EIGHT

January 15th
2:26 A.M.

DÉJÀ VU.

It was happening all over again.

What had she been thinking staying here alone?

Scarlett didn't hesitate this time like she had the night she'd been kidnapped. Even as she wished she'd listened to her team when they suggested she come and stay with one of them, or listened to her gut when she faced her bedroom and realized she couldn't stay in there and should go to a hotel, she was already sliding out from under the covers.

It was too late for wishes. She hadn't gone to stay with one of her team when they'd asked—begged really—and she had stubbornly refused to go to a hotel, so now she was stuck here, and if she didn't want to wind up kidnapped and tortured again then she had to be smart this time.

No panicking.

No pretending she was imagining things.

Because she hadn't imagined the sound of footsteps passing her room.

Someone was inside her house.

Her need for some time alone, to try to process her ordeal, was once again putting her in danger. That need to shut herself off from others—because although she understood her team had been ordered to stay away, they had still stayed away when she needed them—had left her alone and vulnerable.

Not that she could do anything about it.

Was it Raul Castillo sending more of his men after her? Scarlett had known that might be a possibility, but she hadn't really thought he would try to make a move this soon. Surely, she was being watched by some government agency, the suits or some of their colleagues. And if Prey thought she was in danger, they'd have someone watching her, too … wouldn't they?

Problem was, her faith in the people she worked for had been shaken.

Weapon in one hand, cell phone in the other, she crept to the door, inching it open just in time to see a black, shadowy figure step inside the master bedroom.

Thankfully, the thought of sleeping in that room again had her nauseous enough she'd almost thrown up and decided not to push herself. The carpet had been thoroughly cleaned and you could never tell that someone had been shot dead in there less than a week ago, but it didn't matter. Scarlett kept seeing the events of that night play out in her head, burned forever into her mind's eye.

Not wanting to engage, because for all she knew it wasn't Raul's men who had broken in here, but instead someone from the government come to put her in handcuffs, Scarlett slipped out into the hall and crept toward the stairs.

It would only take moments for the intruder to realize she wasn't in the bed, so there was not time to waste a single second.

Regardless of whether or not the intruder was from some agency or part of a criminal organization, it wasn't likely that they had come alone.

There had been six men the night she had been abducted, and law enforcement always worked in groups.

Either way, she was almost certainly outnumbered.

Her palms were so sweaty that she almost lost her grip on both her cell phone and weapon as she reached the stairs.

At least the spare bedroom was closer to the staircase than the master, which was down the end of the hall. And whoever the intruder was, he was probably going to think she was hiding somewhere in the bedroom because Raul's men knew that's what she'd done that night, and law enforcement knew too because it was in her statement.

Maybe if someone had actually listened to her and believed in her, she wouldn't be in danger all over again.

Well, her team believed, and they said no one at Prey thought she had done what she was accused of, but Scarlett was still struggling to believe them. They seemed sincere, but every time she tried to believe she remembered how she felt when she was sitting alone in that interrogation room, hurting, tired, and scared, and not a single person she cared about had been there.

Somehow, she made it down the stairs without tripping over her feet or dropping something and alerting everyone to where she was.

The bottom of the stairs was only steps away from the front door, but she wasn't sure if she should go out that way or around the back. Her backyard had a huge fence and lots of trees and vines, she liked her privacy and she loved to hang out there in the summer and pretend that she was way out in the woods nowhere near another living soul. It would provide better cover for sneaking away, but then again, it would have provided better cover for anyone sneaking in.

Her best bet was to get out of the house, get to someplace she felt safe, and then call someone to see if it was law enforcement who broke in. She wasn't going to make herself look guilty by running, but she also wasn't hanging around and letting those men get her in case they were Raul's.

A shudder ripped through her as she remembered the look on his face as the drug he gave her began to take effect and she started panting and writhing as unbearable pressure built up inside her.

The memory cost her precious seconds and she heard footsteps above. Hurrying toward the front door, deciding to risk it and make a run for it, if someone was waiting out there for her then she would scream her head off and hopefully wake the neighbors.

Just as her hand closed around the handle something

moved behind her.

Lifting her weapon as she spun around, she was too slow to dodge the fist that came towards her.

Connecting squarely with the side of her head, pain flared out from her temple, and her head snapped to the side, slamming into the door hard enough she saw stars. A clunk told her that was her weapon hitting the floor and she knew her chances of escaping just plummeted to pretty much zero.

"Got her down here," the man in front of her called out as a large, meaty hands wrapped around her throat, squeezing just enough to make it difficult to breathe.

Footsteps thumped down the stairs and she saw another man appear beside the one holding her.

Tattoos.

At the hollow of their necks.

Raul's men.

Not law enforcement.

Why they would risk coming after her again so quickly she didn't know, and she didn't care. All that mattered was getting away. If they got her out of her house, she would never be seen or heard from again, and everyone would just assume that the accusations were true and Raul's men had come to whisk her away to safety.

How anyone could look at the marks on her body and think she had been working with Raul was beyond her. And even if he hated her, Tate surely must have told them in his reports that she had been tied to a rock when he found her, about to be shoved into a pool to drown as motivation to talk and tell Raul what he wanted to know.

"Raul always gets what he wants," the man gripping her throat told her with a smarmy smile that made her skin crawl.

If she got taken back to Raul, she would be tortured again and again until she broke. While the thought of the physical pain she would endure was terrifying, it was that drug she'd been given that scared her the most.

How long could she hold out if it was administered again?

What if they kept giving it to her in a never-ending loop, not giving her time to recover in between?

Scarlett knew the answer to that question.

She would break, give over the formula, anything to get relief from the clawing need that had possessed her body.

When the hand around her neck tightened, cutting off her air supply, every cell in her body screamed at her to fight. It was what the man thought she would do, what he wanted her to do if the amusement in his eyes was anything to go by.

But fighting wouldn't help.

He was bigger and stronger, she wouldn't get away by fighting the hand at her neck.

Fighting against her instincts, Scarlett didn't claw at the man's hand. Instead, she focused every bit of her fading energy and rammed her knee up and into the man's groin.

Doing the unexpected worked to her advantage, and suddenly the pressure on her neck was gone as the man doubled over. She'd gotten in a direct hit, and when her would-be strangler staggered sideways, he bumped into the other man, buying her enough time to fumble with the lock and throw the front door open.

Terrified there might be more of Raul's men out there somewhere, she fought against her natural instinct, which was to run, and instead crept out into her front yard, scanning the street as she went.

Unfortunately, she didn't even make it to the sidewalk before a huge body connected with hers and she was slammed onto the hard, cold ground, and pinned in place.

* * *

January 15th
2:47 A.M.

As soon as he saw Scarlett come creeping out of her house Tate knew something was wrong.

The benefit of the doubt he'd been willing to give her was gone.

She was trying to run.

Only guilty people ran.

Shoving open the car door, he ran toward her before she got away. Reaching her before she even got off her front lawn, Tate tackled her, taking them both to the ground.

Predictably she fought him, thrashing about with more strength than her small frame should have had. Still, she was a tiny thing compared to his six-foot-two, two-hundred-pound frame, and he easily pinned her in place.

"I don't think so, little traitor," he murmured as he

straddled her thighs, keeping her legs pinned, while with one hand he held both her wrists and pinned them to the ground above her head.

Stretched out as she was beneath him, he absolutely should not be thinking about how good she'd look just like this only in his bed.

Sex with a traitor was not on his radar.

Yet almost without realizing it, his thumb brushed across the inside of Scarlett's wrist as though they were lovers.

Beneath him, she'd gone still, and the sound of her ragged breathing drew his gaze to her heaving chest. She was wearing black leggings that clung to her toned legs and an oversized sweater instead of pajamas, further fueling his belief that she was going to run.

In the thin moonlight her dark eyes looked like two bottomless pits of pain, but he fought against their pull. He wasn't getting sucked in again. Already he had been willing to consider the possibility that she had been framed, that she was innocent. He'd wanted proof one way or the other and now he had it.

The only reason to run was if you were guilty.

Only ...

She didn't have a bag and her feet were bare.

If she was planning on disappearing, she'd be more prepared.

Indecision warred inside him. Was he only painting her with a guilty brush because of the mess he had inadvertently caused with his father? Was he the one with the problem here? Doubting Scarlett because it was actually himself that he didn't trust?

"T-Tate?" she stammered, blinking up at him with her huge doe eyes.

"Not your lucky day, sweetheart," he muttered. Regardless of her reasons for sneaking out of her home, he wasn't going to just let her go. Someone with a clearer head needed to deal with this because he had no choice but to admit to himself that clear was the last thing he could be around this woman.

"It definitely is," she said, surprising him. "They're inside. Two men. They thought I was in my bedroom, but I couldn't sleep in there after what happened. I was almost out the front door when they got me."

While his traitorous heart wanted to believe her, his logical mind screamed at him that she was leaving. He'd seen no one breaking in and he'd been there the entire time. Plus, nobody had come running out after her, and as far as he knew, nobody but Eagle even knew he was there, although his team might suspect.

"Sure, sweetheart," he mocked.

Instead of the anger he'd been expecting, Scarlett just deflated beneath him, until she looked completely and utterly defeated. "Believe me or don't, but two men were in my house. The second one got me as I was about to sneak out of the door. If I'd been in my bed where they thought I was I'd be dead or kidnapped again."

As though saying the words out loud had made them that much more powerful her entire body began to shake. Not fine little tremors, but full body-shuddering enough that he could both feel and see it.

There was no way she could be faking that kind of reaction.

Yet the little voice in his head screamed at him that he'd also believed the woman he encouraged his father to move on with would be good for him, and he'd been spectacularly wrong on that account.

It was like there was a war raging inside him. One side insisted that Scarlett was innocent, that she didn't act in the least like someone with anything to hide. The other taunted him that you couldn't trust anybody, especially yourself.

"No one is killing you today, sweetheart," he said, voice cold as ice as he reached for some zip ties he'd had on him just in case he needed them.

Although he had hoped he wouldn't.

Because regardless of everything he knew about Scarlett Madden and what she had done, his body still reacted to hers with an intensity unlike anything else he had ever experienced. Not just his body, but his heart reacted to her, too. The craziest thing since he had never wanted, even from a young age, to fall in love. He'd seen the flip side of love with his parents, how it could morph into co-dependent obsession, and he'd wanted no part of it.

Even less so now after what had happened with his father and his second wife.

But whether he wanted it or not, he couldn't deny that he had been unable to forget about this woman. Her laugh, her smile, her sweet and somewhat shy persona, her openness and joy, the way she seemed to brighten a room just by stepping into it.

A small smile curled her lips up. "Thanks to you. I don't know why you're here, Tate, but I'm so glad that you are. If you weren't …"

"Then you would have gotten away," he finished for her, confused by her smile and the gratefulness emanating from her.

At least it had been emanating from her until she saw the zip ties.

Then her brow furrowed into the most adorable frown.

"Tate?"

"No one was in your house, Scarlett," he said firmly, but when he went to bind her wrists he found he couldn't do it.

Because you don't need to.

You can trust her.

"There was," she insisted as his hand fell away and he shoved the ties back in his pocket. "He grabbed me and put his hand around my neck. He was going to squeeze until I passed out and take me, but I kneed him in the groin. He wasn't expecting that." Despite the fear lingering in her eyes, there was a note of triumph in her voice, and in spite of himself he felt a flush of pleasure that she'd defended herself.

Keeping hold of her, Tate pulled her up to her feet with him as he stood. He'd put her in his car, then he'd check out her house, confirm that nobody else had been in it, before driving her back to Prey. They could hold her there until someone figured out what to do with her, because if he stuck around he was going to lose his mind.

"Whether you believe me or not, Tate, someone broke into my home. Raul isn't going to just let me go. He wants the formula to the Reactivator and he's not going to stop until he gets it. Just because no one wants to believe me doesn't make it any less the truth," Scarlett said quietly as he led her to the car.

There was sincerity in her voice, but acceptance as well.

Tate found he didn't like that.

Didn't like knowing that Scarlett had somehow accepted that she was on her own in this. The visit from her friends didn't seem to have convinced her that Prey was on her side, and he had to assume it was because she was used to nobody being on her side.

No matter how many times he ran over the evidence against her in his mind, his gut continued to insist that this woman who offered no resistance as he opened the passenger door of his car and helped her inside was in fact innocent.

Again, the idea that she was being coerced flashed in his mind. It was obvious she cared about her team. If they were threatened, would she agree to give Raul the formula for the drug?

"Look, Scarlett," he started, prepared to have a conversation with her if it got her to open up. Maybe if she confessed now and agreed to help them trap Raul Castillo, she could negotiate her sentence down. "If you just—"

The sound of gunfire abruptly cut him off and he slammed Scarlett's door closed, then dove across the hood of his truck and into the driver's seat.

Someone was shooting at them.

Not any of the many agencies who could have been watching Scarlett's house because they would talk first and shoot second.

Had to be Raul's men.

As he tore off down the street, tires screeching, he had no choice but to believe Scarlett's story that there had been intruders in her house. There had been no time for her to alert anyone that she was being taken in, and they were shooting at her as well.

He was beginning to hate himself for the lingering doubt. Just because he'd messed up with his dad didn't mean that he was messing up now. He knew how to read people even if he'd been wrong a grand total of one time. It was just the consequences of that one time were so severe that it was hard to let it go.

But he had to.

Because if he didn't then it was going to be the woman huddled in the passenger seat of his car who paid the price.

Taking off down the street, Tate didn't even make it to the next corner before he saw the black vehicle on his tail.

"Do you have your phone?" he asked as he took a corner so fast he almost lost control.

"It's in my—"

Scarlett's words were cut off when a bullet hit his tires, and the car went careening sideways, throwing both of them about.

As they hurtled across the road, Tate tried desperately to regain some control.

But he couldn't.

Briefly, he wished he'd put their seatbelts on.

Then they slammed into a pole, and the world was swallowed up into a pain-filled black hole.

CHAPTER NINE

January 15th
3:04 A.M.

PAIN.

Why was that always the first thing to register?

Scarlett dragged open heavy eyes as she heard the sound of voices.

After all the abuse her body and her mind had taken in the last several days, it was hard to summon enough energy to do much of anything, but the first thing she caught sight of was Tate.

Lying as he was, slumped in his seat, half draped over the steering wheel, he looked so vulnerable. So not like the Tate she had met and spent the night with, or the Tate who had saved her life even if he believed her to be a traitor.

Maybe she shouldn't care what happened to him, he'd

been a jerk to her even before she'd been framed, but jerk or not, he was one of the good guys, just not a guy who was good for her.

If their positions were reversed, Scarlett honestly couldn't say that she wouldn't believe he was guilty.

Didn't mean his automatic rejection and willingness to believe the worst of her like they hadn't had sex and slept tangled in one another's arms hadn't hurt. Because it did hurt. A lot. More than it should since she had already known he was a jerk.

Why couldn't her stupid heart get with the program?

Or maybe it wasn't her heart so much as her deeply ingrained desire to find love and happiness, and her interpretation of the connection she and Tate had shared that night.

The connection wasn't real.

All in her head.

The man unconscious beside her didn't even like her, much less feel any sort of connection to her, but still keeping them both alive was the right thing to do.

The only thing to do.

She wasn't a traitor, and she wasn't a killer.

"Yeah, she's in the car," a voice outside spoke.

There was no doubt she was the "she" in question. The voice had a slight Mexican accent and who else would be shooting at them?

Just because Tate was intent on making her the villain didn't mean it was so.

She hadn't written any email to anyone offering to sell the Reactivator, and she would continue to repeat that to everyone until it finally sunk in.

"No, she's not alone," the voice spoke again. Then after a short pause continued, "No idea who he is. Some guy. Doesn't look like they're friends, though. He put her in his car and drove off with her. I'm guessing he's from whatever agency was watching her house. What do you want me to do with him?"

Since she hadn't done more than open her eyes, whoever—and however many whoevers—were outside Tate's car didn't yet realize that she was awake.

Problem was she didn't have a lot of options here. They already knew that the men chasing them were armed, they'd been shooting at the car and must have managed to hit the tires from the way Tate seemed to lose control. Fighting wasn't an option, she didn't have a weapon and she was too weak to do much in hand-to-hand combat right now. Running was out, she wouldn't get far, there was a chance that if she ran, she could lead them away from Tate though. Once they caught her, he'd just use it as further evidence to convict her but at least he'd be alive.

"All right. I'll kill him, grab the girl, and we'll be gone before the cops show," the man continued speaking.

Kill Tate?

No.

She couldn't let that happen.

She wouldn't let that happen.

Whatever it meant for her she didn't care. Chances were, she'd be spending the rest of her life in a prison cell unless she could somehow prove her innocence, the least she could do was keep the man who had saved her life alive. He might not like her, might believe she was a traitor, but nonetheless, Tate *had* saved her in Mexico, and he had saved her again tonight.

Throwing herself over Tate's limp body just as a loud crack sliced through the night, the searing pain near her right shoulder blade told her that the bullet had got her.

Had it got Tate, too?

At this close range, it could easily have passed through her body and into his.

While Raul had a reason to keep her alive, he had no such reason for Tate.

"What the—?" Tate's angry growl filled the car, and the next thing she knew, Scarlett was being shoved sideways back into the seat she'd just jumped out of, and a series of pops echoed through the car.

Then silence.

Blessed silence.

When light suddenly flooded the car, Scarlett winced. It was too bright, and now that she thought about it, the silence was too quiet.

Everything seemed magnified.

Light.

Sound.

The thump of each beat of her heart.

Was it supposed to be that loud?

Was it supposed to be that painful?

Or was the pain coming from her back and not her heart?

"Are you *shot*?" Tate demanded as a featherlight touch whispered over her back right across the epicenter of her pain.

Sucking in a breath, she flinched away from the touch.

Light as it was, it felt like a burning poker aggravating her bullet wound.

"They were going to kill you," she mumbled as a way of explanation.

"You don't ever do something so stupid," he raged, and she wondered why he was yelling at her.

Was she supposed to let him get shot?

That seemed mean even if he had been nothing but nasty to her. Two wrongs didn't make a right, and in this case, they would have made a dead body.

Tate's dead body.

Why was she even surprised that she'd just saved his life and he was still angry with her?

Didn't seem to matter what she did, that man she'd spent the best night of her life with had vanished, and she was no longer sure he had ever even existed at all.

"You were unconscious," she reminded him. With great effort, she shifted in her seat so she was upright again instead of sprawled across it. Catching a glance at his face as she sunk down into the soft leather, Scarlett was surprised by the fear in his stunning eyes.

Was he angry or afraid?

"Doesn't matter." Tate blinked and the fear was gone, replaced by what she was used to seeing, cold disinterest.

"So, I should have just let you die?" Maybe pushing him wasn't the best move to make right now, but she was hurting, she was sick of being accused of things she didn't do, she was sick of Raul sending people after her, and she'd reached her limit. Apparently, at the end of her limit was a whole big pile of anger just waiting to be ignited.

Tate was the match.

The spark that was going to set her off if he didn't stop saying stupid things.

“Did you kill them?” she asked when he didn't respond. Instead, he tried to get the car to start up again.

A grunt sounded like an affirmative so she relaxed a little.

Only a little. The cops would be here soon, the gunfire would have woken neighbors who would have called it in. Once they got there, she’d be taken back into custody. Probably not by the local police department, but some agency would take her in.

“I don’t think your car can drive,” she said when he managed to get the engine to start.

Ignoring her as he always seemed to—unless he had more insults to hurl at her—he merely jerked the car into reverse, and it stuttered backward.

“Why are we leaving? The cops will be here any moment.”

“Because the cops will be here any moment,” he said.

Scarlett frowned. “Right, I just said that. I would have thought you wanted me arrested,” she said.

All she got was another growl, and then he was somehow driving the mangled car.

“I don’t get it. Where are we going?”

“My place.”

“Why aren't we waiting for the cops?”

“Because I don’t want you arrested.”

“Afraid they won't be hard enough on me?” she mocked because one thing she was sure of was that Tate Laurier wanted her to suffer. Why? She wasn’t sure. It was fine he hadn't felt the connection she had, but he seemed to hate her. Like actually *hate* her, and that made zero sense.

"You took a bullet for me," he said, sounding shocked by the idea.

"Of course. I wasn't going to let them kill you."

"Why?"

"What do you mean why? I'm not a killer." Did he have to keep offending her? Thinking she was a traitor was bad enough, but now he thought she was okay with cold-blooded murder?

"What are you then?" This one time he seemed to be genuinely seeking an answer.

"Doesn't matter what I say, you've already made up your mind." Suddenly bone weary, Scarlett let her head fall back against the seat. "You know what? I think I'd rather wait for the cops."

If she didn't know better, Scarlett would have been certain that his growl was possessive. "You're coming to my place."

She didn't get this man at all. "Why?"

For a long moment the only sound was of the ruined car creaking and groaning its way down the street. Then his quiet, anger-free, almost confused voice answered, "I don't know."

* * *

JANUARY 15TH

3:19 A.M.

. . .

SHE'D TAKEN a bullet for him.

A bullet.

Scarlett was currently sitting in the passenger seat of his car bleeding all over the place because she had thrown herself in front of a bullet meant for him.

Meant to end his life.

Tate knew he wouldn't have been able to stop it from happening. He'd woken up just to hear a man's voice saying he was going to kill the man and take the girl. By the time the words had registered through his throbbing head, and he'd gathered enough strength to reach for his weapon, the crack of a gunshot had already sliced through the night.

In that split second, he had been prepared to die.

While he hadn't wanted to leave his dad behind, or his team, he was at peace with death if it was his time. You didn't live the kind of life he did, have the kind of job he did, and then be surprised when death came for you at a young age.

But tonight, he had quite literally dodged a bullet.

Because of the woman sitting silently beside him.

Her question continued to echo in his mind as he somehow managed to get his mangled truck to drive the short distance to his house, only three miles away from Scarlett's.

Why?

Why *was* he taking her to his place?

The answer that rang through his mind was one he wasn't willing to acknowledge.

Not yet.

Maybe not ever.

At the very least, not until this whole mess was sorted out.

But one thing he knew was that a woman who would throw herself in the path of a bullet to save a man who had been nothing but horrible to her and was taking her into custody was not one who would willingly sell a drug to someone who would not use it for its intended purpose. Athena Team had created the Reactivator to save the lives of their colleagues in the field, and the lives of American men and women serving in armed forces across the globe. Not so a weapons trafficker could get his hands on it and sell it to one of their country's enemies to give those seeking to destroy democracy the upper hand.

The only reason Scarlett would have made that deal with Raul was if she had no other choice.

All he had to do was gain her trust enough to get her to open up to him and tell him what she had been threatened with, so he knew how to help her. Maybe if she was open and transparent from here on out, given that she had taken a bullet for him, they could even work out a deal, so she didn't serve any prison time.

For now though, he wanted to keep her somewhere safe, where neither Raul nor any of the agencies who wanted her would find her. There was a bullet wound to take care of, and he wasn't sure whether she'd had any chance to rest after her team left her last night, but that was also a priority.

After that they'd talk.

Honestly this time, and when they did, he had to find a

way to keep his own trust issues under control and not keep using them as a weapon against a woman who didn't deserve his anger.

He had to prove to her that she could trust him. But how Tate was going to do that when his ability to trust had already been so badly damaged he had no idea.

One problem at a time though.

Thankfully, they'd managed to get away from the scene before the cops arrived. The last thing he wanted was to be explaining why he, a Navy SEAL, had just killed three people on US soil.

Not when time was of the essence.

Tonight had made it perfectly clear that even if Scarlett had been coerced, Raul had no intention of letting her go until he got what he wanted from her. It was pretty ballsy to make another attempt on her life, right out in the open on a public street, even if it was in the early hours of the morning, immediately after Scarlett was released from custody.

Once he'd pulled into his driveway he turned to Scarlett, who hadn't spoken a single word after he'd told her he didn't know why he was taking her to his place. Even if he told her that was a lie and he knew exactly why he wanted her close he doubted she would believe him.

Her eyes were closed, and even though he could see the rise and fall of her chest, Tate reached out and touched two fingertips to the base of her throat. It wasn't until he touched the smooth, silky skin that he saw the bruises marring it.

Scarlett had told him she'd been attacked in her home,

and that was why she'd run, and he'd had trouble believing her.

Which now that he had calmed down a little sounded ridiculous even to his own ears.

The evidence of her innocence was right in front of him, his own issues just kept blinding him to it.

Obviously, someone had attacked her because she didn't have those bruises when he'd delivered her to Prey, and no one had laid a hand on her during the time she'd spent there.

He knew. He'd watched her the entire time, and if anyone had done anything close to hurting her physically, he would have … done something that would have ruined his career.

Tate hadn't even realized he was stroking his fingertips over the darkening marks as though he could somehow erase them and the pain and terror Scarlett must have suffered when they had been inflicted.

Each one was fingertip-sized and shaped, and even if she hadn't told him that someone had wrapped their hand around her slender neck and squeezed he would have known that was what had happened. He sincerely hoped that whoever had tried to strangle her was one of the men he had killed.

"I kneed him in the groin," Scarlett's soft voice spoke, and when he glanced up, he saw her eyes were open and she was watching him somewhat warily. "That's how I got away. I know you don't believe me but—"

"I do," he interrupted. Maybe if he had believed her at the time, she wouldn't have gotten shot.

Because being this close to her, touching her so intimately, was likely to make him do something he shouldn't, Tate abruptly pulled back, ignoring the hurt that flared in Scarlett's beautiful big brown eyes.

"Let's get you inside so I can assess the damage," he said briskly, already reaching for his door handle. Since it was so badly damaged, the door creaked and he had to shove at it to get it open.

Not making any progress with her door, Tate could tell from the way it was caved in that it wasn't going to open, he reached over the driver's seat and grabbed Scarlett under the arms, pulling her over and out into the cold night, doing his best to ignore her muted grunts of pain.

She swayed, and he locked an arm around her waist, holding her tightly against him. For a moment their eyes met and he felt that same spark that he had that first night. As much as he knew he never should have touched her, Scarlett had the romance vibe down to a tee, and he was happily single, Tate found he didn't have it in him to regret the night they had shared.

He should.

And he shouldn't have her here now.

But he couldn't let her go yet.

That one night of light, peace, and happiness was going to have to last him a lifetime.

Scooping her up, he carried her inside and set her down on the couch in the living room. He laid her on her stomach so he could examine her wound, then left her there while he went to grab his first aid kit. It was well stocked, and he had the supplies to stitch the wound, he just hoped the bullet wasn't still inside her.

Once his supplies were laid out, he knelt beside the couch and ripped at her sweater where the tear from the bullet was, exposing a ragged, bloody wound. From the angle, it looked like the bullet had scraped along her shoulder blade, deflecting off the bone rather than actually passing through her body.

That was something, and although she'd bled a fair amount, she hadn't lost even close to a dangerous amount of blood. A few stitches, a shot of antibiotics, more bandages, some painkillers, and she'd be fine.

An easy fix.

Yet the wound would leave a scar that would join the marks from the whip that scattered across her back, and those that circled her wrists and ankles. Then there were the psychological scars that would last a lifetime and take much longer to heal.

"You don't take a bullet for me again, Scarlett, you hear me? It's my job to protect you," Tate said as he began to clean the wound. Although he hadn't thought about the words before he said them, he realized he'd never spoken truer words.

Somewhere along the way he had taken on the job of Scarlett's protector.

There was no answer, and when he leaned over so he could see her face he saw that she had already passed out. Exhaustion had sunk its claws into her, and she no longer had the strength left to keep her eyes open.

In sleep she looked so innocent, so young, so vulnerable, and so very beautiful.

"What am I going to do with you, little fighter?" he whispered as he smoothed a lock of hair off her pale face.

The problem was, he truly didn't know the answer to that question, but he feared even if the insidious voice whispering inside his head was right and she was guilty he was going to have a hard time walking away.

CHAPTER TEN

January 15th
7:38 P.M.

"MMM," Scarlett moaned as she woke slowly.

That had been a great sleep.

The only good sleep she'd gotten since she woke up to the sounds of an intruder in her house.

It wasn't even necessary to open her eyes to know why she'd slept so well.

Tate was here, and somehow that meant she was safe.

Just because he didn't like her and hadn't felt the same things she did when they spent the night together, didn't make him a bad man. A jerk, yes. He'd been unnecessarily cruel to her afterward when a simple, hey it was a fun night but I don't want more would have sufficed, but he wasn't the kind of man who would physically hurt her, and he would throw himself between her and a threat the same way she had when Raul's men had been going to shoot him.

Now she could feel his presence beside her and knew he had watched over her while she slept.

The thought brought a smile to her face. Despite what her mind knew about him, her body still thought he was sexy, and desperately wanted a repeat of their night together. Never had sex been better than that night. Afterward she'd thought it was because there was some connection between them, but now she just assumed it was because he was really good in bed.

The connection might not be real, but the chemistry was.

It was undeniable.

Tate felt it, too, even though he didn't want to. She knew because she could feel it in the gentle way he touched her, the fiery passion deep in his eyes. He might not want her, but his body did, same as hers wanted his.

Wanted him right now.

Needed even.

For a few minutes, Scarlett just wanted to forget everything that had happened, the kidnapping, the torture, the drug she'd been given, the accusations, the second break-in, and the gunshots, all of it.

She wanted it gone, even if only for a short time.

When she blinked open her eyes, she saw Tate right where she knew he had been, sitting in the armchair right beside the couch he'd laid her down on after carrying her inside. Exhaustion must have hit the moment she was lying down, and her subconscious knew she was safe because she didn't remember anything after that, not even Tate cleaning and tending to her wound.

Now he was watching her with an inscrutable expression and she had to know.

Had to know if he finally believed that she was innocent.

It shouldn't be important or matter to her at all what he thought, but for some reason it did. Because even though he didn't feel the same way, she had felt a connection that night and his opinion of her *did* matter to her poor, lonely, scarred little heart.

This could very well be the stupidest thing she had ever done, but in this moment, Scarlett didn't care. All she needed was a connection to someone who wouldn't hurt her.

Well, Tate, unlike anyone else, did have the power to take her heart and crush it beyond repair, but he would never lay a hand on her to cause her pain. Even when he thought she was a traitor he had been gentle with her.

Did he still think that?

Please believe in me.

The words whispered through her mind as she straightened and stood. Rejection in this moment would hurt even more than when he'd pretended not to know her that day at the grocery store.

But she didn't stop.

Couldn't stop.

Forces she didn't even understand were driving her toward this man who was lounging in an armchair watching her with a desire that already had her body responding.

She wanted his touch.

Craved it.

Was desperate for the high she knew he could give her.

One moment, just to forget, was that too much to ask after everything she had been through?

He didn't stop her as she walked the few steps toward him. Didn't reach for her as she straddled his lap. Didn't do anything as her palms touched his abs and smoothed up his chiseled chest and then back down again.

Dressed in only gray sweatpants and a black T-shirt he looked good enough to taste. If he let her, she'd devour him the same way she had that night, matching him orgasm gotten for orgasm given. Tate's sex drive had been insatiable that night, and she wondered if he was always like that or if he had felt the same connection she had only to him it wasn't a beautiful thing but something to be shut down.

While he was still in a relaxed position, Scarlett could feel the tension in his body, his muscles bunched beneath her hands as they continued to stroke up and down his chest. Although she had replayed that night many times in the lonely nights she'd spent alone in her house, Tate felt even better than she remembered.

Bracing her hands on his shoulders, she shifted, lifting her hips so she could grind her center against his rock-hard erection.

There was still no movement on his part, no attempt to participate, and for the first-time doubt entered her mind.

What if he really didn't want her?

What if she was trying to take something from him, he didn't want to give?

Shame burned through her. She was trying to use him to forget. If he wanted sex with no strings, too, then that was okay, but if he didn't then she was no better than the men in Raul's dungeon torture chamber who would have raped her if they'd been given permission even though it wasn't what she wanted no matter how many times she had begged for relief.

Humiliated, Scarlett tried to withdraw, and quicker than lightning Tate's hands gripped her hips, holding her in place.

Her eyes snapped up to meet his. What did that mean? Was he about to accuse her of being a rapist on top of everything else?

"I-I'm sorry," she stammered. "I thought …" she trailed off because she wasn't really sure what she thought. She hadn't been acting on logical thinking only on instinct.

Regret filled his unusual eyes, and for a moment, she wanted to silence him, not sure she could take another blow right now.

"Scarlett, I—"

"It's okay," she cut him off. "You don't want me. I get that. You don't like me. I haven't forgotten how you treated me after the night we spent together. I just …" How did she admit to a man who loathed her how badly she needed a human connection right now?

"I can't … give you what you want," Tate said, and the regret in his eyes was echoed in his voice. There was pain there, too, and stupid romantic at heart that she was, she wanted to soothe it all away.

"All I want right now is sex, to forget, to pretend my world hasn't been totally destroyed, to feel instead of think," she whispered.

"There can't be—"

"I'm not asking for more," she said, cutting him off again.

"Just sex?"

"Just sex."

"Just sex," he repeated, not sounding as happy about that as she thought he would have. When he blinked the regret was gone, and the hands on her hips tightened. "You're injured, so we do this my way."

"Pretty sure we did it your way all night that night," she said, heat pooling low in her stomach at his words and the memories of what they shared.

A low chuckle reverberated through her hands, which were pressed against his pecs. "I didn't hear you complaining."

A shiver coursed through her as she remembered she had spent the night begging for more orgasms, not a single complaint had been uttered. "I didn't have any need to."

What could only be described as an alpha smile of satisfaction curled his lips up, and warmth blossomed inside her chest. This was the man she remembered. Funny, sweet, protective, attentive … perfect.

"Hands stay on my shoulders, and I do all the work," he said as one of his hands shifted so it could brush across her center, where her panties and the leggings she still wore were already soaked with the evidence of her arousal.

No one had touched her in months, and already her body was responding to the featherlight caresses.

What was it about this man that drove her so wild?

"Scarlett?" Tate's thumb found her already throbbing bud and pressed hard against it. "I didn't hear your agreement."

Because her brain was frazzled and all she could do was feel, not think. "Umm … what … what was the question?"

Another chuckle vibrated through her hands. "I do all the work and your hands stay on my shoulders unless I tell you otherwise. Okay?"

"Okay," she quickly agreed. Anything so that he would keep touching her.

Keeping her hands still turned out to be harder than it should have been. Tate took his time, stroking her through her clothes, alternating between mere wisps of touch she could barely feel, to working her until she was so close to coming before he eased back again.

She remembered the back and forth from their time together and both loved and hated it. Because as much as she wished he would hurry up and give her an earth-shattering orgasm, she also never wanted this moment to end.

Here, right now, with this Tate who wasn't cold and hard, she felt safe, protected, even treasured.

Too bad it couldn't last.

"Lift," he ordered, his hands on her hips lifting her off him. When she balanced on her feet, he quickly shoved her leggings and panties down over her hips. Then instead of settling her back on his lap, straddling his massive thighs, he leaned her back a little so he could lift one of her legs, freeing it from the leggings, then hooked it over his shoulder. When he did the same with her other leg, tossing the clothes aside, it left her wide open and bare to him.

Maybe she should be embarrassed considering how he'd treated her, but the pure fire of desire burning in his eyes muted everything else.

He wanted her.

Wanted her more than he wanted to breathe, if his sharp intake of air was anything to go by.

Those huge hands of his cupped her now bare backside and lifted her, then his nose was buried against her center, and he was breathing her in. Small puffs of air accompanied each kiss as he pressed one to each of her inner thighs, and then one against her opening.

Then, finally, that hot mouth of his was on her.

He licked, he nipped, he sucked, his tongue plunged inside of her.

There was no hesitation, no holding back now, he worked her higher, and higher, and higher until it felt like she had taken up residence in the heavens themselves.

His mouth latched onto her bundle of nerves and when he sucked hard, and his teeth raked across the sensitive bud, pleasure exploded inside her.

Tate didn't let up, he continued to suck, flicking her bud with the tip of his tongue, then swirling it across the trembling little bundle of nerves, bringing her another powerful explosion.

Still, he wouldn't stop.

Her hands tangled in his hair, and Scarlett wasn't sure

if she was trying to push him away or beg for another orgasm.

Words tumbled from her lips, but she couldn't even understand them.

He'd given her exactly what she wanted.

Right now, there was no room for thoughts, all she could do was feel.

A third orgasm slammed into her, and her entire body was shaking from the force of it as Tate lifted her like she weighed nothing at all and slammed into her in one thrust.

Because he was the kind of man who cared enough about a woman to make sure sex was good for her, even as he thrust into her at a near frenetic pace his fingers worked her towards a fourth orgasm, which fired through her at the same time she felt him find his own release.

As delightful aftershocks continued to pulse through her, Scarlett sunk against him, content to stay right where she was, in this perfect pleasure-filled little bubble, for the rest of her life.

"Sorry, babe, I've got to get rid of the condom and clean you up," Tate's voice murmured by her ear as one of his hands swept the length of her spine.

Honestly, she didn't remember him putting the condom on, had no idea where it had even come from, she'd been too stuck in post-orgasm haze, but she loved that he had been careful, and that he wanted to take care of her now. Not only did it warm her heart, but it gave her a sense of peace because now she knew that Tate was on her side.

He no longer thought she was guilty.

* * *

JANUARY 16TH
1:19 A.M.

SEX WITH SCARLETT had been stupid.

Letting her fall asleep on his lap stupider still.

Tate couldn't deny that the sex they had shared earlier had been out of this world good. Watching Scarlett come apart so totally that complete gibberish had been coming out of her mouth as she begged and pleaded simultaneously for him to stop and to give her more, was intoxicating.

Far too easily he could allow himself to get addicted to her.

To her sweet scent, her breathy moans, her soft touch, her lyrical voice, and her big doe eyes.

But he couldn't let himself forget the facts.

Scarlett was messed up in something dangerous. Just because if she was guilty at all it was because she had likely agreed to sell Raul the Reactivator out of desperation because she had been coerced, it didn't mean she still hadn't done it. Instead of trusting all of Prey's resources to keep her and her team safe, she'd picked the wrong road, and now she was so far down it there was a chance she could never find her way back.

There was zero future for them.

Zero.

None.

Nada.

Wasn't going to happen.

This woman who snuggled so trustingly against him, deep in sleep, completely vulnerable, wasn't his to keep.

Even if fate hadn't brought them back together there had never been a chance for them. Nothing had changed, he still wasn't looking for marriage and forevers. He didn't want to fall in love, and he wasn't going to keep using Scarlett for sex knowing he wasn't going to ever be able to give her what she wanted.

Wishing things were different wasn't going to change anything. They wanted completely different things out of life, were on completely different paths, had had completely different childhoods and models of what love looked like.

So why, when he held her sleeping form tucked against his chest, did everything feel so right?

Denying her sex would have been the right thing to do. Scarlett wasn't thinking clearly, had been traumatized, and might very well have been trying to distract him so she could escape. Only deep down he knew she wasn't, that she just wanted to forget for a while, but he should have been the clear-headed one. He'd taken advantage no matter that Scarlett had been the one to initiate things.

"What am I going to do with you, little fighter?" he whispered as he stroked her back. He kept asking himself that question, but he was no closer to figuring out the answer.

A beep on his phone had his attention snapping away from the sleeping woman.

The alarm for his security system had just been tripped.

Reaching over, he snatched up his cell phone from the coffee table beside the armchair where they were sitting—Scarlett had suggested the couch, but he thought he had a better chance of remaining awake in case she tried anything in the armchair—and looked at the alert.

Someone was in his driveway.

The entire property was rigged with sensors that would allow him to know the second anyone set foot on a single inch of his property. Call him paranoid, but his ex-stepmother knew that he knew his father was innocent and that she was the one dealing drugs. There was a chance that she or one of her gang friends would try something stupid to silence him. So, he had upgraded his system with cameras and sensors everywhere.

Better safe than sorry.

Now the camera showed four men slinking down his driveway.

Not law enforcement or men from any of the agencies.

Raul's men.

Had to be.

But how had they found him?

Throwing a gaze at the sleeping woman. There was no way she could have alerted anyone that she was here, he'd been with her the entire time. Even if he hadn't, her luring Raul's men here to kill him didn't vibe with the incident in his car earlier, she could have let them kill him and gone with them.

Even though doubts tried their best to shove their way into his mind he did his best to shove them right back out again. He'd brought her here because deep down he knew he could trust her, knew she needed protection, that was what he had to focus on. Nothing else.

Gently he shook her awake, then set her on her feet before him.

"Tate?" she asked sleepily, her hands grabbing onto his forearms to steady herself as she swayed, still half asleep.

"Get dressed," he ordered. There was no time to talk anything through with her, they needed to get out of there while they still stood a chance.

"What? Why?"

"We got company," he growled as he shoved past her to grab his weapon. Thankfully, no lights were on, and there was every chance that whoever was about to break in believed both he and Scarlett would be upstairs in bed.

"Company?" Scarlett whisper shouted as she lunged for her leggings and sweater.

That move wound up saving her life.

The roar of gunfire combined with shattering glass as his front windows were destroyed filled the night.

Throwing himself to the side, he grabbed Scarlett's wrist, ignoring her pained yelp as he pressed too tightly on her wounds and dragged her with him behind the couch. Not much protection but better than nothing.

Or was it?

Scarlett was still there, and wherever she went gunfire seemed to follow.

She hadn't been lying when she'd said someone had been in her home right before she went running out of it. The bruises on her neck corroborated that story. And it was true that she had saved his life in taking that bullet, yet here they were again, same story, different page.

The problem was, he couldn't get a read on Scarlett because his emotions kept getting in the way and that allowed the only crack it needed for his issues with his dad and the role he'd played in them to creep in.

From the first moment he laid eyes on her, he'd known she was different and had the power to shake up his life and change everything. He just hadn't known she was going to wind up shaking up his life like this.

"Put your clothes on," he ordered as he ran scenarios through his mind. He didn't have enough weapons on him to handle a full-scale assault. He had to get himself and Scarlett out of there. That was the priority. Get Scarlett someplace safe and then he and his team could go and hunt down Raul Castillo and every single one of his men.

Raul deserved to die, and not just because he was a notorious weapons trafficker, but because of everything he'd done to Scarlett.

As soon as Scarlett had her clothes back on, he grabbed her hand. The shooting had stopped which meant the men were either gone or they were going to come inside to assess the damage they'd caused. Likely the shooting was to flush him and Scarlett out. They had no vehicle since his was mostly destroyed, and while drivable it wasn't going to be any use as a getaway vehicle.

If the men thought they were going to exit the building from the ground floor then they'd do the opposite.

Dragging Scarlett along with him, Tate headed upstairs, then down the hall to the stairs that led to the attic. Pulling on the hanging rope, the steps appeared from the ceiling, and he pulled Scarlett up with him.

She came willingly, not fighting him, and her fingers had curled around his tight enough to hurt. Again, she wasn't acting like someone who wanted to get away, she was acting like someone scared and clinging to the only thing they trusted to keep them safe.

In the attic, he opened the small window down the end. It was just big enough for them to climb through it. From there, they could climb into the tree beside the house, jump from it to one in the neighbor's yard, climb down it, jump some fences, and get back onto the street on the other side of his block.

Then he and Scarlett were going to talk, and she was going to tell him how she'd been pulled into all of this, and so help him, he was going to do whatever it took to get the truth out of her.

No more lies.

No more games.

No more distractions.

Scarlett Madden was going to tell him what he wanted to know, and then he'd decide what to do with her.

CHAPTER ELEVEN

January 16th
2:00 A.M.

When was this going to stop?

Was Raul still trying to kidnap her or did he just want her dead now?

And what about Tate?

Was he in danger too?

How did Raul even know that she was staying at his house?

Wasn't like it was planned or anything. Tate had been watching her house, probably because he thought she was guilty, and wound up saving her life. When he could have just handed her over to the authorities he hadn't. Instead, he'd taken her to his house, tended to her, made love to her, held her while she slept, all because … Scarlett didn't even know why.

She didn't think he did either.

Tears threatened to spill down her cheeks, but alongside the fear, there was a huge dollop of anger.

Raul Castillo didn't get to blow up her life like this.

He'd ruined everything, made her doubt her team and the people she worked with, tainted her home, got her accused of betraying her country and branded a traitor. Whether they believed in her innocence or not, Prey would surely fire her, she'd lose her dream job and the people she had built a family with.

Everything was ruined.

But he wasn't going to take her life.

Nope.

In fact, she was going to do whatever it took to see that he was caught. Heck, she'd rather he was dead. He deserved it for what he'd done to her, and countless numbers of people who had been killed with the weapons he had trafficked to people he knew were going to use them for evil.

Finally, they ran through the front yard of a house at the back of Tate's block and six houses down, and out onto the street.

There had been no more gunshots after the ones that had destroyed Tate's living room. Were the men still there? Checking the house to see if they were inside? Or were they already being followed?

Scarlett turned to ask Tate what he thought and what the plan was when he whirled on her.

"Do you know how they found you?" he demanded, grabbing her by the shoulders and leaning down so they were eye to eye.

The softer Tate that had just been emerging back at his place was gone, the cold, hard, angry Tate was back.

Pain tore through her heart, but again along with it came an arrow of anger.

Tate didn't get to hurl more accusations at her.

He didn't get to blame her.

He didn't get to keep treating her like she had done something wrong.

She was sick and tired of all the accusations.

Enough.

Reaching her breaking point, Scarlett acted without thinking. The crack of her hand connecting with Tate's cheek and the sting in her palm caught her by surprise.

Tate, too, if the way his eyes widened in shock before narrowing was any indication.

"Don't you *dare* accuse me of being a traitor again," she snarled, surprising herself at the venom dripping from her every word. All her life she'd been shut out, left out, told to just get over it, and that wanting her own parents to actually care about her made her weak. All her life she'd just taken it. She hadn't raged at her parents, she hadn't raged at her grandparents, she hadn't raged at her brother when he joined the military and left her behind.

But now she was so consumed with anger there was no way she could keep it inside.

"I've already told you—told everyone—a hundred times already. I didn't write any email, I didn't make any deals, I wasn't selling the Reactivator to anyone, I didn't do anything wrong," she seethed, so angry she was actually vibrating with it.

How dare Tate accuse her all over again after everything they shared last night.

Stupidly, she had believed that him having sex with her proved that he believed she was innocent.

What an idiot.

A man who lied right to her face and pretended he didn't know her had no scruples. Of course, he would take sex when it was offered even if it was with a woman he considered to be a traitor.

Pain speared through her heart again, but instead of allowing it to control her, she took control of it, used it to fan the flames of her rage.

When his gaze softened and the grip on her shoulders loosened a little, she didn't allow her guard to drop.

Right now, Tate was as much the enemy as Raul and his men were. Anyone who wasn't going to listen to her or hear the truth, was working against her. They were trying to prove she was guilty without even looking into what she had said and being fair and impartial.

"Look, I believe you weren't trying to sell the drug. I know you're a good person. A kind and loving person. You wouldn't willingly sell a drug that you and your friends created to save the lives of the people you care about to someone who would use it against them. I do truly believe that. Maybe I had some doubts at first because of the email, but I know you wouldn't do something like that."

There was a but coming.

There was always a but coming.

"But you got involved with Raul somehow. Did he threaten you? One of your friends?"

Her hand was moving before she realized it again, only this time Tate was prepared, snagging her wrist before her palm could make contact with his cheek.

How dare he continue to throw accusations at her.

Hadn't he heard a single word she'd said?

"Yeah, *jerk,* I got involved with him when he sent his men to break into my house and kidnap me. I got "involved","—she made air quotes with her fingers—"with him when I had to shoot one of his men to try to survive, not knowing there were more men already in the house. I got involved with him when I woke up in a small, cold, stone cell. When I was cuffed to a chair and beaten. When I was strung up by my hands and whipped. When I was …" Scarlett trailed off, realizing in her anger she'd almost blurted out about the drug. "When I was dragged out to the pool, and had a rock tied to my leg, and told I was going to be shoved into the water and fished out when I passed out. What about any of that makes it sound like I was any sort of willing, or even unwilling participant?"

By the time she finished her rant, Scarlett was breathing hard, her pulse throbbing loudly, all the aches and pains that had seemed to dim when she was in Tate's home were now screaming at her so she couldn't ignore them.

Tate was staring at her in shock, but by now she was done caring what he thought about her.

Arrogant jerk.

Like he was so perfect and everyone around him was beneath him.

What had she ever seen in him anyway?

Was she so desperate for love that she was inventing

connections now with the first man who looked at her with a hint of interest in his eyes?

No more.

No more going out on dates every chance she got hoping that this time she was going to find the one and fall in love. No more dreaming of big weddings filled with love and laughter. No more pretending happy endings existed.

She was done.

Done with men, done with looking for love, done with caring so much about what others thought because she always felt like such a failure.

From here on out, she was focusing on learning to love one person and one person alone.

Herself.

How could she ever expect to actually find something that would last when she doubted everything about herself? When she felt like she wasn't good enough, that she was a failure, that she was too weak to ever be taken seriously.

She'd survived being tortured, she hadn't told Raul what he wanted, and she wasn't weak. If she could make it through that then she could make it through anything.

You're not weak.

You're not pathetic.

You are strong.

A survivor.

You know how to love and care for others.

You know how to make them smile and laugh.

You learned love even if it wasn't at the hands of the people who were supposed to raise you and teach you everything you needed to know about life.

You have nothing to be ashamed of.

The internal pep talk worked. Sure she'd probably have to repeat it a few hundred times, but Scarlett already felt stronger and more sure of herself.

Determined to bring Raul Castillo down, Scarlett shoved away from Tate, surprised when he let her go. They couldn't stay out here, cops would be coming, alerted by calls of gunshots, and by now, Raul's men had to know they weren't in the house. If she was going to bring down the weapons trafficker, then she had to get to Prey. Her team said they believed in her and told her that everyone else did, too. At the time she wasn't sure she believed them, but that was her insecurity talking.

Her people had her back.

Tate Laurier just wasn't one of her people.

"I want to go into Prey, then I want you to get the heck out of my life," she told him, deadly serious. Any connection she'd thought she felt toward this man had fizzled and died when he accused her all over again of being a traitor just hours after he was buried inside her.

JANUARY 16TH
2:10 A.M.

HE'D MESSED UP.

Possibly beyond repair.

The sense of desolation Tate felt knowing that Scarlett had just slipped outside of his reach came as a shock.

If he'd wanted her, he could have had her, but he'd made his choices, decided that risking falling in love was too great a chance to take, and taken the easy way out, pushed her away before he could develop feelings. He'd been ruthless in how he'd gone about it because he'd panicked at the strength of his feelings after just one night.

Coward.

There was no other way to describe his behavior.

Now, even if he changed his mind, he'd lost his chance with her.

Lost it as soon as he'd accused her of bringing Raul's men to his front door.

The sting on his cheek from where her palm had connected ran deeper than surface level. Not in a physical sense, she hadn't inflicted any injury, no broken bone, not even any bruising, if there was even a red mark at all it would quickly fade. But the sting of knowing that he'd hurt her, pushed her too far away from him to ever get her back, that would leave a lasting mark.

What could have been now never would.

Taking a step away from him, Scarlett pulled her cell phone from a small pocket in the side of her leggings. He hadn't even realized she had it on her. When he thought about it, he recalled her having her cell in her hand when she crept out of her house, but so much had happened in the last twenty-four hours that it had slipped his mind. He'd been preoccupied with the idea of Scarlett taking a bullet for him to think of anything else.

Rookie mistake.

Scarlett hadn't been alone while in his house other than one short trip to the bathroom, she hadn't made a phone call, and while she could have sent a text with the phone on silent so he didn't hear the tapping of keys, there was another much more likely scenario.

The cell phone was bugged.

It would explain why Raul's men knew when she was back home and then knew she was at his place. She was being tracked.

Since her cell phone had been left behind when she was kidnapped, he didn't think Raul's men had a chance to put the tracker in her phone.

Which meant …

Maybe somebody at Prey was setting Scarlett up.

They might have access to her phone, and they'd know about the drug. Was it possible she really had been kidnapped and someone else had set up the email trail in case she was found so nobody would be looking at them?

Was it possible that someone was one of her teammates?

Who else would know enough about both Scarlett and the drug and have access to her cell phone?

She wasn't supposed to be found. She was supposed to have died in Raul's remote jungle home, never to be seen or heard from again. That would leave the true traitor in the clear and make sure suspicion never landed on them.

"No," he said, knocking the phone from Scarlett's hand when she tried to make a call. If the phone was compromised, he had to destroy it. Then he was going to have to keep Scarlett someplace safe, away from Prey, while he figured this out. He needed input from someone who wasn't messed up when it came to this woman. Someone who could think clearly and logically when she was around because those were things he absolutely couldn't do. If that didn't tell him everything he needed to know about his feelings for her then nothing else ever would.

"What are you doing?" Scarlett growled, giving him the most adorable little death glare he'd ever seen.

Fighting a smile—he didn't think Scarlett would appreciate him thinking she was cute when she was clearly furious with him—he lifted a foot and slammed it down onto the phone which had landed at their feet.

"Are you crazy? Do you think I was going to call Raul right in front of you? Newsflash, Tate, I don't have his number because we're not buddies," Scarlett snapped.

"I think your phone is bugged," he explained.

That took a little of the wind out of her sails. "Oh. I mean, I never thought of that, but it makes sense. Why did *you* think of it?" she asked, suspicion raging in her huge doe eyes. "After all, you already have a convenient target standing right in front of you. I'm the epicenter of all that is evil, aren't I?" she taunted.

Was he ready to set aside all hints that she was guilty, even if it was because she had been coerced, and fully embrace the notion that she had been innocent all along?

Was he ready to set aside the evidence against Scarlett and look at it from a different perspective?

Was he ready to allow his gut to lead him rather than constantly trying to override it with what he thought was sensible logic but was really just his guilt over getting his father thrown in jail?

Was he ready to trust the woman whom he suspected if he let her have the power to wriggle beneath his defenses and lodge herself in his heart, a place he wanted to protect from love at all costs?

Before he got a chance to make up his mind one way or the other—and once he did, there would be no going back, no matter which side he picked—he saw shadows moving down the end of the street.

Not willing to hang around and find out if they were Raul's men, not when he had Scarlett with him, he grabbed her hand and pulled her along with him as he darted into the front yard of a house with a huge hedge fence. It should give them a place to hide unless the men were searching each and every yard.

"What are you doing?" Scarlett snapped, trying to fight her way out of his grip.

Not happening.

Yanking her up against his body, he pinned her arms to her sides with one of his across her chest and covered her mouth with his other hand. If she really tried, she could still make enough of a sound to alert the men of their hiding place, so he leaned down to whisper in her ear.

"Shh, Scarlett, I think it's Raul's men."

Tate knew his words penetrated because she stopped fighting him and instead went completely still.

They both seemed to hold their breaths as the footsteps grew louder, whispered voices accompanying them.

"They should be here," a voice with a Mexican accent muttered.

"You sure this is the right spot?" another asked.

“Yeah, tracker says the phone should be here,” the first replied.

“Oh, it’s here,” a third said, and Tate didn't have to be able to see them to know they’d found the wrecked phone.

“They know,” the second man said.

“Boss won't be happy,” the third added.

“They can't have gone far, they’re on foot,” the first reminded them. “We can still find them before the boss even knows we lost them.”

The footsteps faded as the men hurried off further down the road, searching for him and Scarlett. There was no doubt what would happen if they were found. He’d be killed, they wouldn’t allow Scarlett to take another bullet for him—not that he wanted her to—and she would be taken back to Raul.

Where she would be tortured until she gave up the formula.

Everybody had a breaking point.

Didn't matter how much training you had, exert enough pressure, and everybody broke.

No way could he allow that to happen to Scarlett.

Releasing her slowly, he turned her around to face him. She was pale in the moonlight and shivering, not dressed properly to be out on the cold winter night, not even wearing any shoes. Her eyes were wide, and although fear shone brightly in them there was something else as well.

Determination.

She’d taken her anger at being accused of being a

traitor and was using it as fuel. Proud as he was of her for standing up for herself, he was equal parts scared.

Because that determination meant she was prepared to take risks. Risks that might well get her killed, because she already felt like she didn't have anything to lose.

Somehow, he had to convince her that wasn't true.

She was smart and beautiful, strong and kind, sweet and funny, any man would be lucky to have her.

That man just couldn't be him.

If things were different, if he was different, he'd snap up what she was offering in a heartbeat.

But some things just weren't meant to be.

That didn't mean he wasn't going to do everything he could to keep her alive, and hope that one day she found the happiness and place to belong she deserved, even if it couldn't be with him. He wasn't that selfish, even if his entire body reacted violently to the thought of her with another man.

CHAPTER TWELVE

January 16th
2:22 A.M.

"I'M sorry I didn't believe you," Tate whispered as they slipped back onto the sidewalk.

Did he really think one little apology was going to be a balm for her anger?

If he did, he wasn't as smart as she had given him credit for.

Scarlett was in full-on fury mode. Just because she was following Tate without argument didn't mean she wasn't still furious with him. A simple apology just wasn't going to cut it. She was thinking something more along the lines of getting down on his knees and begging for her forgiveness for accusing her of being a traitor and refusing to listen.

For having sex with her when he still thought she was guilty.

That was the biggest gut punch of all.

A part of her kept whispering reminders that he was only basing his decision on her guilt or innocence on the evidence he had. That email was damning, she got that, she really did, but maybe she'd just expected more from him. Thought their night together meant more. At least meant enough that he would give her the benefit of the doubt.

Still, she shut that thinking down real quick.

She was entitled to her anger, and more than that, she *needed* it. It was either be angry at everything and everyone who hadn't been on her side from the beginning or fall apart because everything that had happened really was too much for one person to handle, especially when the end didn't appear to be anywhere in sight.

If Tate was surprised that she didn't accept his apology, he didn't let on. Just kept his hold on her hand as they walked through the quiet streets. With the early hour, there was no one else about. The occasional car passed, and every time it did, Tate would pull her into his arms and pretend to kiss her.

At first, she just closed her eyes, kept her head down, and held her breath. Silently counting the seconds until he let go of her. It was a different kind of torture, being held so intimately by a man that she had at one time craved with every atom of her body, heart, mind, and soul.

When she thought about it like that it made her sound extra stupid.

One amazing night and she had been already planning what an amazing future they'd share.

No more being that naïve.

Love didn't really happen that way in real life. Movies, sure, books, absolutely, and songs too, but not in real life. In real life, people just took what they wanted from you and then left. You had to fight on your own to make something of yourself. Which is why she was sure there would be no more dating, and no more letting men get close until she learned to love herself, be happy and content with her own company.

By the fourth time Tate drew her into his arms for a fake kiss, Scarlett could no longer kid herself into believing she didn't want his touch. Didn't relish it. Wasn't counting down the seconds until he could let her go but rather counting the seconds until he would hold her again.

She really had to be a glutton for punishment.

His touch soothed, comforted, and heated her blood, even though she was pretty sure he still had doubts about her and was yet to make up his mind if she was a criminal, a woman coerced into doing something wrong, or the innocent victim that she was.

Get over him.

He's over you.

Was from the moment he snuck out of your house without so much as a goodbye.

Even if he thinks you're innocent he doesn't want you.

Never did.

Yet, as the taillights of the car disappeared around the corner, Tate took his time releasing her. His fingers trailed down her back, making her shiver, and it had nothing to do with the light touches against her wounds. Sure, they hurt, but his touch ... warmed. It was so gentle, so tender, and the way he looked down at her like he wanted to kiss her until both of them forgot their own names, and then wrap her up in bubble wrap and stash her someplace safe, told her that he felt more than he let on.

Was he running because he was afraid?

They hadn't talked a lot about their pasts so she didn't know much about Tate Laurier or his life.

If he had pushed her away out of fear, she could understand that. Didn't mean that hurting her because he was scared was okay, but she could understand it. There would even have been a time when she would have helped him with his fears if he would have just let her in.

But now …

Now she wasn't sure she had the energy to take on more problems than the ones already on her plate.

Another lifetime and they could have been really happy together. In this lifetime … it was already too late.

Still, when his fingers curled around hers again, she couldn't help the giddy little thrill she felt at holding hands. Was she really so desperate for love and attention that holding hands with a man who had made no secret out of not liking her and believing the worst without even giving her a chance was enough to make her heart race and her stomach cartwheel?

Pathetic.

"The park is right around the corner," Tate said softly. "I'm thinking we hole up there until it's light. Raul wants to stay under the radar, I don't think he'd want his men trying anything in broad daylight. Once the sun comes up, we'll get you someplace safe, and I'll head into Prey."

"Why can't I come with you to Prey?" If Raul Castillo was hunting her then there would be no safer place for her to be.

After a moment's hesitation, Tate's fingers tightened around her own. "Because I think there might be a mole at Prey."

That shocked her enough that she jerked to a stop. "A mole? At Prey?"

That was crazy.

There was no mole at Prey.

Sure, there had been an incident years before she joined the company involving Fox and his now-wife, Evie. A mole at Prey had leaked her location when she was hiding from a crime boss with a hit out on her. Because of that, Evie had almost been killed.

But that was a long time ago, and Eagle was even stricter now when he hired people.

Especially after his own wife—well, now wife, at the time they'd just both been attracted to one another—had been hired under false pretenses. Since Olivia had really been working for Eagle's brother Falcon, everything had worked out okay, and in the end, Eagle had managed to earn Olivia's trust back and win her heart.

"How else do you explain the email and the fact that Raul knew about the Reactivator?" Tate asked.

There was no way she could deny there was some logic to the theory, but still ... a mole at Prey?

Impossible.

"If you have another idea, I'm open to hearing it, Scarlett," Tate continued. "Because as far as I see it, there are only three options. One, you're lying to everyone, and you really did intend to sell the drug to Raul Castillo." When she snarled at him, he smiled and chuckled. "Didn't say I was going with that option. Two, Raul somehow made contact with you and managed to force your hand. If that happened, I hope you would have told someone so they could help you. But even if that's what happened, it doesn't explain how he knew about the drug to begin with. Prey keeps things close to the chest until they're ready. Or three, somebody set you up."

That was the theory she and her team had figured out before they left the other night.

But, somehow, she hadn't really connected the idea to a mole at Prey.

That hurt almost worse than being accused of being a traitor. Because it meant that somebody she loved and trusted had set out to betray her. They had written those emails specifically to make her look guilty, and they had allowed her to be kidnapped and tortured, knowing it would eventually lead to her death.

"You're the one who's been saying all along you were innocent," Tate reminded her. "This is the only theory that supports that. Someone at Prey set you up."

"Who?" she whispered. Who would do that to her?

"I don't know. You're going to have to think about it and make a list. I'm guessing not a lot of people knew about the Reactivator so it's going to be a short list."

The problem was, everybody on that list was somebody she cared about.

Her team.

Fox and his team.

Eagle and probably some of his siblings and their partners, although most of them ran their own teams and left dealing with every single detail up to Eagle.

Prey's lawyer.

A couple of the people who worked in the lab with them.

A couple of other office employees.

Not a single one of them stood out to her.

* * *

JANUARY 16TH

9:13 A.M.

SHE WAS GOING to be mad when she realized what he had planned.

Tate knew he wasn't being fair to Scarlett. She was the one at the center of this mess, and she deserved every chance she could get to prove her innocence, but he couldn't allow her to go walking right into danger.

Someone at Prey was dirty.

Until he knew who, she wasn't setting foot in that building, nor was he going to tell a single person where she was.

Since he still had his phone on him, after they'd walked around the park until the sun came up, he'd suggested stopping at a gas station so they could both use the bathroom and grab something to eat. In reality, he'd wanted to be alone for a couple of minutes so he could set up some meetings without Scarlett knowing.

Yep.

She was going to be *furious* when she found out what he had planned for her.

His team already knew what was going on, he'd called them after Scarlett had passed out at his place in the early hours of yesterday morning. So, none of them had been surprised when he asked if anyone minded if he borrowed their hang-out place for a while. It was an old, abandoned bar that they had originally planned to makeover and run together. In the end, they'd had so much fun just hanging out there that the space was now simply used for that. While the idea of turning it into a bar at some point wasn't off the table, for now, it was quiet, it looked abandoned from the outside, but inside was completely renovated, had a great security system, and the basement had no windows and only one door out.

Perfect for keeping an unwilling guest.

Scarlett could hate him for this, but at least she'd be alive.

"Here we are," he said when they stopped in front of the building. When Scarlett's nose scrunched up in disbelief he laughed. "Trust me, it looks better inside."

"I should hope so."

From the small gasp when he unlocked the front door and guided her inside, he knew he'd proven his point. The walls were painted a dark gray, the hardwood floors stained a dark brown, there was a bar down one end, a couple of tables around it, then the rest of the floor space was taken up with pool tables, air hockey tables, gaming machines, and foosball tables. It was a dream hang-out space for a bunch of single guys.

"Wow," she murmured.

"Best part is the downstairs is a huge apartment. Bathroom with a jacuzzi and walk-in shower, a king-size bed, TV, and fully stocked kitchen."

"Why didn't we come here last night? Would have been way better than wandering the park in bare feet and a ripped sweater," she grumbled.

"Didn't want to risk leading anyone here if they were still out there. Thought we could hang out here for a few days until we get this mess sorted. Why don't you go down and shower and change, and I'll come check your wounds when you're done."

While he would have forcibly put her in the basement if he had to, he knew he wouldn't when Scarlett's eyes lit up at the prospect of a shower.

"I'll be down in a moment," he added, leading her over to the door and opening it, switching on the lights.

Scarlett was a few steps down before she realized what was happening.

"Tate?" she screeched, running back up the stairs, but it was already too late.

He'd closed the door and locked it, trapping her down there.

"What are you doing? You locked me in? Why would you do that?" She sounded so incredulous, so hurt, so betrayed, that for a moment, he second-guessed himself. Just because he was doing this to keep her safe didn't mean she would see it the same way even after he came back later and explained.

"Sorry, sweetheart," he murmured, touching his forehead to the door where Scarlett was hammering on the other side.

Then resolutely, he straightened and walked away, locking the front door behind him. Calling an Uber, he gave the address of Prey's West Coast office building and tried to relax. Scarlett was safe. Angry but safe. For now, he had to focus on finding the mole so that she wasn't going to wind up spending the rest of her life in prison.

Just because Prey was on her side, and he was on her side, didn't mean she wouldn't be charged and sentenced.

Twenty minutes later, they pulled up outside Prey, and he paid the driver and then headed inside. Standing in the lobby was none other than Eagle Oswald himself. With his jet-black hair, piercing blue eyes, expensive suit, and confident posture the man looked every bit the legend he was.

"Laurier," Eagle said in way of greeting, gesturing for him to follow him into a quiet conference room just off the lobby. "To what do we owe the pleasure of your company?"

There was no way Eagle didn't know about the dead bodies left behind just down the street from Scarlett's house. Or that his own place had been shot up. The billionaire didn't look surprised to see him there, so he knew exactly why Tate had come.

Scarlett.

"Was I wrong about you, Laurier?" Eagle asked, a taunting lilt to his tone.

"Wrong about me?"

"When I requested your team go in after Scarlett."

"You requested us?" He had assumed they were just assigned that op because they were the only available team, not that they had been a special request. "Why would you do that?"

"Because I needed someone who cared to go after her. I couldn't risk her being hurt and I knew you would make sure she was safe even if you thought she was a traitor."

"How could you know that?" He had never spoken to a single person about his night with Scarlett.

"You ran a search on her a few months back, right before Halloween. Any time someone searches one of my employees I'm notified. I assumed it was because of a romantic interest so I did a little digging into your background. I don't know why nothing ever happened between you two and I don't care, but when I needed someone I trusted, I asked for you. Was I wrong? Should you bring her in so I can assign someone else to look after her?"

Why did Tate get the feeling the man was playing matchmaker?

And why did the thought of anyone but himself protecting Scarlett fill him with a deep protective rage he'd never felt toward another person?

"I can keep her safe," he replied and was rewarded with a smile as Eagle's posture relaxed. "Wait, you said you needed someone who would keep her safe even if they thought she was a traitor. You never doubted her. How can you be so sure she's innocent?" As far as he was concerned, everyone at Prey was a suspect except Eagle. There was no need for him to sell anything, he was richer than Raul Castillo could ever hope to be. Still, he wondered how the man was so sure.

"Because we only released part of the evidence," Eagle

replied, pulling out a chair at the table and gesturing that Tate should join him. "More than one email was uncovered. Whoever wrote them slipped up. One out of the six emails wasn't signed with Scarlett's name, it was one of the other women on her team."

"So, Scarlett didn't write those emails." Tate waited for the wave of relief to hit having verifiable proof that Scarlett was innocent, but it didn't come. Somewhere along the way, he had come to the conclusion on his own. He'd known it, felt it, understood it even when he didn't realize that he did.

"I'd confirm that, but you sound like you already believed it anyway," Eagle said with a grin, before sobering. "We knew it wasn't Scarlett, but then she was kidnapped, and I knew that if I released everything I had, it would be tipping my hand, putting her and the rest of her team in more danger. Whoever set her up wasn't targeting her specifically. I believe there were emails "written" from all of the women, so whoever they ended up going after could be framed. The timing of us finding those emails suggests we were supposed to find them, supposed to believe Scarlett was guilty so we wouldn't be looking anywhere else."

The same conclusions he'd come to himself even without knowing there were emails in one of the other women's names.

"I have a mole in my company," Eagle said, tone gone dark and cold. "I won't tolerate that. I needed to keep that evidence under wraps because I need whoever really wrote those emails to think they worked. They would have been suspicious if we immediately turned on Scarlett, so I've played everything as though we believe in her, because we do, but that we're also bringing in outside help so nobody can accuse us of covering anything up. We need to keep the mole content. So long as they think the focus is still on Scarlett, they'll become complacent and I can flush them out. When I do, I'll make them wish they never thought of hurting one of my people."

Tate liked that Eagle's main priority was on the people who worked for him and not his company's reputation.

"What do you need me to do?"

"I need to know that Scarlett is safe and being protected. I'm trusting you with her life, Laurier, and I think possibly with her heart. Don't make me regret it."

The threat hung in the air between them, and Tate wished he could say that Scarlett would walk away with her heart intact, but the truth was, he wasn't sure either of them were going to.

CHAPTER THIRTEEN

January 16th
5:11 P.M.

How could he do this to her?

Locking her up like she was a prisoner.

Scarlett was fuming as she circled the room in another futile attempt to find a way out.

Tate had lied to her.

Played her.

Even though it shouldn't, knowing that cut way too deep. It left wounds on her heart. Because it didn't matter how many times she told herself she had imagined that connection and that Tate didn't like her much less feel anything for her, her stupid heart wouldn't get with the program.

It wasn't even that her body found him attractive. That she could definitely ignore. It was the fact that every time she was around him, she got the warmest, flutteriest feeling in her stomach, and her heart felt like it was swelling until it was too big for her chest.

She hated it.

Every time it happened it was like life was taunting her. Like it was whispering in her ear, you know that man you thought could be the one, well he's not, he doesn't even like you.

Did life think she was stupid and didn't know that already?

All those lies he'd told to lull her into a false sense of security so he could convince her to follow him there felt like a dozen knives buried in her back.

Worst of all, he still thought she was a traitor.

Why else would he lock her up?

A scream of frustration bubbled through her and erupted to fill the space, and she took the stairs back to the top, hammering her hands on the door until her throat ached from screaming, and her hands were bruised and bloodied.

Before her mind could spiral down the path of wondering whether her team had been lying to her as well, the door swung open.

Caught off guard, Scarlett stumbled backward.

If it wasn't for a pair of hands reaching out to grab her, she would have tumbled all the way down to the bottom of the stairs.

That moment of relief evaporated in an instant when she looked up to see Tate.

He was back, but what did that mean for her?

What was he going to do?

Was he taking her into custody and handing her off to

whatever agency wanted to deal with her? Or was he going to hand out his own brand of punishment?

Fear and fury warred inside her, but she straightened her spine and met his gaze directly. "I hate you," she said simply.

Did he wince at her words? Scarlett wasn't sure, she was vibrating with anger, breathing hard, and her pounding pulse echoed too loudly in her ears for her to figure out anything else.

"I know you do," Tate said with a weary sigh. His gaze raked over her, taking in her disheveled appearance and her bloodied hands, and his eyes narrowed. "You didn't take a shower. Or get any sleep. Did you eat something? Why didn't you even change your clothes?"

He was kidding, right?

What part about being locked up against her will did he think would be conducive to taking a shower and having a snack?

Just as she was about to spit out every bit of venom that had been growing inside her these last however many hours since he locked her up and left, Tate spoke first.

Spoke the last words she imagined him saying.

"Scarlett, I owe you an apology. Actually, I owe you several."

That took a little of the wind out of her sails. A little. Not all. "Yeah, you do, buddy," she muttered.

When she went to breeze past him, needing to be out of the claustrophobic space before she lost her mind—locking someone who had recently been held captive into a small room was not a good idea—Tate stopped her.

Ready to fight, do whatever it took to not get put back

in that room, Scarlett was already pulling back her arm, ready to strike him when his chuckle halted her.

"Hold up, little fighter, I was just going to give you this." He held up a shiny new key, and when she shot him a confused look he added, "It's a key to the apartment. I'd like us to stay there together so nobody looking for you will find you, but I don't want you to feel like you don't have my trust. This way you know you can't get locked in here again."

Weariness suddenly assaulted her. She just wanted this to be over. She didn't want to have to worry about Raul sending men after her. Didn't want to be considered a traitor. "Wait, you said nobody who's looking for me will find me here. More than just Raul?"

"I'm sorry, Scarlett. There's a warrant out for your arrest." Tate's voice was gentle, and he'd said he wanted her to hide out here. Actually, he'd said that they were going to hide out here together.

Together.

Why?

Rubbing at her temples, she looked up at him through her lashes. "I don't understand why you're staying. Why you're not turning me in. You're risking your career and your freedom."

Why on earth would he do that for her when he didn't even like her?

"Can I make you something to eat while we talk?" he asked.

Curling her fingers around the key when he placed it in her palm, Scarlett weighed her options. With law enforcement, every defense agency, and the weapons trafficker hunting her, she wasn't safe out there. Tate didn't like her, and he'd betrayed her by planning all along to bring her here and lock her in, but he was offering her protection anyway.

And risking a lot to do it.

With a tired nod, she turned and clutched the key as she headed back into the apartment. With Tate here it felt that much smaller, but oddly less claustrophobic. This man threw her system completely out of whack, and she didn't really understand why.

Didn't understand him either.

"What about grilled cheese sandwiches?" Tate asked as he headed for the kitchenette.

Honestly, she didn't care what they ate. It had been ... much too long since she'd last eaten, and yet she had zero appetite. "I'm not all that hungry."

"You need to eat, Scarlett. You haven't had anything since at least the night you went home, that's forty-eight hours ago now, and you've been running on adrenalin ever since. Food, we talk, then you're going to go take a hot bath and get the sleep you need."

There was authority in his tone, and she got the feeling arguing about anything was pointless.

For now, at least, she was going to take the path of least resistance.

"Fine. Grilled cheese is okay with me," she said, sinking into a stool at the breakfast bar.

"Once I've got the food cooking, I'll take a look at your hands."

Glancing down at her hands as they rested on the counter, she saw her knuckles were bloody, more wounds to add to her growing collection. She felt like one big, throbbing, bloody mess, battered inside and out.

"First off I need to apologize to you for blowing you off after the night we spent together," Tate said as he prepared their food. "I shouldn't have done that, and I definitely shouldn't have pretended I didn't know you that day at the grocery store. Truth is, you scare me, Scarlett Madden."

Surprised by Tate's honesty, her gaze darted up to look at him. "*You're* scared of *me*?" she asked incredulously.

"You aren't afraid of anything, Scarlett, not even getting hurt. You put yourself out there, wear your heart on your sleeve, you trust your gut in a way I haven't been able to do. You don't let the possibility of getting hurt hold you back, you just go after what you want, and I respect the hell out of that. Truth is, I've been scared to fall in love ever since I was a kid because my parents loved each other so much they didn't have room in their hearts for anyone else. Not even me. I never wanted to risk being so dependent on another person that if I lost them I could no longer function. But you … you got under my skin."

Unsure if that was a compliment or an insult, Scarlett cocked her head and studied the man cooking in the kitchen. "So, you hate me for that?"

Tate's sigh was as weary as she felt. "No, Scarlett. I never hated you. I resented you for making me feel things I didn't want to and reacted badly. I'm truly sorry for that. No excuses. I was a jerk. And I'm sorry for not trusting what I knew about you to be true and thinking even for a second that you would be a traitor. I let some … family stuff cloud my judgment, and that was unfair to you. I'm sorry that I left you here today. I had to go into Prey, and I couldn't risk taking you there knowing there's a mole. I … don't know what to think when it comes to you, Scarlett. But I know that when you're around, I feel different, and when you're not I can't stop thinking about you. I don't deserve your forgiveness but I'm asking for it anyway. Do you think you can forgive me for treating you so badly?"

* * *

JANUARY 16TH
5:26 P.M.

HE HAD LAID ALL his cards on the table.

After thinking over it all day, Tate had come to the conclusion that he had to find the courage to see through this thing with Scarlett. Wherever it ended up leading him.

Now he had to wait and see if she was willing to give him a chance.

A chance to … what he wasn't quite sure yet.

All he knew was that Scarlett held nothing back. Allowed her childhood of being neglected and abandoned to fuel her and make her go after what she wanted harder. Unlike him. He'd used his childhood as an excuse to wave the white flag of surrender and hide.

Shame.

That's what the comparison made him feel.

While he had no idea what would happen between

him and Scarlett, he wanted at the very least to earn her forgiveness. If he couldn't convince her to risk her heart on him again, after he had rejected it and her at every turn, then he understood. Completely. But he needed to prove to her he was sorry and get her forgiveness. Maybe then he could respect himself again.

Only she hadn't said anything.

Was just sitting there staring at him like she didn't quite believe he was real.

No wonder after the way he'd treated her. The only time she'd seen the real Tate was on that night they spent together. She'd seen the Tate he didn't allow anyone, not even his teammates, to see. But if he told her that he doubted she would believe him. Because the Tate she had the most experience with was the cold, hard man who would do whatever it took to protect himself and his heart from ever being rejected again.

Assuming Scarlett's silence was her rejection of his apology, he turned, ready to go and get the first aid kit. At least he'd make sure her wounds were taken care of. Then feed her and make sure she got the rest she needed. Then he'd do whatever it took to clear her name and make sure she could live her life freely and without fear.

"Tate."

His name falling from her lips stilled him. Did he dare to hope?

"It's easier to forgive you for treating me like a traitor. That I can understand, it's everything else …" her voice trailed off but she didn't need to finish her sentence.

Truth was, their childhoods had been alike in many ways.

Just because he hadn't been pushed to become something he didn't want to be, and his parents had been around, at least physically, they weren't available emotionally. There but not there. Not in any way that mattered.

"Can you give me a chance to make you understand? Show you that I wasn't running from you but myself? That I acted like a jerk out of a sense of self-preservation?" It was a big ask, he wasn't denying that. Nor could he promise her he'd never be a jerk again. But he could promise he would do everything in his power to overcome his fears rather than letting them control him.

"I ... I could maybe ... try ..." Scarlett said slowly, looking up at him with uncertain eyes.

A win as far as he was concerned.

And so much more than he deserved.

"I'll take it," he said quickly, making her smile. Just a tiny smile, but better than the lost look that had been on her face a moment ago. Turning off the grilled cheese, he wanted Scarlett to relax so she could keep her food down, he reached out and took her hand, careful not to press too hard against her battered knuckles. "Can you let me take care of you? Just for tonight."

One night to show her the man he could be.

The man he *wanted* to be.

Was it enough?

No.

That was the simple answer. He'd been a jerk to Scarlett for months, there was no way a single night could change anything. But at least it was a start.

"Umm ... I guess ..." Scarlett said, sounding uncertain,

but the smallest hint of pink stained her cheeks, and his mind immediately went to all the ways he could take care of her.

"Hey." Hooking a finger under her chin, he nudged until she looked up at him. "I don't bite, Scarlett. At least not unless asked," he added with a wink.

Her cheeks went from pink to flaming red in a heartbeat, and Tate threw back his head and laughed.

Damn, it felt good to laugh.

Taking the first step had been hard, but now, earning Scarlett's forgiveness and learning to let someone get close to him was easier than he'd thought it would be. Did he think it was going to be all smooth sailing from here on out? No. But he was at least out on the water, the rest he could figure out as he went.

"Come here." Scooping her up into his arms, he carried her into the bathroom. For a small apartment they'd put in just in case one of them needed a place to crash, they had spared no expense. The room was floor-to-ceiling tiles, with a huge walk-in shower, and an enormous jacuzzi tub.

Now he set her on the counter beside the sink and turned on the tub. Leaving it to fill, he returned to Scarlett, stripping her leggings and sweatshirt off her. She didn't protest him removing her clothes, but when he stripped off his own her eyes grew wide as they roamed his body.

There was no need to worry about their attraction fizzling out, from the looks of things, he didn't think either of them could ever get their fill of the other.

It was earning Scarlett's trust and then her heart that was going to be a challenge.

Grabbing a washcloth, he ran it under the water in the sink, knelt before her, and carefully picked up one of her feet. They were muddy from walking around without shoes, and given the freezing temperatures, she was lucky there were no signs of frostbite.

As he cleaned first one and then the other, guilt swallowed him whole.

He should have made sure she had shoes.

Should have taken her somewhere to buy some rather than having her walk all night in the cold in bare feet.

"I'm sorry, Scarlett," he whispered.

"For what?"

"For letting you down again."

"We were running for our lives," she reminded him.

No excuse.

With both feet cleaned, he turned his attention to her hands. They fueled his guilt just like her poor dirty feet had. Locking her in here might have been the best move safety-wise but it sucked boyfriend-wise.

Boyfriend?

Was that what he wanted to be?

As he smoothed the cloth over her split knuckles, Tate realized that there was a huge part of him that really did want to give things with Scarlett a chance. It was terrifying but kind of in an exhilarating way.

"Sorry for leaving you here," he said, meeting her gaze as he set the cloth down. "I truly believed it was the best move in terms of safety, but it still wasn't fair of me. Not after you'd been kidnapped. Not ever."

"If you'd explained it to me, I would have agreed," she said softly.

"Other than my team on an op, I never trust people to agree with me," he told her truthfully.

Scarlett nodded slowly. "Okay, then apology accepted."

Dropping a kiss to her forehead, he turned to shut off the water, the bath was filled, and he was ready to put her in it and let the hot water soothe her tense muscles. Picking her up before she could stand, Tate carried her to the tub and set her down, then climbed in behind her.

"You're taking a bath with me?" she asked, clearly surprised.

"Miss a chance to touch every inch of your smooth, soft skin? Not a chance, sweetheart."

Her blush was the most adorable thing ever. Everything about her was sweet and adorable and sexy enough that he was already rock hard by the time he settled her between his spread thighs and picked up a loofah.

Taking his time he cleaned her back, careful of the healing wounds from the whip and the gunshot wound that thankfully didn't look red or inflamed. His touch slowed further when he moved to her front, brushing the loofah across her stomach before sliding it up to her chest. He circled one breast and then the other, grinning when Scarlett let out a breathy moan and her head tipped back to rest against his shoulder.

He brushed the loofah across first one nipple and then the other. The contact of the rough material against her pebbled nipples drew another moan from Scarlett and he did it again just to hear the sound.

Then he brushed it down her stomach and grazed it

across her center. Her hips rose to meet the featherlight touch, but he was already moving on to her legs. Bending her knee up so he could reach her foot, he cleaned it again, then moved up her calf and to her thigh. Before he moved onto her other leg, he once again swiped the loofah across her bud.

"Tate," she moaned, the sound a thread away from a desperate plea.

"If you want more you're going to have to say it out loud, sweetheart," he told her. No way was he going to take advantage, but he also wasn't going to deny her anything she wanted. He wanted to be the person Scarlett trusted to always be there for her, to never leave like everyone else in her family had.

"I ... I want you to ... touch me. To make me feel good, to make me feel safe, to make me feel like I matter."

The whispered words made his heart ache. "Oh, baby, you matter. That was the problem. From that first night, you mattered. I've been running from that truth for months, but no more. You matter, and that's a good thing."

With an arm wrapped around her waist, Tate shifted them both so they were on their knees. He knew he had Scarlett positioned in the right spot when she groaned and wiggled her hips.

The flow of one of the jets was aimed right at her bundle of nerves, and his fingers stroked her skin as they gripped her hips. "Are you on birth control?"

"Hmm? Oh, yeah," she said, looking at him over her shoulder through heavy-lidded eyes.

"I'm clean, condom or not?"

"I'm clean, too, I've never done it without a condom before."

"Me either, sweetheart." He'd never wanted to either. But right here, right now, with this woman, he didn't want anything between them.

"No condom," she whispered.

This time not wanting to make her wait for a single thing—Scarlett had been waiting long enough for someone to make her feel important—he lined up and slid inside her.

It felt like coming home.

Like all his life he too hadn't felt important, like he mattered, but with Scarlett, they both ... belonged.

Caught between the jet sending water pounding right onto her bud, and him behind her, gripping her hips as he thrust into her, from this angle grazing the spot inside her he knew would soon have her seeing stars, Tate set a steady pace.

Didn't take long for Scarlett to cry out, her internal muscles clamping around him, setting off a chain reaction as pleasure shot through his body.

Nuzzling her neck as aftershocks of pleasure zinged through his body, Tate touched a row of kisses down the slender column. "You matter, Scarlett. Never doubt that. You matter to a lot of people, and you matter to me."

Absolute truth.

Truth he'd tried to ignore and deny.

But he couldn't any longer.

Didn't want to either.

But even as he fell a little harder for Scarlett, a voice was taunting him at the back of his mind. A dangerous man was hunting Scarlett and there was a warrant out for her arrest.

What happened if he fell for her and lost her?

Would it destroy him as losing his mother had done to his father?

CHAPTER FOURTEEN

January 17th
6:34 A.M.

DID she have enough courage to ask the question buzzing at the back of her mind all night?

Even while she slept it was there.

Even as Tate cooked for her.

Even as he smiled at her.

Even as he made love to her again.

Even as they slept tangled in each other's arms.

Scarlett wanted to ask so badly, but a part of her was afraid of the answer.

The thing was, when it came to this man she no longer trusted her gut. It was easy for Tate to say that he admired her for going after what she wanted in life, but the truth was that fear drove her, not some noble purpose.

Her biggest fear was being alone for the rest of her life.

That was why she looked for love so hard, why she was willing to put her heart on the line, why she didn't hold back.

"Tate?" she asked, deciding to get it over and done with was better than dwelling on it every second.

"Yeah, sweetheart?"

His voice rolled over her like a tidal wave of warmth and safety, and she loved the way he called her sweetheart. There were a few times he'd said it before he decided to trust her that made it sound like an insult, but now it was like a big dollop of sugary sweetness.

"Scarlett?"

"Oh, umm, yeah." She could feel the blush staining her cheeks a bright red, and subconsciously brushed at them. "Yesterday you said that I matter, but you've never treated me like that after the night we spent together."

Since they were still curled up in the king-size bed, Tate rolled her over so she was draped across his body, front to front. Even though the bed was large enough for them to have their own space, he'd held her all night, keeping her close, following her even in his sleep if she rolled away even just so much that their bodies were no longer touching.

Did that mean something?

Or was she clutching at straws?

Did she even *want* it to mean anything?

The way he'd treated her after their night together was hard to forget and … she kept expecting that guy to return. Was that something that would pass? Or would she always be waiting for Tate to panic and lash out?

"Look at me, sweetheart," he ordered, a clear command in his tone even though his voice was gentle.

Lifting her eyes to meet his, she was surprised by the warmth she saw there.

This was the man she'd thought she could fall in love with.

Please let this Tate stay.

"You *do* matter, Scarlett, and I hate that nobody in your life has made you feel as though you do. I hate that I made you feel as though you don't matter."

There was sincerity and regret in his tone.

What world was she living in?

How could the man who had slipped out of her bed without a goodbye, then not just ghosted her but been downright cruel when they randomly met up, also be this man who was so sweet she just wanted to gobble him up like candy?

"I ... I'm not ... it's just ... what changed?" she asked helplessly. Tate had said he wanted to be more open like her, that he had been scared before but hadn't been able to stop thinking about her these last few months, but that's not what she'd seen with her own two eyes. Already once in the last couple of days, she'd mistaken sex as meaning more than it had to him, and she was so afraid she was going to do it again.

Since she was draped over him, Scarlett felt the deep sigh that seemed to come right from Tate's soul.

There was a huge part of her that wanted to soothe his pain, but the other part knew she couldn't jump in with her eyes closed, her fingers crossed, and hope for the best.

Not this time. Tate might have learned something, but she had too. She had learned that looking for love was fine, but being so trusting put both her heart and her life in danger.

What if she'd trusted a man who turned out to be physically violent?

Tate was dangerous to her heart, but he'd never hurt her like that, that she was confident about. He was a protector at heart, it was part of the reason she felt safe with him.

"You want me to be completely honest?" Tate asked, one hand stroking the length of her spine, she wasn't sure if it was to soothe her, or himself, but it did help settle her nerves.

"Yes. Completely." Propping her chin on Tate's chest she waited expectantly.

"I always wanted to give what you made me feel a chance, but I was a coward. Letting you in would have been becoming everything I believed I didn't want to be. So, it was easier to shove you away, then make you out to be the bad guy. When I heard you were suspected of being a traitor my mind immediately went to my dad. After me pleading with him for two decades to get back out there and live after my mom died, he finally met a woman and married her. I pushed for him to give her a chance because I thought she'd be good for him. Turned out, she was dealing drugs, wanted my dad's money, got him addicted then set him up to take the fall when the cops came after her. He's currently serving a ten-year sentence for dealing and she's free. The guilt I feel, knowing *I* pushed him into that, it's been slowly crushing me. I used that to justify me pushing you away, to prove to myself that no good ever comes from loving someone."

Another sigh rumbled through his big body, the hand that wasn't sweeping up and down her back gripped her hip almost painfully tight, but Scarlett relished the tiny bite of pain because it meant he was holding on to her rather than pushing her away. He had been completely forthright with his answer, sharing about his past, and had apologized without making excuses.

It was getting easier to see herself giving him a chance.

"When I walked into Prey yesterday, Eagle was there, and it just hit me how firmly on your side your Prey family was from the very beginning. They didn't doubt you, not for a single second, and suddenly I realized the flip side to what I've always seen. Yes, my parents shouldn't have excluded me the way they did, there was room in their hearts for each other and their child. But there's a positive to having someone love you so strongly they don't even have to question whether you're guilty. That unconditional love must be amazing. I'm so glad you have that from your Prey family, and I want that too. Maybe all these years I haven't been running from relationships because I didn't want to lose myself to another person, but because I thought I would never find someone who could love me that deeply. It was the weirdest thing, but that night … when our eyes met … I felt … I don't even know what, I just felt it, deep inside."

A bright smile lit her face. "You *did* feel it too. I was so sure you did, but then after, when you wouldn't answer my texts or calls, and then at the grocery store, I thought I imagined the whole thing."

"Cowards don't deserve chances, and I can't promise I won't do something stupid, or panic, because this is all new to me and something I was sure I didn't want." Tate grabbed her under the arms and pulled her further up his body so their lips were mere millimeters apart. It was hard to focus on anything but kissing him when he was this close, but his gaze was so serious that she met and held it. "I can promise you that I will always put you first. I'll be open and honest. And when I do feel that panic creeping in, I won't run or lash out."

Wasn't this everything she had wanted for the last almost three months?

To have a chance with Tate, to see if that weird feeling she'd gotten the moment she laid eyes on him was real. To see if they could have something real, something amazing, something all-consuming.

For Tate, that was a terrifying thought, but for her all she'd ever wanted was to be somebody's number one, to matter enough for them to care about her needs. Tate was offering her all of that, and it wasn't like they had to jump into marriage, they had time to get to know one another and maybe fall in love along the way.

This could be the start of the most amazing journey of her life. It could be the beginning of everything she'd ever wanted.

There was only one answer she could give.

"I want to try, to see where things go with us."

No sooner were the words out of her mouth than Tate's lips were on hers as he kissed her senseless.

* * *

JANUARY 17TH
11:46 A.M.

THERE WAS a lightness inside him as they sat side by side at the small kitchen table.

Now that he'd taken that first step, Tate wondered why it had seemed so terrifying.

Hindsight he guessed, and a heavy dose of perspective.

In the end, it came down to the answer to one simple question. Was he going to be happier keeping himself isolated so he never risked loving and losing, or was he going to embrace any chance life gave him to find something wonderful?

Put like that it was an easy answer to find.

Despite the pain it had caused him, his parents' love had been a beautiful thing. Soul deep, all-consuming, the kind of love that fairytales and songs were written about. Maybe all along he hadn't so much been afraid of falling for someone with that same intensity, but that it would consume both him and the woman the same way it had for his parents.

The thing was, though, with Scarlett he knew that could never happen.

Their childhoods had been similar in so many ways, and they both knew the pain of being ignored and shut out. There was no way either of them would ever do that to another person.

Maybe all along he'd just been waiting for the right woman.

Taking Scarlett's hand, Tate entwined their fingers. If fate hadn't tipped his hand and brought Scarlett screaming back into his life, he might have missed out on this chance. Because without this added push, he likely would never have allowed himself to believe that love could be different than what he'd witnessed growing up.

The laptop screen suddenly changed, and up came the same conference room that he'd sat in nine days ago, no idea he was about to learn the woman he hadn't been able to forget had been kidnapped and branded a traitor. So much had changed in those nine days that it was hard to believe it had been such a short space of time.

Actually, everything had changed so much in the last twenty-four hours that it was hard to believe that just over a day ago he'd locked Scarlett in this room and headed into Prey to try to figure out a plan to get the target off his woman's back.

His woman?

Why did that sound a whole lot better and a whole lot less terrifying than he thought it would?

Shoving away those thoughts for now, there was no future for him and Scarlett if she was kidnapped, tortured, and eventually killed by Raul Castillo, or if she wound up convicted and locked away in some tiny cell, in some off-the-books prison where traitors were kept.

Any future he wanted could only start after they found the mole.

Which meant work first. It had to be the priority if he was going to keep Scarlett safe and alive.

Giving Scarlett's hand a squeeze, he focused on the people gathered in the conference room. "Do we have anything?"

Like they were one person instead of a dozen, all sets of eyes seemed to hover over his and Scarlett's joined hands, before blinking almost in unison.

It would be comical if they weren't under more pressure than he'd ever felt in his life.

While he had no intention of hiding the fact that he and Scarlett were a couple, he also wasn't going to do or say anything that she wasn't comfortable with. This was her family, the people who mattered most to her, the people who had her back even if she hadn't realized it at first, they handled this however she chose.

"Umm," she said nervously, obviously sensing the same shock he did. "Tate apologized for being jerky and explained why, and ... we're kind of ... together now." She gave a nervous laugh, and he gave her fingers an encouraging squeeze.

It was the youngest one, genius Cassie, who broke the tension when her face broke out into a huge grin. "That's amazing, I'm so happy for you, Scar."

Like all they needed was for one of them to say something, the rest of the people in the room came to life, offering smiles and encouragement, before the reason for the video call settled on all their shoulders and they grew serious.

"Do we have anything?" Tate repeated his question.

Looking exhausted, Fox dragged his fingers through his dark hair. "We've made a list of every Prey employee who knew about the Reactivator. It's longer than I would have liked."

"There were also two lab workers who have been at Prey during the time Athena Team have been working on the drug," Night added, his silver-gray eyes filled with helpless frustration.

The same frustration Tate felt.

It was the worst feeling in the world to be helpless.

Knowing it had to be one of the people on the list wasn't enough. If they couldn't find the mole in time, Scarlett could pay the ultimate price. He would do whatever it took to keep her safe, but even the best-laid plans could go awry. Especially when dealing with someone so ruthless that would set up an innocent colleague to take the fall for them, knowing what that would entail.

The traitor had allowed Scarlett to be tortured.

Tortured.

And there was more to it than Scarlett had so far admitted if the lie she'd told while taking the polygraph was any indication.

"We've started working our way through the list. Prey's tech people are doing a deep dive into all of their lives," Spider continued. "Looking into all the usual things. Financial troubles, other motives, anyone with a connection, however small, to Mexico. Damn, I hate that place." Spider's now-wife Abigail had been held prisoner by a Mexican cartel leader for over a year before she was found by accident by Spider and his team while they were still in the SEALs. Although the couple had finally gotten their happy ever after, after two previous tries, it was obvious Spider still carried around some guilt.

Tate hadn't realized his grip on Scarlett's hand had tightened until her thumb began to brush softly across his knuckles.

Soothing him.

Reading him so clearly.

He had messed up with her and almost lost her to the Mexican jungle. If that had happened he would have felt some responsibility.

Clearing his throat, he pushed away his guilt, there was no time for it now. "Do we have anyone who's standing out as a suspect?"

"One of the lab workers who was let go is high on the list," Lucy spoke up. "Even though it would have been harder for them to have access to Prey's systems to fake the emails it wouldn't have been impossible. Prey rarely fires anyone. The vetting process is so extensive that it usually weeds out anyone unsuitable. But this guy got through anyway. We all had bad experiences with him," she said, indicating herself and her team. "He was lazy, didn't respect us as a Prey team while he was there just to help us with the workload. He asked all four of us out and was pushy even when we all turned him down."

Ella shivered at that. "Yeah, he was creepy. That kind of creepy women can just … sense. Everything was documented and reported, and when he was drunk one day and almost messed up—a big mess up that would have cost lives—he was fired."

"How did he leave? Did he go quietly? Put up fight?" Tate asked. Drinking problems could lead to all sorts of other issues, and it seemed like he might have a personal grudge against Athena Team, which means he could want to not just get the money for the drug, but also make them suffer.

"It was bad," Scarlett answered. "He lost it, trashed the lab, destroyed equipment, and claimed it wasn't fair. But it was almost a year ago and we never heard anything from him since."

"Takes time to set up a deal with a weapons trafficker," he reminded her. As far as he was concerned, the fired lab worker was top of the list. "Who else stands out?"

"One of the security guards has a brother who recently got himself entangled with a gang," King replied. "People have been known to do crazy things when it comes to family. It's less likely he would know about the drug since he doesn't have direct access to that information, but it's not impossible that he found out, we weren't actively trying to hide it from anyone."

"And the third person who stands out is one of our IT people. She would definitely have the skills to fake those emails, and she would have access to everything that went through the computer system," Chaos explained. "She lost her husband about nine months ago. Terrible car accident, he was in the hospital for almost a month, fought hard, but it wasn't enough. Now one of her two kids is battling cancer. All those medical bills could make her do something stupid."

Three viable suspects, that should make him feel better.

But it didn't.

Because there were no answers yet, just a whole lot of questions.

The only thing that was going to make him feel better

was knowing the woman he was taking the biggest risk of his life on was no longer in danger.

Truth was, he was no closer to making that a reality.

This was one op he couldn't fail on.

Falling in love and losing that person had always been his biggest fear, but maybe falling but never getting a chance for it to turn into love before you lost that person was a worse fate.

CHAPTER FIFTEEN

January 17th
5:35 P.M.

"I CAN'T BELIEVE you've never made your own pasta before," Scarlett said as she ran the pasta sheets through the machine, flatting them out so they could then be cut into spaghetti strips.

Tate chuckled. "I don't think I'm in the minority there, sweetheart."

There was no way on earth her body couldn't respond to that endearment. Never in her life had her parents or grandparents or any of her foster parents ever used one. In fact, there had been a time when her parents and grandparents referred to her simply as girl child, and her brother boy child. Apparently, it was supposed to help both of them prepare for the lives of military service they had planned for them.

Only her parents' view of the military was so very different from those she had met while at Prey.

Serving meant having a new family of brothers and sisters, but it didn't mean you left your family at home behind. The men and women who were prepared to give the ultimate sacrifice to make the world a safer place for the people and country they loved were doing it *for* those families at home.

Unlike her own family who didn't care one little bit about the people left behind.

Shaking off those feelings, Scarlett wasn't going to let her past reach out its tentacles and invade her present or her future.

"You haven't even made your own lasagna?" Surely, he'd at least done that. Hadn't everybody made home-made lasagna at some point in their lives?

Another chuckle. "Sweetheart, I haven't made much of anything. I'm not a cook. Before my mom died, she did all the cooking, so we had homemade meals almost every night, but I never participated in their cooking. Then after, we mostly lived off takeout. In college it was more takeout, and then I enlisted. As an adult, I mostly cook whatever's quick. Throw a steak on the grill, or a premade dinner in the oven. Don't spend my time cooking, much less from scratch."

Staring at him, aghast, she shook her head. "So, you haven't made your own pizza? Or baked cookies? Or made homemade soup in the winter?" How had he never done any of those things before? Was he right? Was she the one in the minority making most things from scratch and spending hours cooking even though it was usually just for herself?

"You're adorable." Tate leaned over the touched a kiss to the tip of her nose. "And, no, I've never done any of those things. But I can tell you've done them and more. What made you get so interested in cooking?"

"Cooking was one of my chores from about as young as I can remember. When I was really little, I used to help my grandmother cook, but then as I got older she left the chore to me. I decided if I had to do it, I may as well make it fun, and so I started looking up recipes, seeing what I could make, and then trying them all out. Some were epic failures, but others were big successes. There was a time when I lived for the compliments I got from my grandparents on my cooking, they were about the only ones I ever got. Lame, I know. I shouldn't need their validation," she said as she laid out the pasta sheets ready to cut.

"Hey." Tate took her shoulders in his hands and turned her to face him. "Look at me, sweetheart." When she lifted her gaze to meet his she found it both tender and firm. "I get it. Trust me I do. Compliments weren't a big part of my childhood either. There's nothing wrong with needing the adults in your life to care about you."

"Once my grandparents died, and Zander and I went into foster care, I never got to cook much," she said softly. Back then as a scared and angry thirteen-year-old girl, she'd missed the one thing that used to bring her joy. "So as soon as I aged out of the system and moved into my own place I started cooking again. As often as I could I'd make big meals, then deliver everything I couldn't eat to neighbors or friends. I did consider for a moment becoming a chef, mainly because I knew it would drive my parents crazy." When she gave Tate a cheeky grin he threw back his head and laughed.

"You would have been amazing as a chef just like you're amazing as a scientist. I'd love for you to teach me to make all the things you love."

"You would?" Just because she loved cooking didn't mean she expected Tate to like it too.

"Of course. I want you to share the things you love with me." The tenderness bled out of his gaze, which grew serious enough that Scarlett eased herself out of Tate's grip, positive that whatever he was thinking was something she didn't want to hear.

Turning, she set up the attachment to the pasta machine so she could cut the sheets into spaghetti. Half of the sheets had been cut before Tate spoke again. Saying the words she had been dreading someone saying to her.

"Scarlett, I don't want you to think I'm angry, or that this means I don't trust you, or that anyone has any doubts about you, but you lied in the polygraph."

Just like that, her heart began to race, and her palms got sweaty. Her entire body clenched in denial as every drop of fear she'd felt in that room when that drug had hit her system came rushing back.

"You can trust me, Scarlett," Tate said gently. "I want you to know that there isn't anything you can't share with me."

Maybe.

But not this.

This she wasn't going to share with anyone.

The last few days, with everything else going on, she'd

managed to forget about those hours the drugs had taken over her body, filling her with that raging need and no way to satiate it.

He couldn't know about that.

Nobody could.

"Scarlett." When his hand touched her shoulder, she jerked away, stumbling backward and crashing into the counter.

"I can't," she whispered, tears blurring her vision. She'd promised herself she would take that to the grave and intended to do just that.

"You can, sweetheart. You're safe here. Whatever you need to say, you can tell me, and I swear unless it involves keeping you safe, I will never tell anyone. Don't hold it in, sweetheart. Let me share this burden with you. Already, I've hurt you so much, let me help you this time instead. Please, sweetheart."

She couldn't let him do that ... could she?

No.

She'd promised herself nobody would ever know.

For some reason, when she'd made love to Tate she hadn't even thought about what had happened to her in that dungeon, but now, the thought of him touching her made her sick and panicky.

"I won't let you down again, Scarlett. I'll carry this load for you if you let me."

He sounded so serious, and he was so strong, would it help to tell him?

Before she could lose her nerve, she blurted the words out. "Raul drugged me. With an arousal drug. Then he and his men stood around and watched while I burned with a need I'd never felt before. It felt like I was going to die if I didn't orgasm even though it was the last thing I wanted to do. They watched and laughed, and some of them got themselves off as I begged and pleaded to be touched. I'm so embarrassed." She wept as tears tumbled down her cheeks. "I asked them to touch me. I didn't want to but it hurt so badly. I didn't tell him the formula for the drug though," she added, worried he would doubt her.

"Oh, sweetheart, I know you wouldn't have. You're so strong, Scarlett. So strong."

Carefully, he drew her against him as though he wasn't sure she would welcome his touch. But she did. She needed it. Scarlett curled her fingers into the soft material of his T-shirt and leaned against his solid frame, letting him take her weight.

"I didn't want anyone to know," she cried, face pressed against his chest, her tears soaking his T-shirt. "That's why I lied. I wasn't ever going to tell anyone."

"I wish I'd known before we slept together, I would have made sure I didn't do anything to trigger anything for you." There was regret in his tone, but he had nothing to be sorry about.

Pulling back, she tightened her grip on his T-shirt. "I wasn't thinking about Raul when you made love to me, Tate, I swear. All I was thinking about was you, touching me, making me feel good, and making me feel important and cherished. You saved me. Even though you thought the worst you still came for me and saved me. Even when your words were angry and you felt cold, your touch was always soft, always warm. I wanted you to be my safe place then, to hold me, and tell me everything was going to be okay because it felt like it wasn't, and I didn't even know then what I'd been accused of."

Tucking her back against his chest, she felt his lips touch the top of her head. "I'm here now, sweetheart. Holding you. Being your safe place. My touch will always be soft and warm when it comes to you, and I won't ever be cold toward you again. I've never been anyone's safe place before, but with you, I want to be, baby. I want to be so badly. I'll learn, I'll learn how to give you everything you need, you won't ever want for anything again. Not attention, validation, or the words or the actions you need. I was an idiot to run from my feelings for you, and it's not a mistake I intend to repeat."

As badly as Scarlett wanted to believe Tate's words, and she did, she knew he would never intentionally hurt her again, and he would be her safe place, but would it be enough to protect her from the danger circling around her?

* * *

JANUARY 18TH

7:52 A.M.

SCARLETT KEPT STEALING LOOKS at him when she thought his focus was on something else.

Too bad for her that if she was in the room, his focus was automatically mostly on her.

It probably didn't make him an ideal bodyguard, but

on the plus side, there was literally nothing he wasn't prepared to do to keep his girl alive.

Things had been … different … between them since she confessed the lie she'd told while taking the polygraph. Not bad, not by any stretch, and Tate was honored that she had trusted him enough to open up and give him the whole truth, even the parts she was deeply ashamed of.

They hadn't had sex last night. Given what Scarlett had been through he wasn't going to push her for anything she wasn't ready and willing to give. Since she hadn't given any indication that she wanted anything other than to just be held, that's what he'd done.

As much as he loved her delectable body, it was her sweet soul that he loved more, and he had been perfectly content just to hold her close, making sure she knew that while she had faced that horrific ordeal alone she never had to be alone again. Whatever it took to help her heal he would do. If she needed time she'd get it. If she needed sex she'd get it. If she needed reassurance she'd get it.

For a guy who had spent a lifetime avoiding anything that even hinted at commitment, it was surprisingly easy to offer those things. His decision to not let a woman get close was his fear and resentment talking. Once he was able to shove those aside and see the good sides of love it was easy to let this woman in.

There was just something about Scarlett that called out to his soul.

Something he was done running from. Done hiding from. Done pretending didn't exist.

Another sneaked glance came from Scarlett as he

scrolled through the files he was supposed to be reading. Prey had sent some to him and Scarlett for them to go through while they went through the rest of the suspects, since time was of the essence they were dividing to conquer.

"You okay, sweetheart?" he asked. Just because he wasn't going to push didn't mean he didn't want her to know that there was nothing she couldn't come to him with. However big or however small, he was there to listen and help however he could.

Her gaze skittered away, back to her own laptop. She was fiddling with a ring on her finger, something he noticed she did when she was anxious or nervous, but not when she was lying. It was a tell he didn't want to let on that he knew because he liked that there was a way he could tell that she needed him even if she wasn't ready to outright tell him that herself.

"Yeah, fine," she mumbled, although she was twisting her ring at a near-frenetic pace now. So fast he was surprised that it didn't go spinning right off onto the floor.

Turning his chair so he was facing her, Tate reached out and grabbed the arms of her chair, turning it, too, so they were facing one another. Wanting to push her just enough to remind her she was safe here, that he wanted to be her safe place, but not so hard that he got her to shut down completely, he tugged her chair a little closer.

"Something is bothering you," he stated, trying not to let on just how badly he wanted her to be able to trust him. Telling himself that trust had to be earned was easier than actually living it. But there was no way he could just wipe away the pain he'd caused her. He had to work to prove to her that he could be trustworthy and dependable. Patience. That's what he needed to have. Not his strong suit but Scarlett was worth the effort.

"I … it's just … umm …" she stammered as he waited her out. He wanted her trust, but he wanted it given freely because it was real, not forced and fake.

So, he waited.

And waited.

Then was rewarded with Scarlett's nervous gaze shifting back to meet his. "Do you think … less of me?"

"Less of you? Why would I?" He wasn't following where she was going with this. There was nothing about Scarlett that didn't make him think she was the most amazing, strong, and determined woman he'd ever met.

"Because of umm … what I told you last night."

He was still not quite sure what she was getting at. "About the drug you were given?"

A shaky nod. "I begged, Tate. *Begged*. For them to touch me. I hated the thought, but I was so desperate for something to release that need clawing inside me. If you hadn't rescued me, I would have eventually caved and given him what he wanted to know." There was so much guilt and pain in her eyes that he couldn't not reach out to her.

Scooping her up, he settled her in his lap. "Sweetheart, that's the goal of torture. To break you. Almost every single person in the world, regardless of their training, is going to eventually break under that much pressure."

"I hate that I begged those disgusting men to touch me," she whispered, pressing her face against his neck.

He could not take away that experience no matter

how much he wanted to. All he could do was be here to help Scarlett deal with the fallout. "You did the only thing your body could in the moment. You don't have anything to be ashamed of, Scarlett. Nothing. Not a single thing."

"Then how come you didn't want to make love to me last night?" There was a thread of self-doubt in her voice he ached to soothe away.

"Because I was trying to do the right thing and not push you into something you weren't ready for." Now, he was having his own major bout of self-doubt.

"You weren't worried about that before." Scarlett lifted her face to look up at him.

"Before I didn't know the whole truth about what had happened to you." As soon as he said the words he realized he had confirmed Scarlett's fears that he did indeed see her differently now, even if that wasn't how he meant them.

"So, you *do* think less of me." There was devastation in her voice, and Tate hated that, once again, he had been the one to put it there.

Before he could offer reassurances that it wasn't what he meant, that he didn't think less of her, he just wanted to make sure he wasn't going to do something that would hurt her, her laptop chimed with an incoming email.

When she went to shift off his lap, Tate tightened his hold, keeping her where she was and instead reached over to grab the laptop and pull it closer so she could see what Prey had emailed them.

Only Scarlett's eyes flew to his when she opened the email. "Tate, look," she said, pointing at the screen. "The email, it's not from Prey. Well, not really anyway. I think it's from the mole."

Shoving away his need to reassure Scarlett of his feelings for her, reminding himself that his priority had to be her life, Tate looked at the email. It was short, an address, an invitation to come and meet to talk, as well as a threat not to alert anyone else. While the person didn't outright say that they were the mole, it was the only logical conclusion, and he wondered if whoever was trying to sell the formula and set Scarlett up had done so under duress. That had always been a possibility and the mole wanting to meet could reinforce that.

"We have to go," Scarlett said, already trying to scramble off his lap.

Instinct had him tightening his hold. "It could be a trap."

The sassy woman rolled her eyes at him. "Of course, it's a trap. I don't need field experience to know that, but it's also the only chance I might have to clear my name. My options are pretty limited, Tate. I can't hide forever, so my only choices are to get arrested and spend the rest of my life in prison for crimes I didn't commit or get abducted by Raul Castillo again and be tortured and then killed. This could be my only chance at getting ahead, at getting something that can be used so I don't wind up dead or imprisoned."

Could he risk Scarlett's safety for a chance at getting answers?

Didn't seem like a good trade-off as far as he was concerned.

"You'll be safe here until we figure this out," he countered.

"I can't stay here indefinitely, and you know it. What if your team gets called out? You've already been blowing off PT to hide out with me. We need to do this to get ahead, Tate, you know it as well as I do. You said you don't think less of me so show me that's true. I know how to shoot, I know self-defense, and you're a SEAL. We can do this. I *need* to do this."

Damn.

She knew just how to tug on his heartstrings.

This would be a big risk, and he wouldn't have his team at his back. Raul Castillo was a dangerous man, and whether the mole was acting out of greed or being coerced, they had proven themselves to be dangerous as well.

Here was safe, but out there ... was anything but.

CHAPTER SIXTEEN

January 18th
8:36 A.M.

"This is the worst idea ever."

Scarlett didn't look over to the driver's seat where Tate was, her gaze instead fixed on the passing scenery. "Never said it was a good one, just that I was out of options."

"It's too dangerous."

"We've been over that." Like a dozen times while they got dressed and did their best to disguise her so she wouldn't be immediately recognizable. With the chilly morning, it wasn't hard. She had on a big coat that pretty much covered her from ankles to neck and a scarf that basically covered half of her face. Unless you were looking directly at her and actually be looking for her, chances were you would have no idea who she was.

"I don't like this."

"You've told me." And she hadn't been able to stop thinking about it.

Was he against this idea just because it was taking a huge risk, or was there more to it than that?

Was Tate secretly worried because he thought she was a liability?

Just because she didn't have anywhere close to the same level of field experience as he did—okay so she had one step up from zero—didn't automatically make her a liability.

While little Tate would have been playing with his friends and learning to tie his shoes, little Scarlett was learning self-defense and how to shoot a target with pinpoint accuracy. No, her skills didn't come anywhere close to his, but she wasn't some completely helpless maiden in need of a knight on a white horse.

She'd killed one of Raul's men.

She'd survived being tortured.

She was still standing when everything in her urged her to find a bed, curl up under the covers, and refuse to come out until this problem just disappeared.

"Hey." One of Tate's hands reached out to grasp one of hers. Although she kept it limp in his grip, his fingers managed to lace with hers anyway. "Can you look at me, Scarlett, please?"

The childish part of her wanted to say no. It wanted to pout and complain that he'd held her last night like she was a friend who needed comfort instead of the woman he said he was interested in. All night there hadn't been so much as a stray hand brushing against her breasts.

Nothing.

Nada.

Zip.

Zilch.

Zero.

And her confidence had taken a serious beating. Things with Tate were so new, and their history, while short, was extremely bumpy, and they weren't at a place yet where she could just trust in him.

Still, she looked up and met his gaze as he glanced away from the road and over to her.

“Do you want me to be the kind of man who would have sex with you after you told me how you were assaulted without you giving me the green light?”

“I … uh … umm … didn't think of it like that,” she finished lamely. She’d been too busy thinking of how Tate must think less of her now because he hadn't tried to make any moves on her. But he was right. She’d confessed to him how she’d been violated, made to feel things she hadn't wanted, and while no one had touched her, men around her had been getting themselves off and coming on her.

That was a violation.

An assault.

And she’d been too wrapped up in it to be able to think clearly about what might be going through Tate’s mind.

That was unfair of her.

If she’d wanted to make love to him then she could have made that clear. It was just that …

Asking for what she wanted was never something that was encouraged in her childhood.

As a kid, nobody cared what she wanted. She was expected to be the good little soldier. Get perfect grades, do her chores, work hard, not cause problems, not answer back. There had never been a time when she was encouraged to speak up.

A habit that needed to be broken.

"I just assumed that you were … I don't know … repulsed maybe by what I'd told you," she admitted.

"Repulsed?" Tate sounded both shocked and horrified by the idea. "Not repulsed. *Never* repulsed. I was angry, furious, with Raul and that he would do that to you. I felt sick that you were subjected to that. I was helpless that I couldn't erase it from your mind and make it like it never happened. And I was filled with this need to hold you, soothe you somehow, maybe make things a little better just by being there. But instead, I failed you again."

"No," she said quickly, squeezing the fingers tangled with hers. "I got stuck in my own head, because maybe … I'm the one who's … repulsed by what happened."

"You don't have any reason to be, sweetheart. You didn't do anything wrong."

"In my head I know that, but part of me is still back in that room, naked and chained to the chair, pleading for a touch I didn't want because I knew it was the only thing that would make the pain and need go away. I don't … I don't know how to get past it," she whispered, embarrassed to be having this conversation with a man she barely knew and who just a couple of days ago, would have sworn hated her.

"Time. I know it sounds overly simplistic, but the thing is, it really is only going to take time. It won't ever completely go away, but time will give you perspective and that will help. You're also not alone. I get that we don't know each other that well yet, and that I've given you no reason to trust me so far, but you have a team of friends who have your back and a whole family at Prey who believe in you. You don't have to go and tell them everything but don't shut them out. I hope you won't shut me out either. I'm trying. I might not be good at this, and I'll probably keep messing up, but I am trying."

He sounded so sincere that she immediately felt even worse for being mad at him when he was only trying to handle a situation neither of them had been prepared for.

"I know you are." The smile she shot him was genuine, and she hoped he knew how much she appreciated him traversing this road with her. "I'm trying, too. I guess this is new for both of us. I might have been in serious relationships before, but this feels so different. Feels so big."

"Huge," he agreed.

For a while, they were content to just hold hands as they drove through the wintery morning. The location they'd been told to meet at was a park on the outskirts of the city. It was a regular with dog walkers in particular, but also runners, walkers, and cyclists. Scarlett had been out there a few times with Lucy, taking her friend's fluffy poodle for walks.

The place was packed in the middle of summer, but as they approached the parking lot on this cold, blustery winter's day there wasn't another car in sight.

A weird feeling settled in her stomach.

And not a good feeling.

Something was wrong.

Of course, she knew they were walking into a trap, she just didn't care. Between Tate and her, she was sure that whoever the mole was they'd be able to take them. Even if a few of Raul's men were there, too.

Now she realized she may have been a little overly confident. Or more likely, too desperate to find answers to bring this to an end.

"Tate—"

"I know, I feel it too," he said, even before she could express her concerns that maybe she had been too hasty in insisting they come rushing over here.

It had been a mistake.

More than that though, if she had underestimated their opponents, she wouldn't be the only one to pay the price for that mistake. Tate would pay, too.

Was she willing to risk his life for answers?

No.

She wasn't.

More than she wanted to find evidence to clear her name, she wanted Tate to be safe. It would be selfish to insist he continue when they both had a bad feeling and she'd been selfish enough already demanding he bring her here.

"We should go," she said, nervously looking around.

"I thought—"

"I don't want you to get hurt because of me."

But it was already too late.

The next thing she knew, the world around them was exploding, and the car was picked up and thrown through the air, landing with a bone-jarring thud that tossed her into unconsciousness.

* * *

JANUARY 18TH
9:09 A.M.

LUIS WAS GOING to kill him.

That was Tate's first thought as he made the slow swim back to consciousness.

After returning to join Scarlett in the basement apartment, he'd put in a call to his team and asked if anyone could lend him a vehicle since his was destroyed. Luis had agreed to loan him the old Jaguar he'd bought and intended to restore.

Now the car was a mangled mess, lying on its side, yards from the entrance to the parking lot close to where they'd been instructed to meet with whoever had sent that email to Scarlett.

Of course, they had both known it was a trap, but he'd been expecting something more along the lines of an ambush. While he hadn't given Scarlett all the details of his plan because he hadn't quite been sure that she would be cooperative—he knew how desperate for answers she was—he hadn't ever planned on getting out of the car. His theory had been sooner or later, the mole would get antsy and come down to check on the parking lot to see if they'd arrived.

All he needed was one glimpse and this could all be over.

Instead, what he'd gotten was blown up.

Two cars ruined in three days, that had to be some sort of record.

Groaning as pain shot through his head, Tate shoved it aside and shifted in his seat, thankful for the invention of seatbelts. Without them, it was likely both he and Scarlett would have been thrown from the car and killed.

He'd survived, but had she?

"Scarlett?" he called out as he blinked to clear his vision.

When the car had been blown up, it had landed on its side, there was no fire—yet—but he could smell gas, so there was every chance that if they didn't hurry up and get out of there they would wind up dead.

Thankfully, the explosion hadn't been quite big enough to kill them outright.

Amateurs.

"Scarlett," he called her name again when she didn't answer him.

Fear sliced through his veins.

Was she already dead?

Every single reason why he never wanted to risk falling for someone flashed through his mind as he fought with his seatbelt.

His side of the car had landed on the ground, which meant he was resting against the driver's door, but with Scarlett's side in the air, the only thing keeping her in her seat was her seatbelt.

"Answer me, Scarlett," he ordered, harsher than he should have, but panic was beginning to bubble up inside him.

Why had he agreed to this?

Years of training, years of experience, years of honing his skills, and he went and did something this stupid.

If Scarlett was dead, there was nobody else to blame but himself.

No matter how badly she wanted to come here, he should have insisted they either call in backup or send someone else from Prey. If they lost this chance to catch the mole there would be another, and Scarlett wouldn't have been in the firing line.

Checking his weapon was still in the holster at his side, Tate planted his feet against the driver's door and scanned the empty parking lot ensuring the mole wasn't moving in to check that they'd been successful.

The car creaked ominously, and he was painfully aware that one wrong move could set the whole thing alight. A little friction could light the tiniest of sparks, which could be all it took.

Carefully, he straightened then reached over to press his fingertips to the slender column of Scarlett's neck. His relief at the thud of her pulse was tampered by the blood streaking her face.

Damn, he was sick of seeing his woman covered in blood.

She'd been through enough, this had to stop.

"Hold on, sweetheart," he murmured as he smoothed a lock of dark hair away from the blood on her forehead and tucked it behind her ear. "I'll get you out of here, and I swear to you I will do whatever it takes to end this. To keep you safe. I didn't fight against the fears I've had since childhood to take a chance on having you in my life only to lose you now."

Taking one of her arms, he draped it across his shoulders, then balancing her weight against his chest, he slid an arm around behind her back and unsnapped her seatbelt.

Immediately, her entire weight rested against him, but she was small, and other than bumps and bruises, he wasn't injured. Slipping his other arm under her knees, he cradled her against him, taking a moment to touch his lips to the top of her head and be grateful they were both still alive.

Then he knelt and set her at his feet. Using the steering wheel to brace himself so he didn't step on Scarlett, he grabbed the passenger side door handle. As much as he wanted to yank on it and get his girl out of there, he forced himself to go slow. There was every chance the door had been damaged and wouldn't open.

If that happened, he'd have to try the back door, and if that didn't work, he'd have to risk kicking out a window.

But luck was on his side for once.

The door handle turned, and he shoved it as open as he could get it.

As he reached down to pick Scarlett up, she began to stir. "Tate?"

Her voice was a mere hint of a sound, but it was the most beautiful one he'd ever heard. Scarlett was alive, and while the last thing she needed was another injury, at least she was cognizant and aware, and that was more than he could ask for.

"Right here, sweetheart," he assured her, sweeping his fingertips across her cheek before gathering her into his arms. "We have to get out of the car. I'm going to climb out, all I need you to do is hold onto me. Can you do that, little fighter?"

Wincing, she nodded her head. Although Scarlett looked weak, her grip was strong as she wound her arms around his neck and held on just like he'd told her to.

With his height and Scarlett's small size, it didn't take much effort for him to get them both out of the car. Once his feet hit the ground he was running, eyes scanning the trees of the park that surrounded the parking lot and the road in search of anything out of place.

When he felt like they were a safe distance, Tate dropped to his knees, placing Scarlett between him and a large tree trunk, giving her all the protection he could.

"What happened?" she asked, voice trembling as her hands fisted in his shirt.

"Car blew up."

"That was the trap." Despite the likely concussion, the wheels in her head were obviously spinning. "It wasn't to try to kidnap me again it was to kill me."

Framing her face with his hands, he smoothed his thumbs across her cheekbones. "I won't let him."

Hands moving to grip his wrists, her grasp tight, she looked up at him with big, scared doe eyes. "This is my fault. I'm sorry. We shouldn't have come. I was being self-ish, thinking only about what I wanted, what I needed, and it almost got you killed." Tears rolled down her cheeks, mixing with the blood and leaving pink trails in their wake.

"I came because I wanted the same answers you do," he reminded her, caressing her silky soft skin with his fingers.

"But you didn't want to do it like this. I'm sorry, Tate, I won't be reckless again, I promise."

He believed her.

Only not for the reasons she would have thought.

Already a plan was forming in his mind, the only one he could think of given what had happened here this morning.

"What's our next move?" Scarlett asked so trustingly that what he was about to do was going to break her sweet heart.

But he didn't have a choice.

Things had changed.

Wrongly, he had assumed that the purpose of this meet-up was to flush Scarlett out so that Raul could kidnap her again and try to force her to givc up the formula for the Reactivator.

But that didn't seem to be true.

They'd been lured out of hiding so Raul could have Scarlett killed.

Obviously, now he considered her to be more of a liability than an asset, and he was cleaning house, cutting his losses, and either moving on and giving up or regrouping and coming up with another way of getting his hands on the drug.

Either way, it wasn't good for Scarlett.

Hurting her was the last thing he wanted to do, but more than that, he wanted her alive and safe.

Which meant he was willing to hurt her if it was for her own good.

He would just have to pray she forgave him.

CHAPTER SEVENTEEN

January 18th
9:31 A.M.

"I WISH we'd at least got a glimpse of something," Scarlett said, running her hands through her hair and wincing when that tugged on the gash by her hairline. Other than a killer headache and some new aches and pains she'd been lucky.

They both had.

Tate hadn't received any serious injuries either. Things could have so easily gone the other way. Dead or in the hospital fighting for their lives, either could have been the outcome of this morning's events.

If Tate had been killed because of her, she never would have forgiven herself.

It was her fault they'd been at the park. Her selfish actions could have cost her everything. Too late, she had realized that she'd rather have Tate than answers, but by then they were already caught in the trap and blown up.

Worse than the new bruises littering her body and their accompanying pain was the anger at herself. Why had she been so selfish? Why hadn't she listened to Tate when he had so much more knowledge than she did when it came to things like this? Why had she been so arrogant as to think she had what it took to help him take down the mole?

Tugging on her hair again, this time she welcomed the sting. It didn't feel like enough though. She could have gotten a man who was very important to her killed.

Killed.

"Stop doing that." Tate's hands closed around her own, untangling them from her messy brown locks and lowering them until they rested in his lap.

Sitting in the back of one of his teammate's cars, they were on their way back to the little apartment where they would regroup and catch Prey up on what happened this morning. Maybe there were cameras at the parking lot that had captured something useful.

At least then she wouldn't feel like she had risked Tate's life for nothing.

Everything.

That's what he was risking for her.

Now that a warrant was out for her arrest, he could be charged with harboring a fugitive. He'd lose his career and his freedom. And for what?

Her?

Didn't seem like a good trade-off. Especially since

she'd gotten him shot at, his car ruined, his house shot at, and gotten him blown up.

Yet he hadn't complained.

Not even once.

Even when he'd had doubts, he had done everything in his power to keep her safe.

And that was what convinced her that she was doing the right thing giving him a chance. He hadn't gone about it the right way, but he'd been trying to outrun his fears when he'd been a jerk to her, and now he was facing them head-on. All for her.

Warm fuzzies renewed her determination to make this morning's efforts worth something.

"They must have been there watching," she said, thinking aloud. "To make sure we got blown up. Do you think they saw us get out of the car?"

"I didn't see anyone, and I didn't feel eyes on us," Tate replied.

"Still, they *had* to be there, at least until we got blown up."

"We'll get this all sorted out. I promised you that, Scarlett, and I intend to keep that promise."

There was a determination in his voice that hadn't been there before. As soon as he started believing in her innocence, he'd been determined to help clear her name, but it hadn't been quite like this. This felt like the kind of all-consuming determination that would wind up getting him killed.

Not what she wanted.

"Don't do anything crazy, Tate," she begged, latching onto his hands like she never wanted to let go. Because she didn't. She was one hundred percent committed to giving this tiny, little fledgling relationship everything she had. There were no guarantees of where it would go, but she didn't want regrets.

His gaze shifted from her to the rearview mirror, where it met with his friend's before returning to her. "I will do whatever it takes to keep you safe, Scarlett. Never ever doubt that."

"I know," she said, brow furrowing in confusion. Why did he sound so desperate for her to believe that? If him going with her to the park this morning, even though he didn't think it was a good idea, wasn't proof enough then what was?

Tate nodded slowly like he had doubts, but then he wiped them away, clearing his expression. "At least we know whoever the mole is they don't have much field experience. If that blast was supposed to kill us—and I have no doubts that it was—then they didn't add enough explosives. No one with even the slightest bit of training would make that mistake. If you have a target you need to get rid of you get the job done because you might not get a second chance."

"What if they *do* get a second chance?" Just because she had no intentions of doing something as selfish and stupid as running into a trap ever again, that didn't mean she was free and clear. Raul was determined and he had resources, he could pay someone off, do a deep dive into her life, and find her connection to Tate—which wouldn't be hard since he already had to know she'd been at his house—and find the guys' hangout spot and the apartment where she was hiding.

"They won't." Tate said it with such confidence that, for a moment, she faltered.

How could he know that for sure?

He couldn't.

Yet, there had been no room for doubt in his words.

"I know you'll do whatever you can—"

"Whatever I have to," Tate corrected.

"But that doesn't mean ..." Scarlett's words trailed off as she saw where they were. Panic gripped her in a vice. "This isn't the way back to the apartment."

It looked like ...

But no.

It couldn't be.

Could it ...?

No.

Tate wouldn't do that to her.

He wouldn't.

But the conviction in his words rang through her mind.

Maybe ...

"This looks like the way to Prey," she said nervously. Tate wouldn't take her back there when he knew exactly what would happen to her if he did. There was absolutely zero chance that the building wasn't being watched by every law enforcement, and security agency in the country. As soon as she set foot out of the car, she'd be in handcuffs.

Tate wouldn't do that to her.

He wouldn't.

He couldn't.

Betraying her like that would damage the fragile trust

they were building possibly beyond repair.

"Whatever it takes to keep you safe, Scarlett," he said, voice hard and uncompromising, reminding her more of the man from the Mexican jungle than the one she'd spent the last couple of days with.

"But they'll arrest me as soon as we get there," she whispered, already knowing she was fighting a losing battle.

"You said you understood that your safety was my top priority," Tate said.

"That was before I knew you wanted to get me arrested."

His jaw clenched together so tight she was surprised his teeth didn't crack. "I don't want you arrested, but I do want you safe. Raul's orders have changed, now he wants you dead, at least, this way you'll be safe."

"Until he uses a contact in prison to kill me while I'm alone and unprotected." She wasn't going to be any safer in prison than she was out of it. And in there she wouldn't have anyone at her back. She'd be truly on her own.

Again.

Always alone.

"You'll be kept in solitary away from the other prisoners."

"Yippee." Like that made it any better. If he thought she was going along with his plan then he was crazy. Totally crazy.

Yanking her hands free from his grip, she unsnapped her seatbelt at the same moment she lunged toward the door. She'd rather take her chances running on her own than be arrested and imprisoned.

But the door handle didn't move.

Apologetic blue eyes met hers in the rearview mirror as Tate's arms curled around her, holding her tight against him.

"Sorry, Scarlett. I hope you know how much I hate having to do this. But I want you alive so I can have a future with you."

"There is no future if you do this," she said, meaning it with every ounce of her being.

For a second, his grip loosened, and she felt his fear, but then it locked tight again. "I hope you don't mean that. I hope you'll see I'm doing what I have to in order to keep you alive."

Maybe in his mind, but not from where she was standing.

She'd fight, but it all seemed so hopeless.

Minutes later, they pulled up outside Prey's office building.

Just like she expected, the second they were out of the car and walking toward the building they were approached by men dressed in black suits, their hands hovering over their weapons like they truly believed she was some criminal mastermind.

Like he wasn't breaking her heart in the process, Tate handed her right over to them, stood there impassively watching as her hands were yanked behind her back and secured with cuffs.

She didn't look back as she was led to a car and shoved in the backseat.

Didn't spare him a glance as she was driven away.

What would be the point?

It seemed like there was always something more important than her, and for Tate, like everyone in her family, it was his job. He could say all he liked that he was doing this for her, but he was doing it for himself, so he didn't lose everything.

She wasn't worth more to him than his job.

* * *

JANUARY 18TH

8:22 P.M.

HIS ENTIRE BODY was so tense that his muscles were actually aching.

Tate didn't think that for as long as he lived, he would ever get the look of complete and utter betrayal on Scarlett's face out of his mind.

It was etched in there, a permanent reminder of the fact that he had hurt her in a way that might not be able to be undone.

All he could do was pray that Scarlett would understand that nothing was more important to him than keeping her alive. He got that she didn't see it the same way. Already he'd done the whole locking her up for her own good thing, and he hadn't intended on doing it again.

But this was different.

Things had changed.

No longer was it just Scarlett's freedom on the line, but her life.

Trapped between two terrible options, her sitting in a

prison cell or her dead body sitting in the morgue—or worse, buried in some shallow grave never to be found—he'd done the best he could. There was no way he could guarantee a mole at Prey couldn't find a connection between him and the apartment.

Put in this position there was no good choice, but Scarlett wouldn't see it that way.

Still, even if she never forgave him—although he'd fight like hell for a chance with her—at least she'd be alive. Alive trumped dead every single time. It trumped everything. Including Scarlett's feelings. Including his own happiness.

Trumped everything.

Had to.

Because the alternative was a world without Scarlett's bright, shining presence.

As far as he was concerned that was unacceptable.

Even though he would make the same choice every single time, none of this was easy. Focusing enough to be any help at all as they'd worked on narrowing down their suspect list until they could zero in on the most likely had been next to impossible.

It was only knowing his entire future was resting on this that gave him the strength to do it.

And now they might be moments away from getting the proof he needed to free Scarlett once and for all. Then he'd beg, grovel, plead, get down on his knees, whatever it took to make her understand that hurting her hadn't been his goal, but he cared about her enough to do whatever it took to protect her.

"Hey, relax, man, we're going to get this mess sorted,

keep your girl safe," Blake "Rocco" Wise told him.

Looking over at the man seated beside him on the helo as they headed out to check out a lead on the mole, he had to fight not to scoff. The only thing that held him back was the fact that these men weren't strangers to knowing what it felt like to have the woman you would do anything to protect in trouble.

Rocco and his team were SEALs, and every single one of them had gone through something with the woman they now called their wife.

To that end, his retort died on his tongue.

"Not sure I can still call her my girl," he admitted honestly. "She doesn't understand why I had no choice but to let her get arrested. At least there I know she's alive."

"Sometimes you have to lay it all on the line, regardless of the consequences," Forest "Phantom" Dalton said softly. The man had risked his career, and ultimately, his freedom by going off on his own to rescue the woman he hadn't been able to forget. Now Kalee was his wife, and the two were happy together, but in saving her he'd put everything on the line, and Tate had heard that it had caused relationships to be tense between the team for a while.

"Easier to say when your woman isn't sitting in a jail cell hating you," he muttered. The thought of Scarlett hating him was eating him alive. Slowly devouring him from the inside out. How was he going to survive if he couldn't get her to forgive him?

Big picture.

Each time he doubted that he'd made the right choice,

that's what he had to remind himself of. The big picture was going to keep Scarlett alive.

"She doesn't hate you," Cole "Rex" Kingston assured him.

What did Rex know about his woman hating him?

The man had saved Avery's life, believed in her when she'd been written off as a deserter. He'd gone above and beyond to track her down and save her from being buried alive as a prisoner of war.

Completely the opposite of what he'd done to Scarlett.

Rex had been Avery's savior, but he had been Scarlett's villain, responsible for getting her arrested.

"Pretty sure she does," he argued. It had been written into her voice and her face as soon as she realized he had no intention of taking her back to the apartment, and that instead, he was taking her to Prey where they both knew she'd be arrested as soon as they got there.

"Nah, man," Mark "Bubba" Wright countered. "I've known Scarlett for a while. She's sweet as they come. She doesn't hate you. She's scared and she's hurting, and she thinks you messed up. Right now, she can't see the big picture but she will." Bubba and his now-wife Zoey had rekindled the attraction between them when their plane crashed leaving them stranded together in the Alaskan wilderness. Again, there was nothing Bubba had done to betray his woman.

These guys had all been their women's heroes, and in this moment, he was resenting the hell out of all of them.

"What do you guys know about failing your women?" he snapped. Including Rocco, Decker "Gumby" Kincade, and Beckett "Ace" Morgan in his glare. Gumby had rescued his now-wife Sidney when she was trying to save a dog, and Ace had saved his now-wife Piper, when she had been fleeing civil unrest in Timor-Leste with three little girls in tow after an attack at an orphanage.

Heroes.

Every last one of them.

So why couldn't he be Scarlett's hero for once?

Instead, he let her down at every turn.

From pushing her away when he should have held on to her, to not believing in her and giving her the warmth and comfort she needed when he rescued her in Mexico, to sleeping with her when he still had doubts.

For all his fears of losing the woman he loved, and it destroying him, he had been the one to cause himself to lose Scarlett. While he admitted that at every turn he'd made the wrong choices, he couldn't deny that this time, he knew he'd done the right thing despite all the doubts and fear.

"Sorry," he mumbled before anyone could offer any retort.

Lashing out at these guys wouldn't change anything, and it wouldn't help at all. These guys had dropped everything when Eagle called them in, and they were coming with him to check out the boat where they hoped Warren Barone was hiding out. The former lab worker at Prey, who had been fired for being drunk and unreliable, was the best lead they had for the mole, and thankfully, he appeared to have taken a boat out into international waters, meaning Tate, as a SEAL, could be involved.

"I'm grateful you're here, and you're right," he said to Bubba. "Scarlett is amazing. If anyone can forgive me it's her. It's just ... I keep letting her down, right from the beginning. And now I've done it again."

"To keep her alive," Ace reminded him.

"Any one of us would do the same thing," Gumby said.

"You would?" Tate asked.

"I love my wife more than anything in the world," Rocco said. "But her life and safety would absolutely come before her happiness if I had to make the choice. Caite is amazing. Brave and smart. She risked everything to save me before she even really knew me. I'd protect her with my life, and I don't think there's anything I wouldn't do to keep her alive. I'm not saying it doesn't suck to be Scarlett right now, but at least Raul Castillo can't get to her where she is, and I believe that once everything is over, she'll realize that you were trying to do what you thought was best in a no-win situation."

And if she didn't ...?

If Scarlett couldn't get over her feelings of betrayal, the happy ever after he'd just reached out to try and grab hold of would go up in smoke.

It was all well and good to say he was prepared to lose her so long as she was alive to be angry with him, but if it came down to that, he didn't know what he'd do.

In just a few short days, he'd allowed all the feelings that had been building inside him for the last three months to finally bubble to the surface. Scarlett had become the most important person in his life, and letting her go would be next to impossible.

Tate would fight for her, for them. With everything he had.

But that didn't mean he'd win.

CHAPTER EIGHTEEN

January 18th
8:52 P.M.

WHY WAS she so used to being alone and yet it still hurt so badly?

Scarlett sat huddled on the bed in her cold, lonely cell. It was possibly the most uncomfortable mattress she'd ever had the displeasure of sitting or lying on. Worse even than the one she'd had as a kid. That one had been secondhand, the metal springs were starting to poke through, and when she'd timidly asked if maybe she could have a new one, she'd been told that the men and women serving their country—protecting her—slept in worse places.

The military weren't the only ones who slept in worse places than that bed.

Prisoners did, too.

And while she wasn't comparing those who had

committed crimes and were suffering the consequences of their choices to the men and women of the military, there were innocent people in prison, too.

Like her.

She wasn't paying the price for her choices, she was paying the price for someone else's.

She hadn't asked to be targeted by some greedy colleague who cared only about themselves. She hadn't asked to be kidnapped by a weapons trafficker who bought and sold weapons for fun and thought he could do whatever he wanted. And she hadn't asked to trust the man she could so easily fall in love with to turn on her and hand her over to the authorities.

In the hours since she'd been driven to the police station—she had no idea why she was at the local precinct instead of some defense agency—Scarlett had had a lot of time to think.

Too much time to think.

Enough time to have started doubting everything and everyone.

There had been crickets from Prey. She hadn't heard a peep from Eagle, or Fox and the guys, or her team.

None of them had come by.

None of them had called to check on her.

Well, not as far as she knew.

Wasn't like she had her phone here, that had been confiscated from her as soon as they arrived, and she was led down to this quiet cell. There were no other prisoners here, so at least she guessed she ought to be grateful that Tate had carried through on that promise.

Guards hadn't come other than to bring her food, and

the doctor who had checked out her head wound and other assortment of injuries and then given her a pair of scrubs. There had been no interrogation, she hadn't been fingerprinted, or had a mug shot taken, she'd just been brought here and left here.

It was strange, and Scarlett desperately wanted to believe that it was because this was all just some big game that was being played, and she hadn't really been arrested, but then she looked around the cell she'd been kept in for the last several hours and ...

It didn't feel like a game.

It felt like being arrested.

It felt like being imprisoned.

It felt like everything had shrunk until all that existed was her and this cell and her fear which seemed much too big for the tiny space.

Too big and growing.

And growing.

Consuming her.

Memories of being locked up in Raul's dungeon, dreading whatever was coming next tumbled through her mind. The pain of being whipped, her skin splitting, warm blood dripping down and puddling on the floor under her feet. Blows striking her all over while she was powerless to do anything to block them because she was restrained.

The absolute horror of begging for an orgasm she didn't want but needed.

Breathing accelerating as memories mingled with her current situation, she pressed a hand to her chest, above her heart, in a feeble attempt to slow its racing beat. Were any of the guards here on Raul's payroll? It might sound crazy, but no crazier than someone from Prey working with the weapons trafficker. Was it really his game she was tangled up in and not Prey's? Had he organized for her to be isolated and vulnerable?

With a small whimper, the only sound other than her own ragged breathing, Scarlett shoved to her feet.

She couldn't sit still any longer.

She had to move before her panic swallowed her whole.

Prey said they believed in her, the guys, her team, and they were on her side, but then why had they just left her here?

Were they working on a way to get her out?

Was this just Prey's way of keeping her safe and attempting to draw out the mole?

Had they turned on her and now thought she was guilty?

Since she was locked up, there was no way she could get any answers, and it was making her doubt everybody, even the people she thought were her family.

Doubting Tate, too.

How could he do this to her?

And why was she being so unreasonable about it when she knew exactly why he was doing it?

His job.

It meant a lot to him. He'd told her about his dad and how the man was serving a sentence for a crime he didn't commit, so she knew this had to be hard on him. If nothing else, she did actually believe that Tate believed in her innocence. It had been evident in the guilt and remorse in his tone when she figured out his plan to have her arrested.

He believed in her, and it didn't change anything.

It wasn't enough.

Even though he knew she was innocent, he was still prepared to hand her over to protect himself.

How could she blame him for that though?

They hadn't known each other long. They'd only met just before Halloween, not quite three months ago. Was it fair for her to hope that he would prioritize her over a career he'd been building for years? Just because he wanted to go out with her didn't mean he was prepared for the risks continuing to protect her would come with.

It was understandable that he would walk away to protect his job and freedom.

Why should she be angry about it?

"Because it's *not* fair," she hissed, beginning to pace around the small cell feeling like a caged animal.

It wasn't fair.

Not really.

Because she would have risked everything to save someone she loved. As much as she loved her work at Prey, she would have risked it if their positions had been reversed and Tate had been the one who needed her. Risking her freedom would have been scary, but again, she would have done it. She would have put Tate above her job and her freedom. Why couldn't he do the same for her?

Wishing that he had, especially when they had really only connected in the last couple of days, might be wildly unfair of her but she couldn't help it.

Being here, knowing the man who she was falling for was responsible, it was driving her crazy.

"Why did you have to do it, Tate?" she whispered into the silence. "Why did you have to go and be like everybody else in my life and make your job your number one priority? Why couldn't you have just let me go and then honestly told everybody you didn't know where I was? I could have taken care of myself."

Story of her life.

For as long as Scarlett could remember, she'd been taking care of herself.

Sure, her grandparents had provided for her physical needs, clothes to wear, food to eat, and shelter. But that was it. There was more to caring for someone than providing them with the bare necessities.

Why did no one ever want to give her those things?

Even her own twin brother had eventually walked away, followed in their family's footsteps, leaving her behind like she didn't matter.

Footsteps told her a guard was coming, and while she knew these weren't the same as the guards in Raul's house, Scarlett couldn't help but tense and shrink in on herself, attempting to become as small a target as possible.

The man slid a tray through the opening in the door and she crept over to collect it. "Umm, excuse me," she said softly, unsure if she was allowed to speak to the guards or if she'd be punished for it.

"Yes?" The guard sounded impatient but not angry, so she asked the question she'd been dying to since she got here but hadn't had the courage to.

"Umm, has anyone tried to come to see me?"

"No. You've had no visitors."

The next words were even harder to get out. "Has anyone called, to ask about me?"

"No phone calls," the guard said, his footsteps echoing in the quiet corridor as he walked away, leaving her alone with nothing but her thoughts, her doubts, and her fears.

"The answer to why no one is ever there for you, Scarlett, is a simple one," she told herself, brushing at a stray tear that rolled slowly down her cheek as she stumbled back toward the bed. "Because you're not enough. Not for your parents, not for your grandparents, not for your brother. And not for Tate."

Not for anyone.

* * *

JANUARY 18TH
9:03 P.M.

THE COOL WIND whipping past him was the only thing keeping Tate together.

Each brush of the wind against his skin made him think of Scarlett and the way her fingers felt as they caressed him.

As soon as they had the mole in custody, he was going to put his entire focus into doing whatever it took to gain Scarlett's forgiveness. Nothing was off the table. But first this.

They'd gotten off the helo about fifteen minutes ago and were going the rest of the distance on a zodiac. The boat they were heading toward hadn't moved in all the hours since they'd managed to track Warren Barone to it.

The anger raging inside him was desperate for an outlet and he was about to find the perfect target.

On paper, there was nothing suspicious about Warren. He had a high IQ, no criminal history, and graduated at the top of his class in high school and college. Had an exemplary reference from his prior job, came from a good family with no history of substance abuse. The man was even in a committed relationship before taking the job at Prey although he had broken up with his girlfriend only a couple of weeks after starting his new job.

There had been no indication the man would have done something like this. No way to predict it. Tate had no idea what had changed, if the man had been jealous of Scarlett and her team, of their permanent positions at Prey, or the drug they were working on. If he had a problem with women in general, or if he felt he should have been promoted and was angry that he had been overlooked. If the pressure of working for such a big company had set off his drinking, and he'd simply spiraled.

Whatever the reason it didn't matter.

Warren Barone thought he was going to get away with this. That he could try to sell a drug he hadn't created and take the money that rightly should have gone to the four women of Athena Team if they decided to sell it. That it was okay to set someone up to take the fall for him so he could take the money and be in the clear.

Not going to happen.

Nobody messed with his girl and got away with it.

Thankful for the overcast winter night, and the rough seas, since both would help to disguise their approach, he locked his gaze on the boat they were fast approaching.

To the best of their knowledge, Warren didn't have any training in hand-to-hand combat, and he had no weapon registered in his name. Not that either meant that the man wasn't going to be armed or try something stupid.

Part of him was *hoping* Warren did something stupid. If he didn't unleash some of his anger and helplessness soon, he was going to lose his mind.

Just because he had never worked a mission with Rocco and his team before didn't mean they didn't move as a cohesive unit. Pulling the zodiac up close enough to board the small boat Warren had fled on when he realized that the walls were starting to close in on him, they jumped onto the deck.

All was quiet.

Almost eerily so.

If the tension rolling through Rocco's team was anything to go by, the guys felt it too.

This was not a boat meant to be driven long distances, so he had no idea what Warren's plan had been. If he'd been hoping to just hide out long enough for the heat to die down, or if he'd thought it could make it all the way to a country he could hide out in. Maybe he thought he'd wait out here a couple of days and then head down into Mexico to meet up with his buddy Raul, who they hadn't been able to track since he'd fled his jungle estate.

Since Warren hadn't done a particularly good job of covering his tracks, Tate half expected this to be some sort of trap.

But no one shot at them as they approached the cabin, and there were no explosions like the one that had almost killed him and Scarlett this morning.

Just silence from the boat and the roar of the wind and waves around them.

Because these guys knew how personal this was for him, they had his back as he made entrance to the boat's living quarters.

Nothing moved as he took the few steps down below deck. Weapon ready, he scanned the area, but when he didn't see signs of Warren, he moved further into the space, Rocco and the others at his back.

Something felt off, and he was beginning to wonder if this wasn't a trap so much as a false lead. Something to focus everyone's attention on so that Warren could slip away somewhere else. The man might be a scientist, but he was working with a wealthy weapons dealer, surely, people would have made sure he didn't leave such an obvious trail.

Too obvious.

With the small living and kitchen area cleared, Tate headed for the closed door at the other end of the room. It likely led to a bedroom and a bathroom, there was no space for anything else, and if Warren was on this boat, and it wasn't a red herring, he had to be in there.

As soon as he opened the bedroom door, he knew why he'd had such a bad feeling.

Warren *was* on the boat, but he wasn't hiding from them or preparing an assault for the second they stepped through the door.

He was lying on the bed bleeding out.

The man must have realized they were onto him because he'd slit his own wrists.

Blood was everywhere, and it was already drying in places so he hadn't heard them board the boat then rushed in here to end his own life before they could arrest him. How had he known he'd been discovered? Not many people had been briefed on this mission. In an attempt to keep closed any avenue the mole might have set up to keep apprised of the goings on at Prey, they had limited the number of people being kept informed on this op.

Still, despite their best efforts, Warren had been expecting them.

And tried to outsmart them.

Trusting the men at his back, Tate lowered his weapon and ran toward the bed. Kneeling on the mattress beside Warren, he pressed his fingertips to the man's neck and felt the faint throb of a pulse.

"He's still alive," he called out to the others, then grabbed one of the pillows on the bed, yanked off the pillowcase, and wrapped it around Warren's left arm. Clamping a hand over the wound to keep pressure on it, he muttered, "Oh no you don't. You're not getting out of everything this easily."

If they were going to clear Scarlett's name, they needed proof. Proof that only Warren could give them.

"Hey, wake up," he yelled, slapping Warren's face. On the other side of the bed, Rex stripped the other pillow of its case and used it to wrap Warren's right arm.

A moan was all the response he got, but he wasn't giving up.

Another slap had the man's eyelids fluttering, and a third had them finally opening.

"Who …? What …?" Warren whispered weakly.

"We know what you did, Warren. You sold something that didn't belong to you to a very dangerous man, and now Scarlett is paying the price for that," Tate growled. "You're going to fix it." Nothing else was possible. Because if he'd gotten Scarlett arrested to keep her safe, only to be unable to get her out again, he would never forgive himself.

"Did …?"

"Tell us what you did," he demanded. "Give us something that can clear Scarlett's name."

"Was …"

"Was what?" They were running out of time. There was no way they could get Warren to help in time to save his life, he'd already lost too much blood. A field transfusion might work, and Tate was a universal donor, but the idea of giving blood to the man who had destroyed Scarlett's life made him feel ill.

Near vacant eyes stared up at him, and from Warren's labored breathing, he guessed they had a couple of minutes at the most until the man died.

"Didn't do it … wasn't me … not mole …" Warren mumbled.

About to scoff at the man's audacity, lying on his death bed and telling lies, Rex's dark eyes met his. "There are bruises on his arms, around his elbows, looks like he could have been held down while somebody slashed his wrists."

If Warren was just another patsy, then that meant

somebody in the small group of people in the loop had leaked that information to Raul. There had been three names at the top of their suspect list, and Warren was one of them. Raul must have sent his people after Warren, set up a trail to lead them all right here, and once again outmaneuvered them.

"Who was it, Warren? Who did this to you?"

But Warren didn't answer, his eyes drifted half closed, and a gurgle rumbled through his chest as he took his final breath.

No.

Not happening.

Abandoning his grip on the man's wound, Tate shifted so he could start CPR.

"Who was it, Warren? Who killed you? You tell me right now," he shouted as he started chest compressions.

They couldn't lose this lead.

Scarlett couldn't afford for them to lose it.

Without proof someone else was the mole, she'd be kept locked up indefinitely. Letting her get arrested might have cost both of them a price that could never be paid.

What had he done?

CHAPTER NINETEEN

January 19th
10:28 A.M.

IF SHE KEPT THIS UP, she was going to have no fingernails left intact.

Scarlett had always been a nailbiter when she was nervous. As a kid, she used to get in so much trouble from her grandparents and her parents when they came home from deployments for doing it, but she couldn't seem to break the habit.

The more they yelled, the more pressure they put on her, and the more they threatened the worse it got.

They didn't seem to understand it was her instinctual reaction to stress. If they wanted her to stop doing it all they had to do was remove the stress they kept heaping on her shoulders.

It wasn't until she aged out of the foster system and

struck out on her own that she finally was able to break the habit. That was when she realized she hadn't been biting her nails and gnawing on her cuticles because her parents put so much pressure on her, it was because she was so desperate to be loved that she had internalized everyone else's lack of care and blamed herself.

Because she wasn't good enough her parents didn't want to raise her.

Because she wasn't good enough her grandparents hadn't loved her.

Because she wasn't good enough, no one wanted to adopt her, and no foster family wanted to keep her.

Because she wasn't even good enough for her twin brother to stay.

That was the moment she knew she had to stop looking to others for their validation. She had to be good enough for herself.

For years, she thought she had learned that lesson, but now, looking back at all the failed relationships and two engagements that had never gone through to marriage, Scarlett knew all she had been doing was lying to herself.

Still, she was trying so hard to get someone to love her.

Doubt was her constant friend. Worry that she might say or do something to make one of her teammates or someone from her Prey family turn on her was constant. She tried so hard to find love, but she kept looking in all the wrong places, that's why she failed. You couldn't force real love it just … was.

Maybe it was just time to accept that she was never

going to be loved. Not the way she wanted to be. That sense of belonging that remained constantly out of reach was never going to happen for her.

She had to be enough for herself.

If she didn't learn that lesson, she was going to wind up losing herself.

There was no way she could keep going through the pain of convincing herself she was in love with a man, that they were the answer to all her prayers, that she was going to have forever with them.

It had to stop.

Now.

No more.

So, she huddled in her cell, wondering if this was going to be what the rest of her life looked like, trying to figure out how she could be enough for herself, and chewing on her nails because right now, there was too much stress piled on her shoulders to make herself stop.

When footsteps outside her cell caught her attention, she straightened.

She'd already been given breakfast, and although there was no clock, there was no way it could be lunchtime already.

Scarlett was even more surprised when instead of a meal being pushed through the slot, the door was unlocked and opened. A guard stood there, his expression unreadable, and she warred between hope that she was finally being let out, and fear that it was time. Time to be booked and processed, time to be sent off to join the rest of the prisoners.

Or worse, time to be shipped off to some hidden prison that housed traitors and terrorists.

"Let's go, Ms. Madden," the guard said.

There were no handcuffs in his hands, and she faltered slightly as she got to her feet, unsure what that meant. Too many hours of sitting curled up in the corner of the uncomfortable bed had left her muscles stiff, and she swayed a little as she walked uncertainly across her cell.

When the guard merely turned and started walking, Scarlett followed.

They walked back the way they'd come when she was brought in, stopping in a small interview room. It was empty, and when the guard left her in there she stayed where she was, frozen in the middle of the room, no idea what was going on.

It was that unknown that had her fear ramping up.

What was going to happen to her?

Was her life about to get better or a whole lot worse?

She was still standing right where she was when the door opened again. Only this time, it wasn't a guard or a cop who walked through it. It was the lawyer Prey kept on retainer. She'd only met him once, but she'd liked Walter Gunnerman. He was an older man in his early fifties, quiet, calm, professional, and a steady presence.

Now he was here, and her hope soared.

Did this mean what she hoped it did?

"Walter?" she asked, taking an uncertain step toward him.

His smile was warm and reassuring. "You ready to get out of here?"

Relief literally stole her strength and she dropped to her knees as tears streamed down her cheeks. "I … I'm … free?" she asked through her tears.

When he knelt before her on the dirty linoleum floor, no concern for his expensive suit, Walter's smile was so gentle that her weeping intensified. It had been so many hours that she had been without a soft smile, and the wounds of Tate's betrayal were so raw that, without thinking she reached out, wrapped her arms around the lawyer's neck, and held onto him as she sobbed.

Walter didn't stop her, he just held her until she cried herself out, then helped her stand and held out a bag to her. "Why don't you change and I'll take you home."

Home.

Not to Prey.

She wasn't sure what that meant.

This was a Prey lawyer, so it had to mean they'd been working this whole time to get her out. But why wasn't he taking her straight there so she could find out what evidence they had that had proven her innocence?

Deciding she'd wait until she was dressed and they were out of there before she started peppering Walter with questions, she nodded and took the bag, opening it as he left the room to give her privacy. As badly as she wanted answers, she wanted out of there more. There was only so long she could take being trapped in a small cell, memories of being locked up in Raul's dungeon mingling with the horrors that could be awaiting her in prison, and she had well and truly reached that limit.

It didn't take her long to change into the jeans and

sweater that someone must have packed for Walter to bring with him. The clothes were hers, as were the sneakers she shoved her feet into, and the coat she shrugged on.

It warmed her a little to know that her friends hadn't given up on her. They'd packed her clothes, and she bet anything that Lucy, Ella, and Cassie were waiting for her at her house.

Just because she might not ever wind up with a husband and kids of her own didn't mean she had no family. By the time she was dressed and opening the door, she was sorry she'd ever doubted her Prey family.

Of course, they wouldn't give up on her.

"You ready to get out of here?" Walter asked.

"More than," she replied.

Half worried this was all some dream or some sort of trick and expecting the worst, Scarlett was surprised when nobody stopped them as they walked through the precinct and out the back door into a quiet parking lot.

The fresh air felt so good against her cheeks, and she dragged in a huge breath.

Free.

She was free.

If she was out, that meant the real mole had been identified and she was in the clear. While she didn't have to worry about being arrested again, she did still have to worry about Raul Castillo. The man would remain a threat until he was apprehended.

Anxious to help in whatever ways she could to make sure that happened, Scarlett turned just as Walter jammed something into her neck.

Just like that, the terror beginning to ebb roared back to life.

"What did you ...?" her question trailed off as the world began to spin around her and she lost control of her body, slumping forward into Walter's arms.

"I'm sorry, Scarlett. I didn't want it to end like this, I truly didn't."

The words were cold comfort as unconsciousness swirled around her, and she knew that the next time she opened her eyes she would once again be a prisoner. This time of Raul Castillo.

* * *

JANUARY 19TH

10:37 A.M.

"DEAN WEBSTER GOT HIS BROTHER OUT," Gumby announced, looking up from his laptop.

"Got him out how?" Tate asked, rubbing at tired eyes. He hadn't gotten any sleep last night. The only time he'd tried to lie down and get a little rest, dreams of Scarlett weeping and asking him why he'd betrayed her had haunted him. He'd functioned on less sleep than this during an op, but he knew he wasn't running at the top of his game.

That could get Scarlett killed.

So, he was grateful that he had all of Prey, his team, and Rocco's team all at his back.

Together they would sort this mess out and keep his

girl safe.

"Sold his house and paid the gang to let his brother go," Gumby replied. "He just put in his resignation to Prey, said he wanted to move away, and make sure there was no fallout for either of them. Not like gangs are known for sticking to their word and being honorable."

"Why would he sell his house to pay off the debt if he knew he had a huge payout coming from selling a drug to a weapons dealer?" Bubba asked.

"He wouldn't," Tate answered. "If Dean Webster sold his house and paid off his brother's debts, and they're moving, then he's out as a suspect. I mean, we can keep an eye on him, but there's no reason to sell the house unless it was the only way he could get the money."

"Unless he just sold it in the last couple of days, after Scarlett was rescued," Ace suggested.

"House has been listed for the last three months," Gumby told them. "So, he had this plan in motion for a while now."

"Definitely out," Rocco agreed.

"That still leaves us Amy Jenkins as a suspect," Tate said, trying not to sound as desperate as he felt.

Which was next to impossible.

It had been over twenty-four hours since he'd allowed Scarlett to be arrested, and he was aching to take her in his arms and soothe the pain he himself had inflicted.

Soothe every pain she'd ever suffered.

Punish every person who had ever hurt her.

Unfortunately, her grandparents and brother were all deceased, but he had half a mind to track down her parents and give them a piece of his mind. They had started the ball rolling when they decided that their twins weren't ever going to be a priority in their lives. Giving them up and having them put in foster care rather than giving up their careers had them right near the top of the worst parents ever list as far as he was concerned.

"Uh, I think we might be able to clear Amy as a suspect, too," Phantom announced.

"What? Why?" he asked. Of their two remaining suspects, his money had been on the IT specialist. She had the skills to track down a weapons dealer on the dark web, she had the skills to plant the emails, and she was desperately in need of the money.

If they had cleared both their suspects, and they believed Warren when he said he hadn't been involved, then where did they look next?

"Her GoFundMe hit its goal and then some, which means she's going to have all the money she needs to pay off her husband's medical bills, and those for her son, and still have plenty left over so that she won't need to work while she takes time to care for her dying child. Money was the only motive we had for her. We were going on the assumption that she wouldn't hit her fundraising goals and therefore would get nothing, but she did," Phantom said.

"But she couldn't have known that she would. She still could have done it," Tate argued.

"Maybe, but to be honest, I'm not sure how she'd have the time," Ace said. "I've got kids, they keep you on your toes, there's barely time to blink. Not only is Amy grieving, but she's a single mom to two kids, one of whom is in and out of the hospital. She's also got to work, get her daughter to and from school, and her son to and from appointments. I just don't think she had the time or energy to set something like this up. Desperate people do desperate things sure. But this woman seems completely focused on taking care of her kids. Plus, she has a great support system. I don't think it was her."

"Then who was it?" Tate demanded, shoving away from the table and dragging his fingers through his hair, enjoying the sting as it tugged on his scalp.

Good.

He should hurt.

Should hurt as badly as Scarlett had when she realized he was going to allow her to be arrested.

It was killing him that he couldn't go to her, plead with her to understand why he'd made that choice, and beg her to forgive him.

When Rocco's phone buzzed with a message all attention focused on the man. From his expression as he read it, whatever the news was it wasn't good.

"What happened?" Tate asked. Good news or bad he was desperate for something. The more intel they had, the more they learned, and the more they learned the closer they got to ending this once and for all.

For a moment, when Rocco's brown eyes lifted to meet his, Tate was sure that the other man wasn't going to answer.

To hell with that.

He'd fight for the intel if he had to. Scarlett was his, and he was going to get her name cleared, and the weapons dealer off her back so she could finally be free to live out her dreams.

Dreams they shared.

Dreams she'd made him realize he had even if he refused to allow himself to acknowledge them.

"Easy, man," Phantom murmured, and Tate realized he'd curled his fingers into fists and started stalking toward Rocco.

"Not going to keep it from you," Rocco assured him. "Eagle just wants me to be sure you can handle this before I tell you."

Then it was bad.

If Eagle was worried about what he was going to do, it had to be even worse than he was thinking, and there were already a dozen worse-case scenarios forming in his head.

"I can handle it," he vowed. He had to. Simple as that. Because if he couldn't it would be Scarlett who would pay the price.

Rocco studied him, expression inscrutable, but then he nodded. "Scarlett was just released from jail."

"Huh?" How could that be? Much as he had hated it, they'd decided against allowing anyone outside the small circle of people he was sure were trustworthy to learn that Warren Barone had claimed innocence. It meant leaving Scarlett in prison until they had a name of who had set both her and Warren up, but in the end, he was the one who had set this in motion by allowing her to be arrested and they had to play through the hand he had dealt.

"How did she get out?" Rex asked.

"Eagle had a pretty tight rein on things," Bubba added.

"Who got her out?" Phantom asked.

"Walter Gunnerman," Rocco told them.

Sifting through all the names of Prey employees he'd learned over the last couple of weeks, Tate placed the name as being one of the lawyers Prey kept on retainer.

From what he knew, the Reactivator was almost complete, and Athena Team had contacted the lawyer to discuss filing for a patent.

"No way, man, he's loyal to Eagle and Prey," Ace said.

"We rescued Walter's daughter several years back after he got himself into some trouble. It was a joint mission with Prey's Charlie Team. A loan shark sold off all his client's debts to a human trafficker looking to make a quick buck by clearing the debts in flesh. Walter's then thirteen-year-old daughter was taken along with a bunch of other girls and women. We were able to recover all but one of the girls, and the trafficker and most of his key men were killed. Walter was so grateful he vowed to stop gambling. It's been over a decade, and he's been clean ever since. Family first. Job second. There's no way he would betray Eagle after everything the man did for him and his family."

But that wasn't quite true.

There was always a limit.

Everybody had one.

And when you reached that limit there was nothing you wouldn't do.

Walter Gunnerman might have reformed and gone on the straight and narrow, but he knew about the drug, and he obviously knew that Warren had been suspected of being the mole because he had to have used something to get a judge to sign off on getting Scarlett out.

There was only one thing Tate could think of that would cause the lawyer to turn on a man who had helped him when he was at the lowest point of his life.

"If Walter relapsed, got himself in debt again and panicked, needed an out, he might have thought selling the drug was an easy option," Tate said. "And if Raul Castillo threatened his daughter, his family, then I'm guessing there isn't anything the man wouldn't do to keep them safe. We have to bring him in, get him to talk."

"We can't," Rocco said, stopping him in his tracks when he had already started heading for the door.

Dread pooled in his stomach. "Why not?"

"Because Walter and Scarlett have disappeared," Rocco replied gently. "Eagle got wind of what was going on just as it was happening, but he was too slow getting someone to the jail. Walter and Scarlett were already out the door. He reviewed the security footage, hoping to get a lead on their direction, since Walter wasn't answering his phone."

"And?" he prompted when Rocco didn't continue.

"And the footage shows Walter drugging Scarlett and shoving her into the trunk of his car," Rocco finished.

Scarlett had been kidnapped.

Again.

Because of him.

He was the one to put her in a position where she was alone and vulnerable, not surrounded by the people who would have her back. He'd thought he was keeping her safe, away from the mole at Prey, instead, he'd left her open to an attack.

What happened to her now was all on him.

The images of Scarlett's bruised and battered body

assaulted his mind, along with what she'd told him Raul had done to her.

There was no way he was ever going to forgive himself for this.

CHAPTER TWENTY

January 19th
2:41 P.M.

How could this be happening to her again?

Scarlett lifted her fuzzy head and scrunched her eyes tightly closed as the room spun in sickeningly fast circles all around her.

It wasn't just the lingering drugs in her system that had her head swimming, it was the mass of overwhelming emotions mixed in along with it.

Fear of course, that was topping the list.

Hopelessness, too.

Betrayal. By everyone and everything.

But there was anger there as well.

A whole lot of it.

She was sick of feeling like she wasn't good enough. She was sick of being ignored or shoved aside. She was sick of allowing her self-worth to depend on other people.

And most of all, she was sick of people playing games with her life.

There was no way she was going to give Raul Castillo what he wanted.

On principle alone, she'd keep her mouth shut. No matter what he did, she wasn't going to give him the satisfaction of breaking her.

She wasn't breakable.

If life had proved anything to her it had proved that.

Crackable, yes. Bendable, scratchable, chipable, sure. But after everything she had been through, she was still standing, and like Tate had said, she was still willing to put her heart on the line in the hopes of finding what she wanted, what she craved above all else.

So, Raul didn't get to change that. He didn't get to break her.

"Whatever happens you can do this, Scar. Believe in yourself. Just because nobody else ever has doesn't mean that you can't. Doesn't mean you haven't. You got yourself this far. And even though your emotions are telling you to feel betrayed, you know your Prey family loves you. Whatever is going on they're doing their best to save you. Hold onto that."

Pep talk done, she forced away her fear enough that she could open her eyes. The room still felt like it was spinning, but it had slowed down enough that she no longer felt like she was going to throw up.

Blinking her eyes to try to clear her vision, she planted her hands on a wall—which felt like scratchy concrete—and pushed to her feet. As she looked around, she saw her accommodations were even worse than last time. The room was tiny, barely six feet by six feet, the floor was torn linoleum and the walls concrete. There were metal shelves on the walls above her, and she assumed she was in some sort of pantry or storage shed.

The door was wood, and while she was sure it was locked it didn't look all that sturdy. Still a little wobbly, Scarlett took the two steps to it and immediately reached for the handle. It was indeed locked, but she gathered all her strength and rammed her shoulder into the wood.

Jarring pain speared through her body, and the impact sent her stumbling back, but she was sure she felt a little give in the door.

Not allowing herself to think ahead, of how she'd get out of wherever she'd been taken even if she got through the door, of how she'd find her way back home, because if she did then she'd get so overwhelmed she'd just sit in the corner and shake and cry.

No.

That wasn't what she was going to do.

If she was going to die there then she was going to go down fighting.

Lining up, she slammed her shoulder into the door again.

This time, since she was prepared for the impact, she managed to absorb most of it, and quickly regained her balance, then hit it again and again.

The final time she was rewarded with the door groaning and splintering slightly.

Just as hope began to soar inside her, the door was yanked open and an irritated man stood there glaring down at her. “Did you really think you would get out of Mr. Castillo’s house?”

“He knew I was going to try,” she shot back. No more was she going to cower. Just because she was terrified out of her mind didn't mean she had to give in to those feelings. “If he didn't want me to try to escape, he shouldn’t have put me inside such a pathetic excuse for a prison cell.”

Shooting her another glare, the man grabbed her bicep and began to drag her along with him. Turned out they were in the back corner of a large garage, big enough to hold at least six cars. There was no time for her to try to get a glimpse of outside or anything that might help her identify where she was being held because she was pulled along to an interior door that led into a laundry room, and then through a house. It was nice, expensively furnished, but not quite as big as the mansion in Mexico.

They ended up in a bedroom, so she guessed this place wasn’t kitted out as well as the Mexican mansion and didn't have its own dungeon and torture room. Of course, it occurred to her to fight, to try to escape, but the man was armed and wasn’t alone. Another three had been waiting along with him in the garage, and there was no way she could get away from that many armed and trained men.

After all, she wasn’t a superhero.

She wasn’t Tate.

Could he find a way to get away from these men?

Probably.

But he was a SEAL, and she was just a scientist with some training that had been forced on her.

Quickly, she shoved away thoughts of Tate. They were not what she needed right now. Since she knew that Raul had already changed his mind about keeping her alive and forcing her to give up the formula, she knew she didn't have much time. Probably not even enough for Prey to find wherever she was and mount a rescue.

If they even knew she was missing.

Which meant her best bet at making sure she couldn't be forced to talk was to find a way to take herself out of the equation.

That was her plan.

And as she glanced around, she spotted the huge glass doors opening up onto a balcony.

Perfect.

While the four guards were still in the room, no one held on to her, and she knew she might not get another chance.

This was not how she figured on her life ending. She was only in her twenties, she wasn't thinking about death at all. But the bottom line was, she had no intention of giving up the information Raul wanted and she knew she might be forced into it against her will.

Before she could run, the door opened again and Raul stalked in.

Unlike last time, he wasn't all cool and calm and in control. The opposite, he was every bit the menacing weapons dealer he was.

"I've had enough of you," he snapped like this was all her fault. But he was the one who had set this in motion by kidnapping her in the first place. "I lost the home I had specially built because of you, and you've been nothing but trouble since. I should just kill you and be done with it, but I've invested too much time and money in this, and I don't like to lose. So, you get one more chance to tell me what I want to know or I'm just going to kill you and be done with it."

Yeah …

No.

If she was dying today it was going to be at her own hand.

"I'm not telling you anything, and I'm not going to give you the pleasure of getting to kill me." With that, Scarlett ran toward the door, prepared to make the ultimate sacrifice rather than risk something she and her friends had created for good to be used against them.

As her hands reached the doorknob arms circled her body, dragging her back, away from the only freedom she would find.

"I won't tell you," she screamed, kicking and thrashing in the man's grip as she was carried toward the bed.

"Then the last few hours of your life won't be very pleasant," Raul sneered. "You're going to be injected with the same drug you had the pleasure of trying out last time, only this time my men are going to listen to your pleas. They're going to give you everything you beg for and more. And if you're still stupid enough not to tell me what I want to know then they're going to keep injecting you, keep taking you until there's nothing left. I should warn you, Ms. Madden, that my men won't be gentle, and you won't survive it."

At the bed, she was held down by one man as another prepared a vial of the drug that haunted her dreams.

The syringe delivered the drug into her body, and almost immediately, she began to heat inside as arousal took hold. Scarlett wished she had made it to the balcony so she could have ended her life on her own terms and spared herself this horrific death.

* * *

JANUARY 19TH
3:39 P.M.

"I'M NOT WAITING to go in." For Tate it was as simple as that.

Scarlett was in there.

She needed him.

Already she had been through so much. There was no way he was going to wait until nightfall before mounting a rescue op.

Not when he knew that she was already living on borrowed time.

Just because her body hadn't been found at Walter Gunnerman's house along with his and those of his family didn't mean that she was even still alive.

They knew that Raul had ordered her death because the bomb the other day was supposed to kill her, and anyone with her. The only other option was that the mole had gone rogue. Not an impossibility, but even if that was true and it was no longer Raul Castillo who was calling the shots, it hardly put Scarlett in a better position.

She was a loose end that needed tying up.

"We don't know how many men are in there, what they're armed with, or even if Scarlett is in there," Rocco said, far too calmly considering the frantic way Tate's heart was hammering in his chest.

"Walter said she would be here," he reminded the man of what they'd found when they had searched a mountain cabin owned by the man and his wife. They'd found Walter's dead body, executed with a simple bullet to the back of the head. Evidence on the bodies of his wife, and three kids, including the daughter Prey and Rocco's team had rescued years ago, suggested that the wife and kids had been held and tortured before being executed along with Walter.

Marks on their wrists and ankles similar to those Scarlett had from being bound, bruising on top of bruising going back several days at the least, wounds that had partially healed along with fresher ones. Their theory was that Walter wasn't the mole but another scapegoat to keep the attention off whoever the true mole was.

This theory was backed up by the fact there was a tiny scrap of paper in Walter's pocket with Scarlett's name on it and an address.

Since there was no way Tate was wasting time trying to figure out if Walter was the mole, and if he intended to lead them into a trap, he had insisted they go and check out the location immediately.

So they were back in Mexico, outside a house in the remote jungles. This one much smaller than the one they'd rescued Scarlett from last time, but just as grand. From their hiding spot in the trees outside the fence, there didn't appear to be any cars in the driveway, and there were no lights on inside the house.

But this was where the last person to see Scarlett said she was, and he wasn't leaving until he searched it from top to bottom.

"I'm going in with or without you," he told the others. If it cost him his job, so be it, if he wound up court-martialed then he'd deal with it. Whatever consequences he had to suffer he would gladly accept so long as he knew that Scarlett was safe. "Come on, man, you should get me even if they don't," he said to Phantom. "You went off on your own to Timor-Leste to go after Kalee. How can you ask me to do anything less than you did when we're talking about the woman I could fall in love with?"

While in his head he kept telling himself Scarlett was just the woman he *could* fall in love with, he knew it was more than that.

He was already falling.

Hard and fast.

Knowing that the landing might not be the softness and safety of love, acceptance, and belonging, and instead could be cold, lonely, and unforgiving was terrifying.

But knowing he could lose Scarlett was worse.

This was a leap of faith he had to take. Like it was already written in the stars, Scarlett had consumed him since that very first second, and no matter what had happened, or where things would end, he had to try.

Had to let himself fall.

There was no time to worry about what the landing would be like.

His girl was counting on him.

"We should go in," Phantom agreed, his dark eyes so full of understanding that there was no way Tate couldn't nod in acceptance of his support.

"If it was Caite in there, you'd risk it all," Rex reminded Rocco, whose brown eyes seemed to darken at the thought.

"All right, let's do this," Rocco agreed.

Adrenalin was pumping through his bloodstream, the only thing keeping him on his feet after several days of not more than a couple of snatched hours of sleep here and there. Still, that and fear for Scarlett were the only things he needed to function as he and the rest of his team, and Rocco's team gained entrance to the property.

Unlike last time when bullets had been flying in all directions, this time, it was silent as they breached the perimeter and headed across the manicured gardens toward the house.

Deadly silent.

The kind of silence that had his skin crawling and the hairs standing up on the back of his neck.

That silence continued as they entered the house. It was obvious it had been recently inhabited. A stack of dirty dishes sat on the counter above the dishwasher, the fridge was fully stocked, there was a book, open and upside down, on the table, and a TV was on.

"Blood in a storage room off the garage," Bubba's voice came through the comms.

While there was no way to know for sure that it was Scarlett's blood, his gut told him that it was.

"Sounds coming from upstairs," Ace said moments later.

The only signs of life in the entire house. From the looks of things, it seemed like everyone had left in a hurry, and he couldn't help but wonder whether once again, something had tipped off Raul Castillo that his place was about to be raided.

If he'd fled in a hurry, he had no reason to leave Scarlett alive. He wanted her dead and she wasn't going to give him the intel he wanted.

No matter what he did.

His stomach muscles clenched and twisted at the thought of what Raul would most likely do to her to try to get her to talk before he counted her a loss and eliminated her.

Heading for the stairs, he took them three at a time, no longer concerned that someone was going to start shooting at them or launch any kind of attack. For whatever reason, Raul was gone, and while he was praying that it was Scarlett making the sounds Ace had heard there was every chance it wasn't.

"Tate, get in here. Now," Ace's urgent voice came through the comms.

The tone amped up his fear several notches. "What's wrong?" he demanded, quickening his pace.

"It's Scarlett," Ace replied.

He could hardly make himself say the words. "Is she …?"

"She's alive. But she's … look I can't explain, just hurry up," Ace ordered.

Panicking was the last thing he should be doing right now, but it was exactly what he was doing as he reached the top of the grand staircase and headed in the direction of the whimpers and moans he could now hear clearly.

Nothing could have prepared him for what he saw when he located the room where Ace and Scarlett were.

In the middle of the bed was Scarlett. Her skin was flushed, her hair a tangled mess of thick brown waves around her head, her eyes wild.

Ace was trying to approach her and calm her down, but it only made things worse.

It was clear something was wrong with Scarlett, and because she'd confided in him about what Raul had done to her last time he feared he knew exactly what it was.

"Back off," he whispered to Ace as he approached the bed.

"Tate, she has—"

"I know. I see it," he gritted out as he held his hands out, palms up, and continued slowly approaching the bed. "Scarlett, baby, it's Tate," he said gently, drawing her wild gaze in his direction.

Her hands clawed low on her stomach, and he could only imagine the horror of her current situation. Because not only had she been given a drug to induce an arousal so powerful it was painful for her, but there was a suicide vest strapped to her chest.

"It's going to be okay," he soothed.

"N-no, it's n-not," she stammered, then moaned and pressed her thighs together as her eyes scrunched closed and she began to rock back and forth.

"It is," he countered as he carefully eased one knee onto the bed.

"He wants to blow us all up," Scarlett said through

clenched teeth. "You have to leave. Now. All of you." Her eyes opened and latched onto his, pleading with him, but he had no intention of doing as she said.

If Scarlett was blown up in this room today, he was going out with her.

"Like hell, I'm leaving you here. Nothing is going to make me leave your side. Not ever again."

CHAPTER TWENTY-ONE

January 19th
4:00 P.M.

"No," the tortured word fell from her lips as a wave of arousal so strong it took every ounce of her willpower not to strip off her clothes, strip Tate's pants off him, and sink down onto him, letting him soothe the burning ache tearing her apart.

Right now, Scarlett wasn't even sure she cared who gave her an orgasm, anything as long as for one second she wasn't consumed by need.

She'd take Ace, she'd take any of the guys on his team who she knew, although not well, she'd take one of the guys on Tate's team who were strangers.

If they were still there, she feared she'd even take Raul's men.

Anything as long as she calmed this beast inside her.

But this she didn't want.

Scarlett would endure the rest of her life plagued by this horrendous clawing arousal if it meant that nobody else died in this room today.

When Tate reached for her, she scrambled back, out of reach, a shaky hand held up between them. "You have to go," she insisted.

"Not leaving you, sweetheart, so get that through your pretty head," Tate said. There was that stubborn look in his eyes, but there were other things there, too. Things she didn't have the energy to figure out right now because all of her energy was being spent on not jumping either of the two men in the room.

Or taking matters into her own hands.

This time she wasn't tied up, and the temptation to throw out the window the fact that she had an audience and just put her hands between her legs and relieve a little of the pressure was strong.

"You *have* to, Tate," she begged. "He wants you all dead. Me and whoever came to rescue me. I … I'm stuck here … but you aren't. Leave, please. I don't want you to die."

"What the hell? You think *I* want *you* to die?" he demanded. "I'm not leaving, Scarlett. So don't mention it again."

"Bubba's on his way," Ace announced, reminding her that the other man hadn't left either. "Trust me, if anyone has a chance at disarming the bomb, it's him."

"If you can't you have to promise me you'll leave in enough time," Scarlett pleaded. The last thing she wanted was to take her dying breath knowing anyone had died because of her.

"Scarlett," Tate warned.

Since arguing with Tate seemed pointless, she turned her attention to Ace. The man had a wife and kids, there was no way he was going to stay in this room and die along with her. "When you leave you have to take Tate with you."

His brown eyes narrowed, and he looked offended. "No one is leaving you, and no one is dying here today," Ace said like it was already a fact.

"But—"

"No buts, Scarlett. Now look at me, did he hurt you?" Tate asked.

It was hard to look at Tate and not grab his face and shove it between her legs, let his tongue work its magic, and bring her at least a couple of seconds of relief.

"N-no," she replied truthfully. All Raul had done was drug her, then he'd gotten a phone call and before he could carry through on the threats to let his men rape her to death, he had ordered someone to strap the bomb on her, told her she was going to die along with whoever was coming for her, and then left.

Almost like he was afraid to touch her, Tate's hand hesitated for a moment before his palm cupped her cheek, and his fingertips caressed her sweat-dotted brow.

If she wasn't so consumed by the drug she'd been given, Scarlett would have sworn it was relief in Tate's eyes.

But he'd made it clear he didn't care about her the same way she cared about him when he'd allowed her to get arrested.

A moan fell from her lips when the drug-induced arousal coursed through her system, and she shoved

Tate's hand away, worried that his touch would lead her to do something she couldn't take back. It was one thing to crave Tate's touch when she was in her right mind, when she could assess the consequences and decide if her heart could take another battering. It was another right now when her mind could focus on only one thing.

"Don't, Tate," she whispered when he reached for her again. Another wave of fire burned through her body, and she moaned and pressed her legs together. Tomorrow, when the drug was out of her system, she'd be mortified to know she'd been moaning and squirming like this, with her eyes dark with desire and her cheeks flushed with arousal, in front of men she didn't know well.

Ignoring her, he leaned over and scooped her up, shifting so he was sitting on the bed with her on his lap facing him. In this position, the thick ridge of his length nestled between her legs, pressing against her soaking-wet center. It felt so good that Scarlett moaned and rocked her hips for the moment, forgetting they had an audience.

"Tate, please," she begged, her fingers curling into his clothes so tight her hands ached. But not worse than the gnawing feeling low in her belly that screamed at her to do something about it.

"Shh, baby, I can't, not like this, not when you can't consent," he whispered against her ear as he drew her closer. His arms locked around her like steel bands, and he tucked her face against his neck. One hand rubbed circles on her back, and the other gripped her hip, keeping her close against him.

"I need it," she whispered back, hating how desperate

she was, that she was begging for a man who didn't want her, but that was how far gone she was.

"Oh, sweetheart, I know you do. But I won't touch you while you hate me." His tone showed genuine regret, and it helped a little to know at least he had been conflicted about turning her in.

If lying would get him to touch her, then in this moment, Scarlett wasn't above it. "I don't hate you."

A chuckle rumbled through his chest. "Yeah, you do. You need to get an IV going, she's got drugs in her system we need to flush out," he said, presumably not to her since she couldn't do anything right now but sit here and writhe in blissful agony.

"Timer says we have ten minutes to get this thing off her," Ace said.

Right.

The bomb strapped to her chest.

Somehow, she'd forgotten about it.

That was how badly aroused she was, it was all she could think about.

Ten minutes wasn't long. Certainly not enough time for Bubba to figure out how the bomb was put together and what wires to cut to disarm it.

"You all have to leave," she said desperately. Earlier she had been prepared to die to prevent Raul from getting what he wanted. While she certainly didn't want her life to end here and now, more than that, she didn't want anyone else being taken out with her.

"Nah, honey, I got this." A comforting hand landed on her shoulder, giving a single squeeze before disappearing. Bubba sounded so confident, and she wanted to believe him so badly, but her skin was overheated, and need pulsed through her body with every beat of her heart that it was hard to believe anything could ever be all right again.

"I'm sorry for taking you back to Prey," Tate murmured as she felt his arms drop a little to her waist so Bubba could see the suicide vest.

If she was going to die, she didn't want to do it holding onto a grudge. "It's okay," she mumbled wearily as someone took one of her arms and swabbed the inside of her elbow before starting up an IV. "Your job is important to you. I get that."

"That's why you thought I let you get arrested? To keep my job?" Tate sounded aghast, and when he pulled her back enough that he could look down at her there was shock on his face.

Scarlett shrugged. "Well … yeah. What other reason would there be?" As much as she hated it, she did get it. It just sucked to be her.

"Sweetheart, that's not why I did it. I thought it was the only place you would be safe from Raul and the mole. It killed me to do it, but I wasn't going to let you get hurt. I made sure Eagle organized for you not to be booked or processed, and to be kept away from everyone else. I think I drove all the guys crazy calling to check on you at least every hour."

"But … when I asked, the guard said nobody had come to see me or called to see if I was okay."

"I don't know why he told you that, Scarlett, but it's not true. Maybe he just didn't know, or maybe he was lying on purpose, I have no idea, but I called. A lot," Tate said, his gaze complete sincerity.

"He did, and it did drive us all crazy," Rocco said from somewhere behind her.

"It made me sick to think it, but I was prepared to lose you if you hated me and couldn't forgive me, doing whatever it took to make sure you were alive was more important," Tate told her as he leaned down to touch a kiss to her forehead. "The world has to have you in it. My world has to have you in it."

More confused than ever, Scarlett didn't have the energy to try to process everything. "How many minutes left?"

"Six," Bubba replied.

Because she was looking at him, she caught the disapproving frown Tate tossed Bubba's way before he urged her to lie against him again. "I want you to close your eyes and try to rest," Tate told her like she wasn't suffering from the mother of all arousals.

The fingers of the hand on her hip were so close to the part of her body that was weeping for touch, and with her tucked against his chest again, nobody could see the soft sweeps of his fingers against her center that at least held off the worst of the gnawing need.

For what felt like hours they sat like that. "How many minutes?"

"Two," Bubba replied.

"You have to go now, Tate, please."

"Not leaving you alone, sweetheart."

Lifting her head, she looked at Rocco. "You have to make him leave, please."

"I got this," Bubba insisted.

Tears began to tumble down her cheeks. Why wouldn't they leave her? Everyone in her life left. Her parents, her grandparents, her foster parents, her brother, only Tate and these guys were staying now even though they were risking their lives in the process.

"Why?" she whispered, looking at Tate as she sought the answer she so desperately needed to hear.

"Because you're amazing, Scarlett, and so very worthy of love and devotion," Tate said as his lips whispered against hers.

Bubba suddenly squeezed her shoulder again. "All done," he announced.

"Huh? You did it?" Scarlett asked, hardly daring to believe it.

"Told you I got this," he told her.

There was no time to be relieved that she wasn't going to get blown up because another wave of arousal flooded her system. Her entire body clenched as it tried to find some sort of relief, leaving her seconds away from stripping her clothes off and forcing Tate to have sex with her before she became the first person ever to die from lack of orgasm.

* * *

JANUARY 19TH

4:12 P.M.

. . .

Relief that the bomb was disarmed was short-lived because the look on Scarlett's face said she had reached her limit.

Actually, Tate was surprised she'd been able to hold off for so long given the look of raw desperation on her face when he'd first walked into the room. Probably, the shock of the bomb, and her surprise at seeing him there had helped to distract her enough from the drug coursing through her system.

Now that it was gone, she looked like she could no longer control herself.

"Sedate her," he ordered Phantom who had set up the IV. Fluids would help to flush the drug out of Scarlett's system, but they weren't going to work fast enough.

"No!" Panic laced the word and there was pure fear in Scarlett's wide brown eyes as she looked up at him.

"It's okay, sweetheart, you're safe now. Let us sedate you, then when you wake up at the hospital, the drug will be gone, and you'll be okay."

"No, don't, Tate. I don't want to be drugged," she pleaded, the hands that had already been twisted in his clothes somehow seemed to tighten their grip.

It wasn't that he didn't get her fear, the last two times she'd been drugged against her will, it was as she was being kidnapped, and she'd had to wake up and face torture and unimaginable terror. But this time was different, this time she'd wake up safe and free from the arousal currently tormenting her.

"Please, don't. You said you thought I was worthy, please, just help me."

A growl rumbled through him.

There was never a time when he didn't want to touch Scarlett, to bring her pleasure, to watch her face as she fell apart.

But not like this.

What he'd said earlier was still true. Maybe she didn't hate him, but she also wasn't sure about him either, and he didn't want this between them. It felt too much like taking advantage because she was hardly in a place where she could give anything that could come close to being considered consent.

While she might want him to help ease the pain inside her, she didn't really want him to touch her right now.

"Please," she whimpered, her hips thrusting forward, seeking anything that would bring her relief.

Another growl tore through him.

It felt like being trapped all over again with no good solution to keep the woman he was falling in love with safe.

"Everybody out," he ordered.

All six of the guys gave him wary looks, clearly not liking his decision, but he'd like to see what one of them would do if they were in his position and their woman was begging them to bring her some relief from her suffering.

Still, the guys left, and as soon as the door closed his hands framed Scarlett's face, making sure she was looking at him so he could see the truth in her eyes.

"Tell me this isn't taking advantage of you," he pleaded. "Tell me that you want my touch not just because I'm the only man here who you feel comfortable enough with to have touch you when you're like this."

"Have you ever lied to me?" she asked.

Not the direction that he'd expected her to take this, but it was a question that was easy to answer. "I might not always have told you what I had planned, but the only outright lie I've ever told you was that day at the grocery store when I pretended I didn't know you, and we both knew I was lying."

"Did you mean what you said before? When you said your world had to have me in it?" There was so much doubt in her eyes that it gutted him. She had never had someone in her life who had put her first. She was always bumped down the list, and it had made her doubt her own worth.

He'd never had anyone put him first either, but together they could find that place to belong that neither of them had had before.

Unconditional love wasn't the curse he had convinced himself it was, it was beautiful, special, and something to be treasured.

Just like the woman he held on his lap who wanted to trust him with something so personal that he couldn't not fall harder and faster.

"I meant it. With every fiber of my being, I meant it," he assured her.

Scarlett's hands circled his wrists and tugged gently, guiding his hand down between her legs. "I don't have all the answers right now, and there's so much we need to talk about, and that I need to figure out. But I know that there isn't anybody else I trust to do this, it's not taking advantage. I'm making the choice to have you touch me rather than being sedated."

Unable to turn her down after that, he nodded, slipping his hand inside her pants and past her panties to find her completely soaked. "Okay, baby, then you keep your eyes on me. You watch who's touching you and know you're safe. Watch the man who is completely in awe of your strength and resilience, your bravery in not letting your fears control you, of still going after what you crave even though you know you might get hurt in the process."

A moan tumbled from her lips as he slid a finger inside her. Already he could feel her internal muscles quivering, the drug keeping her so close to an orgasm that it was nothing short of torture.

"There you go, sweetheart," he murmured, trailing a line of kisses down the slender column of her neck, as he slid another finger inside her, his thumb finding her bud and working it hard and fast. This wasn't the time to draw things out, to tease her, to bring her to the edge and then back up so he could build her higher and make her release that much better.

Right now, his girl needed him to bring her relief, and Tate wanted Scarlett to know that she could always come to him for anything, and he would find a way to make it happen.

"Watch me, sweetheart. I need you to know that it's me touching you, that you're safe."

Her eyes latched onto his as he pumped his fingers in and out, his thumb never letting up on her bundle of nerves.

"Come now, Scarlett. I'm here, you're safe, and I am never going to let anyone—including myself—hurt you ever again."

The words were the final thing she needed to push her over the edge, and her hands grabbed onto his shoulders as a powerful orgasm ripped through her. It seemed to go on and on, and he kept touching and stroking, drawing it out, hoping it was going to ease her raging need.

When tremors stopped rocking her body, he removed his hand and she slumped down against his chest, tucking her face against his neck. It was damp, with sweat or tears, he wasn't sure, but he liked that she was snuggling closer rather than pulling away.

More than he deserved considering the mess he kept making with her.

"Thank you," she whispered, words muffled as she pressed her face closer against him.

"You never have to thank me for giving you what you need, sweetheart." Tate touched a kiss to the top of her head and then began to rub circles on her back, hoping he might be able to soothe her into falling asleep. He had no idea how long the drug would last, or when it had been administered, but he prayed the worst was over.

They sat like that in silence for several minutes, a comfortable silence, and the feel of Scarlett's heart beating against his chest was the most amazing feeling in the world. Honestly, he could stay like this, holding her on his lap, forever.

A groan suddenly fell from Scarlett's lips, and he felt her entire body go tense. Before she even lifted her head and spoke, he knew what was happening. "Tate—"

"It's okay, sweetheart, we have as long as you need." His hand went back into her pants, and he didn't hesitate to slide his fingers straight back inside her, once again letting his thumb work over her bundle of nerves.

Scarlett held onto him as he once again brought her the release her body so badly needed, and as he watched her fall apart again, he realized how addicting it was to be able to give the person he cared about what they needed. No wonder his parents had become addicted to this feeling because there was nothing like it in the world.

His girl was always going to be his top priority, but there was room in that number one spot for any kids they might have. While it might be rusty from lack of use, his heart was big and there was a lot of space in there.

Space that was longing to be filled.

This was nowhere close to being over. Raul Castillo was still out there, still a threat, and they had yet to identify the mole, but from here on out, he and Scarlett were going to work this together as a team. Whatever it took to keep her safe was still a good motto, but her mental health was as important to him as her physical health.

Already once he'd promised not to do what he thought was best without discussing it with her and broken that promise. Not a mistake he would repeat.

Broken promises weren't anything he wanted between them.

So, he was going to have to find a way to help Prey neutralize this threat to his girl and her team, because otherwise, the happy ever after he was just opening himself up to would be lost.

CHAPTER TWENTY-TWO

January 20th
11:18 A.M.

ALL IN ALL, everything considering, it had been a reasonable morning.

Yet Scarlett couldn't help but feel unsettled.

Something was missing.

No, some*one* was missing.

Tate.

Where was he?

Yesterday he'd spent ages with her in that bedroom at Raul's house, holding her on his lap, giving her orgasm after orgasm until finally the drug was out of her system enough that she'd passed out into an exhausted oblivion.

But he hadn't left her.

Every time she surfaced into consciousness, his name had been on her lips. She had needed the reassurance of knowing that he was there, that she was safe, and that everything was going to be okay. When they got to the hospital she had still been in his arms. Any doctor or nurse who suggested he set her on the bed on her own was glared at until they backed off.

After a complete thorough exam, she'd begged to be allowed to leave, and Tate had taken her back to his place, bathed her in the bath, then tucked her into his bed where she'd fallen asleep in his arms.

Only when she woke up he'd been gone.

It felt weird to not have him beside her. Weirder still that she was alone at his place. If he was gone it had to be for a reason, and she knew he wouldn't have left her alone and unprotected. The black SUV in the driveway confirmed that theory. So, she knew he was coming back, and she'd taken care of a couple of things that had been high on her to-do list already, but now she was just sitting on his couch, feeling lost and alone, and almost ready to call a cab and go back to her place.

Like he was some sort of mind reader, that exact second, the front door opened, and Tate strolled in, bags of groceries in his hands. As soon as his gaze fell on her with her phone in her hand, his eyes narrowed. "You better not be looking for a way out of here."

Surprised that he'd guessed, since there were a dozen things she could be doing on her phone, Scarlett laughed. "Your mind-reading skills are impressive." The smile faded from her lips as insecurity took hold. "Where were you? I woke up and you were gone."

Setting the grocery bags down, Tate didn't hesitate to walk right to her and draw her into his arms. "There was something I really wanted to do, and I had hoped you might be exhausted enough from everything that's happened over the last couple of weeks that you'd still be asleep when I got back. Guess I wasn't that lucky. I didn't leave you alone, a couple of the guys from my team are watching the house."

"I know you'd never put me in danger," she assured him. Until Raul was caught and the mole identified, she would continue to be in danger, but at least her name was cleared, and she had people she trusted watching her back.

"Never," he agreed. "And I wasn't trying to say I didn't want you here. Because if I didn't want you here, I wouldn't have brought you here."

There was so much anxiousness in the man she was used to seeing as sure, and confident, if a little arrogant and jerky for a while there, that it softened the edges of her own insecurities. "I know that, Tate. I wasn't worried that you had left, I was at your place after all, I just … missed you," she admitted. "I wish you'd been here when I woke up."

"I wish I had been, too. But there was something I wanted to do for you, and I wanted it to be a surprise."

That piqued her interest. "Oh yeah? What?" Surprises were great fun, but not something that was a big part of her life. As a kid, there hadn't been many birthday or Christmas gifts, and what she and Zander got were never fun presents like toys, they were usually practical things like clothes, toiletries, and school supplies. And not fun clothes either, but practical jeans and T-shirts, and sensible sneakers.

"Well, you told me how much you love cooking, and

you know that I don't know how to make pretty much anything other than the basics. So, I went to a cooking class this morning," Tate told her, somewhat nervously, like he wasn't quite sure if she would think that was a good reason for him to disappear for a few hours.

"You took a cooking class?" she asked, thinking it was possibly the sweetest thing ever.

"You've been through a lot, and you've never really had anyone to take care of you, not in the way you should. I was looking up classes while you were sleeping, and I just took the first one I could find."

"What was it?"

"Vegetable soup and bread. I know you already know how to make both but—"

"But it's the nicest thing anyone has ever done for me," Scarlett said, cutting him off. No one had ever done something like that for her before, and for all the reasons Tate hadn't been there this morning when she woke up, this one had to be right up the top of the list. "Thank you."

Now that he knew she wasn't angry with him, Tate grinned and leaned down to press a kiss to her mouth. "I'm glad you're not mad. I have all the ingredients, why don't you go take a bubble bath, relax, and I'll get the soup cooking and the bread … proofing, and then I'll whip us up some sandwiches for lunch."

As nice as a bath might be, right now, she'd much rather hang out with Tate than go off and be on her own. She'd had more than enough alone time to last an entire lifetime. "Actually, I'd love to watch you cook," she said with a grin. Sweet as it was that he'd gone and taken a cooking class just because cooking was something she enjoyed, and because he wanted to take care of her, she doubted he'd picked up many skills this quickly. Watching him in the kitchen was going to be highly amusing, she was sure of it.

Tate's unusual eyes narrowed. "Do you think I'm going to make a fool of myself, Ms. Madden?"

She giggled. "Umm ... no ... of course not."

"I think you do." His lips nibbled at a sensitive spot on her neck, making her moan and arch into his touch. Kissing and nipping his way up her neck, his tongue touched a spot behind her ear that drew another moan from her, and then he kissed his way along her jaw. When his lips touched the corner of hers, a content sigh slipped out this time as she waited for his mouth to claim hers.

Only it didn't.

Instead, he stepped back and smirked. "Come on, my little fighter, let's go give you some entertainment."

"You're mean, you know that?" She pouted, but followed him into the kitchen anyway when he scooped up the bags and headed through the living room.

Tate laughed. A wonderful free sound she hadn't heard from him before. It warmed her heart, and she didn't even hear whatever it was he said because she was too busy feeling such a wonderful array of emotions.

Climbing onto one of the stools at the breakfast bar, she watched as Tate slipped on an apron and began to bustle around the kitchen. His movements were a little clunky and it was obvious that he didn't spend much time cooking. She could have chopped the vegetables in half the time, but she liked watching his large hands and muscled forearms as he worked. Who knew a shirt rolled up to the elbows, showcasing forearms was so sexy?

This was the future she wanted so badly.

Simple things like hanging out in the kitchen cooking. She wasn't after anything extraordinary, she didn't need big gestures or expensive gifts. All she wanted was to be loved, to feel important to someone, and to know that no matter what happened, someone would always be there for her.

"I talked to Piper Hamilton-Eden," she announced.

From the way Tate froze, his eyes lifting to meet hers, she knew he knew who Piper was. "To help you process what you went through?"

"In part. But I also had a lot of time to think while I was sitting in that prison cell, and I realized that I have issues from my childhood I want to address. I've been so desperate to be loved that I've tried to force relationships with anyone, just so I wouldn't be alone."

For a moment Tate looked stricken. "Are you trying to tell me that you're rethinking things between us?"

That shocked her enough that she jumped out of her seat and hurried around the counter to wrap her arms around his waist. "No. Not at all. I knew the second I met you that you were different. I've felt so unworthy and unlovable for so long, that I was prepared to pretend to be in love because it was easier than being alone. But with you … I can't even explain it. It's so … big. So filling. All that emptiness is just gone when I'm with you. I had doubts about you at first, I couldn't believe you would put your job on the line for me, but you did. You pushed to keep your team helping Prey with this situation when you didn't have to, and you're here with me now. I want what we have to be real, I want it to grow, and I hope it lasts a lifetime. For that to happen, I know I have to confront my feelings of unworthiness, and abandonment issues. I want to be my best, for you."

"Sweetheart, you already are the best."

"It's sweet you say that," she said, snuggling against him, resting her head against his chest where she could feel the steady beating of his heart. "But I don't want to have doubts. I want to be able to love me for me. I don't want to feel unworthy anymore. This is something I want to do, and I'm excited to do it."

"Then I'm here to support you every step of the way."

The words she'd hoped to hear. It might feel like it was too soon to say the words I love you, but it didn't change the fact that she knew deep down in her heart that it was true. For some crazy reason, she'd loved this man from the second their eyes met at the Halloween party at the bar three months ago.

It might not have been an easy road getting here, but standing in his kitchen, in the arms of a man who was offering her everything she'd ever wanted, Scarlett knew she was on the cusp of having the family she'd always craved.

* * *

JANUARY 20TH

6:44 P.M.

. . .

"THAT WAS DELICIOUS," Scarlett announced setting down her spoon.

"It was not," Tate said plainly. Somehow, she had managed to eat her entire bowl of soup, and three slices of the bread he'd made.

Well, *attempted* to make, might be more realistic.

Because the food was a disaster.

Flat out.

No other way to put it.

"Was so," she countered.

"Sweetheart, that was not food and we both know it. Somehow, I managed to burn the bread on the outside, yet it's not even cooked properly inside. And the soup ... how does someone even ruin vegetable soup? I mean, it's only cutting up vegetables and boiling them in broth. I have no idea why mine manages to taste so awful."

"I enjoyed it," Scarlett said stubbornly.

And that right there was why he was falling in love with her.

There was no way she could have actually enjoyed the food itself. What she enjoyed was that someone had cared enough to try to take care of her. To prepare a meal just for her, with no other motivation than love.

"Thank you," he told her sincerely.

Her brow did that adorable scrunching thing it did when she was confused. "For what? You're the one who cooked dinner for us."

"For eating it, and actually enjoying it. Come here, sweetheart." Pushing back from the table, Tate patted his lap, already growing hard as Scarlett's tongue peeped out and ran along her bottom lip as she rounded the table and straddled his thighs.

Didn't seem to matter how many times he touched this woman, it was never enough. He was completely and utterly addicted to her. There was just something about her willingness to keep going after what she wanted, continuing to stand up every time she got knocked down, that drew him in.

It showed him what life could be like if only he was willing to give it a chance.

And he was willing.

More than willing.

Anything to keep Scarlett in his life.

Because giving her up and not having her was worse than the possibility of accepting something amazing between them and losing her along the way.

"What do you want, sweetheart?" he asked as he kissed the pulse point in her neck where her pulse was fluttering wildly.

"You," she whispered, tilting her head to the side to give him better access to her neck.

Accepting the invitation, he kissed his way up the slender column just like he had when he'd been teasing her earlier, only this time, he didn't stop when his lips reached the corner of her mouth. His hands lifted, fingers tangling in her hair as he framed her face, and then his mouth was on hers, pouring every ounce of tenderness, admiration, respect, and love he felt for her into that kiss.

When they both needed to draw in air, he pulled back, staying close enough that there were mere millimeters between them. "Tonight is for you, baby. For you to take what you want, what you need, I'm all yours. You want sex, you've got it. You're not ready for that yet, then we can just fool around a little. We can stay here, move to the living room, go upstairs to the bedroom or the bathroom. You tell me what you want, and you got it."

"I'm not scared of sex because of what almost happened," Scarlett told him. "Well, maybe that's not quite true, but I'm not scared of sex with you. I'm not scared of anything with you. When you touch me it's all I can think about. It makes me feel special, wanted, and desired."

"You are all those things, Scarlett. All of them and so much more."

"Only to you," she said, but the smile on her face told him it was enough even before she said the words. "But that's all I ever needed. You're all I'll ever need."

Those words should terrify him considering everything he'd thought he hadn't wanted, but they didn't. Instead, they warmed him and stoked the fire of his desire for this woman who so bravely bared her heart and soul for the world to see, regardless of the consequences.

"The bedroom," she said.

"Your wish is my command. Forever, Scarlett, not just for tonight," Tate promised as he stood, lifting her with him. "I'll always do everything within my power to make you happy. To make you feel treasured. So you never again feel alone and unwanted."

"I know you will."

With her legs wrapped around his hips, her hot center was pressed against the bulge in his pants, and when she began to rock against him, Tate groaned as he carried her up the stairs to his bedroom. They hadn't had sex since before Scarlett was kidnapped the second time, and because he knew what she'd been threatened with, he intended to make sure she had complete control over what happened between them.

Despite her assurances she didn't have any fears about sex, he wanted to make sure that was true. After all she'd been through, he wanted tonight to be perfect for her. Wanted everything in her life to be perfect from here on out.

In the bedroom, he set her on her feet but stopped her when she went to reach for the hem of her sweater. "Let me undress you, baby."

Her smile was sweet and shy, and utter perfection. Scarlett let her hands drop to her sides, and he pulled one arm from the sleeve, touching a kiss to her palm, and then the inside of her wrist, kissing his way up to her shoulder. Then he repeated the process with her other arm, taking his time, keeping the kisses featherlight, enjoying the way tiny goosebumps broke out on her petal soft skin.

With her arms free, he quickly tugged the sweater over her head and tossed it aside, then stripped off her yoga pants and panties, leaving her perfectly naked before him. There wasn't a single part of her delectable body he didn't want to kiss and touch. Those long lean legs wrapped around his waist as he sunk into her tight, wet heat would be pure bliss, and those perfect breasts of hers were practically begging to be licked and sucked.

"Umm, Tate? I can't help but notice things are a little uneven," Scarlett said, voice husky with desire, indicating her naked body and his fully clothed one.

"Then we better rectify that, hadn't we, sweetheart?"

Pulling his T-shirt over his head, it quickly joined her clothes on the floor as did his sweat pants and boxers.

After trailing along his pecs, and abs, Scarlett's gaze landed on his erection and stuck there. She did that cute thing again where her tongue darted out to sweep across her bottom lip, and right now it sent every drop of blood not already headed south zinging straight there.

"The things you do to me," he murmured as he scooped her up and laid them both down on the bed.

"What do I do to you?"

"The craziest things. I didn't know I could feel like this," he admitted as he rolled onto his back so Scarlett was on top.

"I didn't know either. It's almost too much, and yet at the same time, the fullness feels like … perfection. Happiness. Belonging." As she spoke she lifted her hips so they were right above his hard length and sunk down just enough to take the tip of him inside her.

While he was certainly no teenage boy who came before his girl did, just the smallest feel of Scarlett around him was almost enough to make him come.

Not that he had any intention of hurrying her.

Tonight was Scarlett's night, and he was going to let her do whatever she wanted. Even if it was the most exquisite torture.

Instead, as she sank down slowly, one inch at a time, and her head fell back in delight, he claimed one of her breasts that was thrust forward as his other hand found her bud and began to work it over. Her pebbled nipples and bundle of nerves responded to his touch, and he could feel the pleasure beginning to hum through her body in the small tremors that rippled through it.

Each tug of a nipple, each swipe of his thumb across her bud, elicited another moan from her lips. His length jerked and pulsed as Scarlett took more of it inside her, and by the time he was finally buried deep, he was clinging to control so he didn't grab her hips and began to thrust into her, pushing both of them over the edge.

Staying in the moment, focused purely on the expression of bliss on Scarlett's face, he held onto his control as she began to rock her hips, finding a rhythm that worked for her. Lifting her hips until only his tip remained inside her, she sank back down again, then she'd roll her hips bringing him dangerously close to coming, before lifting up again.

Their breathing began to grow choppy as they drew ever closer to the inevitable.

Desperation had his fingers working faster, pressing harder as he tweaked her nipples, and rolled her bundle of nerves between a thumb and forefinger.

"I'm so close, Tate, but I can't ... I can't get there," Scarlett whispered in a tortured voice.

"I got you, sweetheart, always." Grabbing her hips, he positioned his hands so that with every thrust, his fingertips would graze her bud and set a faster pace, a harder pace, shoving everything he felt for her into each thrust.

Her internal muscles began to quiver, each breath more a pant, he felt her getting tighter, and then all of a sudden, she snapped. Her head fell back as a scream of pleasure tore through her and his name tumbled from her lips.

Allowing himself to hit his release it exploded through him with a ferocity he hadn't been expecting, although he probably should have.

As the pleasure began to dim, he pulled Scarlett down to rest against his chest, keeping himself buried inside her. "You're everything I was sure I didn't want, and didn't know I needed, sweetheart. Thank you for giving me this chance to prove to you I can be the answer to your dreams."

With a content sigh, she nuzzled her face against his neck. "Thank you for showing me what it feels like to be treasured."

"Always," he promised, finding it the easiest promise he'd ever made, and one he knew he wouldn't have any trouble keeping.

CHAPTER TWENTY-THREE

January 21st
10:32 A.M.

"I WISH we could have stayed in our bubble a little longer," Scarlett said as she took Tate's offered hand and they strolled toward Prey's building.

Yesterday had been perfect, everything she needed, and she wasn't ready for it to end. A vacation, several weeks away from the real world, where it was just her and Tate, getting to know one another, exploring each other's bodies, that's what she craved. The downtime was desperately needed. The last two weeks had been beyond rough, and both her physical and psychological health depended on time when all she had to worry about was relaxing.

But unfortunately, time was not a luxury they had right now.

Between Raul Castillo and the mole at Prey, there was

no way she could just check out and leave everyone else to handle things.

If her team was in danger then she was going to be there, doing whatever it took to make sure nobody ever got their hands on the Reactivator.

"Me too, sweetheart," Tate said, his gaze constantly roaming the street. Saying he was against the idea of her being there would be a gross understatement. There was no doubt in her mind that he had been about a heartbeat away from sending her away to a place only he knew the location of and keeping her there until this whole mess was resolved. It was only his promises to her that they would face things together from here on out that had stopped him.

If his team had been able to take leave, she was pretty sure the two of them would already be on a plane by now, heading off to some unknown location.

Since that wasn't a possibility, she would stay with him at least until the mole was identified and in custody and Raul had been apprehended. There was no point in going to a safe house since the mole would be able to find the location, same thing with staying at a hotel. So, they'd decided she may as well just stay with Tate. If she was at Prey, she'd be sticking close to someone she trusted, otherwise she'd be with Tate, with some of his team watching over his place.

Not a perfect system, but the best they could do under the circumstances.

It was quiet in the Prey building, and they headed through to the conference room that had been set up specifically to work on this problem. Eagle was in there, along with Fox and the guys, and two of her teammates. With a mole in the building, there was no way to hide what they were doing, their best bet was to keep everything out in the open and hope that it caused the mole to slip up.

"How are you?" Cassie asked, hurrying over to wrap her in a hug.

"I'm okay, better than I was," she assured her friend as she returned the younger woman's embrace. Even though she hadn't wanted to, she'd told them all everything. Including about the drug she'd been given. Since Rocco and his team had been there and seen firsthand what had been given to her it wasn't like it was some sort of secret. Rocco and the guys had been very sweet. In the hospital, she'd been embarrassed to see them, but they had all come and hung out with her for a while, treating her completely normally and she loved them for it.

"We're going to figure this out," Eagle vowed as he, too, came and gave her a hug.

The man might be her boss, but she didn't see him all that often and Scarlett was completely in awe of the man. In the special ops community, he was like some sort of legend, and she would be grateful every day for the rest of her life that he had thought her worthy enough to work for Prey.

"Thanks for believing in me," she whispered, a little embarrassed that tears were blurring her vision.

"I know you, Scarlett," Eagle said, pulling back to look down at her. "And I never doubted the kind of person that you are. I'm sorry you got caught up in a mess because I dropped the ball and hired someone who betrayed us all. I promise you that I will make sure you don't get hurt again."

"It's not your fault, Eagle," she assured him, but from the look in his eyes, it was clear he didn't believe her. Prey was definitely a family and Eagle saw himself as the head of that family—which he absolutely was—and he took that responsibility very seriously.

Ella's phone rang. "That's Lucy," she announced.

"She's on a plane going to collect more of the plant she used to base the healing part of our drug on," Cassie informed her.

"She's on a plane, heading off somewhere on her own?" she repeated, panic thrumming through her. Right now, she wanted her friends here, close, and safe. They had no idea how invested Raul or the mole would be in attempting to follow through on their initial plans. There was a chance they would just give up, cut their losses, and accept they weren't going to get their hands on the Reactivator. Or they could double down their efforts and do whatever it took to get it.

Doing whatever it took to get it meant she wasn't the only one in danger.

"Don't worry, the pilot is skilled, he won't let her get hurt," Cassie soothed.

"Here, check in on her yourself," Ella offered, holding out her phone.

Scarlett's hand shook as she took the phone, but Tate's presence beside her was solid and steady. "Hey, Luce," she said as she saw her friend smiling back at her on the screen.

"I wish I was there to give you a huge hug," Lucy said.

"As soon as you get back the four of us are going to spend an entire day together. Spa, facials, massages, manicures, the whole works. Lunch, more than we can eat, and we're going to talk and laugh, and I'm warning you now, I might cry too," she said, tears already blurring her vision again. She loved these women, they were the sisters she'd always wanted, and she wished she hadn't doubted them, not even for a second. Of course, they wouldn't think the worst of her. They loved her, had always had her back, and she had theirs, too. Forever.

Lucy laughed and the phone moved with her as she did so.

As it did, Scarlett caught a glimpse of the pilot's hands as he flew the small plane.

There was a scar around the man's wrist, a tattoo had been inked over the marks.

A chain of infinity symbols.

No.

It couldn't be.

The world began to spin around her.

The phone fell from her hand.

When her knees buckled it was only Tate's quick actions, wrapping an arm around her waist, that kept her from hitting the floor.

How was that possible?

Surely, she had to be wrong.

Had to be.

There could be no other explanation.

"Scarlett, you okay?" Ella asked as she retrieved her phone.

Snatching the phone, she stared at Lucy, willing this

not to be true because if it was, there was a chance her friend was in danger. "Show me the pilot," she demanded.

"Huh? Scarlett, what's—?"

"Please," she said, cutting Lucy off.

Her friend looked confused, but she shifted the phone slightly so the camera picked up the man's face.

The bottom fell out of her world in that moment.

"Sweetheart, you're scaring me," Tate said, the arm around her waist tightening.

Just drawing air into her lungs was an effort right now, let alone getting out the words she needed to say.

How could her life keep getting worse?

Just when she thought that things were looking up this happened. Another betrayal. She was alive, she had Tate, she had her Prey family, she knew she was going to be so surrounded by people she trusted that there was no chance anyone would get to her and hurt her.

Only now, life had delivered her the most devastating of blows.

Gripping the phone in one hand, her other held onto Tate's forearm, needing him more than ever now that she knew how deeply she'd been betrayed by the only person she thought would never do that to her.

The pilot's eyes met hers, understanding flowed between them, then the next thing she knew an alarm began to sound in the plane carrying Lucy and Zander, Scarlett's supposedly dead twin brother.

"What's happening?" Lucy asked, panic in her voice and the view on Ella's phone shifted to the ceiling as Lucy's phone moved, the camera no longer capturing the face of the person who for the first thirteen years of her life had been the only thing keeping her going.

"We're going down," the pilot's voice spoke far too calmly considering what he'd just said.

"Lucy, whatever happens, don't trust him," Scarlett screamed. "That's Zander, my brother. He's supposed to be dead. If he's there then you're not safe."

Those were the last words she spoke before the sound of the plane hitting the ground filled the room, leaving all of them standing there in horrified silence.

Even if Lucy survives the plane crash, she's still trapped with a man who might be a threat to her safety in the second book in the action packed and emotionally charged Prey Security: Athena Team series!

Fighting for Lucy (Prey Security: Athena Team #2)

ALSO BY JANE BLYTHE

Prey Security: Athena Team Series

FIGHTING FOR SCARLETT

FIGHTING FOR LUCY

Prey Security Series: Artemis Team

IVORY'S FIGHT

PEARL'S FIGHT

LACEY'S FIGHT

OPAL'S FIGHT

Prey Security Series

PROTECTING EAGLE

PROTECTING RAVEN

PROTECTING FALCON

PROTECTING SPARROW

PROTECTING HAWK

PROTECTING DOVE

Prey Security Series: Alpha Team

DEADLY RISK

LETHAL RISK

EXTREME RISK

FATAL RISK

COVERT RISK

SAVAGE RISK

Prey Security: Bravo Team Series

VICIOUS SCARS

RUTHLESS SCARS

BRUTAL SCARS

CRUEL SCARS

BURIED SCARS

Saving SEALs Series

SAVING RYDER

SAVING ERIC

SAVING OWEN

SAVING LOGAN

SAVING GRAYSON

SAVING CHARLIE

Candella Sisters' Heroes Series

LITTLE DOLLS

LITTLE HEARTS

LITTLE BALLERINA

Broken Gems Series

CRACKED SAPPHIRE

CRUSHED RUBY

FRACTURED DIAMOND

SHATTERED AMETHYST

SPLINTERED EMERALD

SALVAGING MARIGOLD

River's End Rescues Series

COCKY SAVIOR

SOME REGRETS ARE FOREVER

PROTECT

SOME LIES WILL HAUNT YOU

SOME QUESTIONS HAVE NO ANSWERS

SOME TRUTH CAN BE DISTORTED

SOME TRUST CAN BE REBUILT

SOME MISTAKES ARE UNFORGIVABLE

Detective Parker Bell Series

A SECRET TO THE GRAVE

WINTER WONDERLAND

DEAD OR ALIVE

LITTLE GIRL LOST

FORGOTTEN

Count to Ten Series

ONE

TWO

THREE

FOUR

FIVE

SIX

BURNING SECRETS

SEVEN

EIGHT

NINE

TEN

Storybook Murders Series

NURSERY RHYME KILLER

FAIRYTALE KILLER

FABLE KILLER

Christmas Romantic Suspense Series

CHRISTMAS HOSTAGE

CHRISTMAS CAPTIVE

CHRISTMAS VICTIM

YULETIDE PROTECTOR

YULETIDE GUARD

YULETIDE HERO

HOLIDAY GRIEF

Conquering Fear Series

(Co-written with Amanda Siegrist)

DROWNING IN YOU

OUT OF THE DARKNESS

CLOSING IN

ABOUT THE AUTHOR

USA Today bestselling author Jane Blythe writes action-packed romantic suspense and military romance featuring protective heroes and heroines who are survivors. One of Jane's most popular series includes Prey Security, part of Susan Stoker's OPERATION ALPHA world! Writing in that world alongside authors such as Janie Crouch and Riley Edwards has been a blast, and she looks forward to bringing more books to this genre, both within and outside of Stoker's world. When Jane isn't binge-reading she's counting down to Christmas and adding to her 200+ teddy bear collection!

To connect and keep up to date please visit any of the following

Email – mailto:janeblytheauthor@gmail.com
Facebook – https://www.facebook.com/janeblytheauthor
Instagram – https://www.instagram.com/jane_blythe_author
Reader Group – https://www.facebook.com/groups/janeskillersweethearts
Twitter – https://www.twitter.com/jblytheauthor
TikTok - https://www.tiktok.com/@janeblytheauthor
Website – https://www.janeblythe.com.au

There are many more books in this fan fiction world than listed here, for an up-to-date list go to www.AcesPress.com

You can also visit our Amazon page at: http://www.amazon.com/author/operationalpha

<u>Special Forces: Operation Alpha World</u>

Christie Adams: Charity's Heart
Elizabella Baker: Challenging Luke
Linzi Baxter: Dangerous Rescue
Misha Blake: Flash
Anna Blakely: Rescuing Gracelynn
Julia Bright: Saving Lorelei
Cara Carnes: Protecting Mari
Kendra Mei Chailyn: Beast
Melissa Kay Clarke: Rescuing Annabeth
Gia Cobie: Saved from Revenge
Samantha Cole: Handling Haven
KaLyn Cooper: Spring Unveiled
Jordan Dane: Redemption for Avery
D.M. Earl: Claire's Guardian
Riley Edwards: Protecting Olivia
Dorothy Ewels: Knight's Queen
Lila Ferrari: Protecting Joy
Nicole Flockton: Protecting Maria
Amy Gamet: Guarded by the SEAL
Lea Griffith: Finding Ava
Desiree Holt: Protecting Maddie
Danielle M. Haas: Crossroads of Betrayal

Bree Hera: Trusting the Team
Jesse Jacobson: Protecting Honor
Rayne Lewis: Justice for Mary
Ireland Lorelei: The Detective
Kristin Lynn: Worth the Risk
JM Madden: Rescuing Olivia
A.M. Mahler: Griffin
Ellie Masters: Sybil's Protector
Trish McCallan: Hero Under Fire
Naomi McKay: Twist
Rachel McNeely: The SEAL's Surprise Baby
KD Michaels: Saving Laura
Olivia Michaels: Protecting Harper
Annie Miller: Securing Willow
MJ Nightingale: Protecting Beauty
C.K. O'Connor: Delaney's Bodyguard
Melinda Owens: Betraying Katie
Victoria Paige: Reclaiming Izabel
Danielle Pays: Defending Sarina
Lainey Reese: Protecting New York
KeKe Renée: Protecting Bria
Taryn Rivers: Savage Cove
TL Reeve and Michele Ryan: Extracting Mateo
Ariana Rose: Chasing Paige
Deanna L. Rowley: Saving Veronica
Angela Rush: Charlotte
E.M. Shue: Discovering Tyler
Rose Smith: Saving Satin
Tyler Anne Snell: Cowboy Heat
Dee Stewart: Fighting for Brielle
Lynne St. James: SEAL's Spitfire

Bella Stone: Rexar
Jen Talty: Protecting Ainsley
Reina Torres, Rescuing Hi'ilani
LJ Vickery: Circus Comes to Town
R. C. Wynne: Shadows Renewed

Delta Team Three Series

Lori Ryan: Nori's Delta
Becca Jameson: Destiny's Delta
Lynne St James, Gwen's Delta
Elle James: Ivy's Delta
Riley Edwards: Hope's Delta

Police and Fire: Operation Alpha World

Freya Barker: Burning for Autumn
B.P. Beth: Scott
Jane Blythe: Salvaging Marigold
Julia Bright: Justice for Amber
Gia Cobie: Saved from Revenge
Hadley Finn: Exton
Danielle M. Haas: Crossroads of Betrayal
Deanndra Hall: Shelter for Sharla
Jenna Harte: Dead But Not Forgotten
India Kells: Game Master
Amber Kuhlman: Protecting Paisley
Reina Torres: Justice for Sloane
Aubree Valentine, Justice for Danielle
Maddie Wade: Finding English

Tarpley VFD Series

Silver James, Fighting for Elena

Deanndra Hall, Fighting for Carly
Haven Rose, Fighting for Calliope
MJ Nightingale, Fighting for Jemma
TL Reeve, Fighting for Brittney
Nicole Flockton, Fighting for Nadia

As you know, this book included at least one character from Susan Stoker's books. To check out more, see below.

SEAL Team Hawaii Series

Finding Elodie
Finding Lexie
Finding Kenna
Finding Monica
Finding Carly
Finding Ashlyn
Finding Jodelle

Eagle Point Search & Rescue

Searching for Lilly
Searching for Elsie
Searching for Bristol
Searching for Caryn
Searching for Finley
Searching for Heather
Searching for Khloe

The Refuge Series

Deserving Alaska
Deserving Henley
Deserving Reese
Deserving Cora
Deserving Lara
Deserving Maisy (Oct 2024)
Deserving Ryleigh (Jan 2025)

SEAL of Protection: Alliance Series

Protecting Remi (July 2024)
Protecting Wren (Nov 2024)
Protecting Josie (Mar 2025)
Protecting Maggie (TBA)
Protecting Addison (TBA)
Protecting Kelli (TBA)
Protecting Bree (TBA)

Delta Team Two Series

Shielding Gillian
Shielding Kinley
Shielding Aspen
Shielding Jayme (novella)
Shielding Riley
Shielding Devyn
Shielding Ember
Shielding Sierra

SEAL of Protection: Legacy Series

Securing Caite (FREE!)
Securing Brenae (novella)
Securing Sidney
Securing Piper
Securing Zoey
Securing Avery
Securing Kalee
Securing Jane

Delta Force Heroes Series

Rescuing Rayne (FREE!)

Rescuing Aimee (novella)
Rescuing Emily
Rescuing Harley
Marrying Emily (novella)
Rescuing Kassie
Rescuing Bryn
Rescuing Casey
Rescuing Sadie (novella)
Rescuing Wendy
Rescuing Mary
Rescuing Macie (novella)
Rescuing Annie

Badge of Honor: Texas Heroes Series

Justice for Mackenzie (FREE!)
Justice for Mickie
Justice for Corrie
Justice for Laine (novella)
Shelter for Elizabeth
Justice for Boone
Shelter for Adeline
Shelter for Sophie
Justice for Erin
Justice for Milena
Shelter for Blythe
Justice for Hope
Shelter for Quinn
Shelter for Koren
Shelter for Penelope

SEAL of Protection Series

Protecting Caroline (FREE!)
Protecting Alabama
Protecting Fiona
Marrying Caroline (novella)
Protecting Summer
Protecting Cheyenne
Protecting Jessyka
Protecting Julie (novella)
Protecting Melody
Protecting the Future
Protecting Kiera (novella)
Protecting Alabama's Kids (novella)
Protecting Dakota

New York Times, *USA Today* and *Wall Street Journal* Bestselling Author Susan Stoker has a heart as big as the state of Tennessee where she lives, but this all American girl has also spent the last fourteen years living in Missouri, California, Colorado, Indiana, and Texas. She's married to a retired Army man who now gets to follow *her* around the country.

www.stokeraces.com
www.AcesPress.com
susan@stokeraces.com

Made in the USA
Monee, IL
21 August 2024

64263510R30190